GOBLINS
VS DWARVES

PHILIP REEVE

■ SCHOLASTIC

Scholastic Children's Books
An imprint of Scholastic Ltd
Euston House, 24 Eversholt Street, London, NW1 1DB, UK
Registered office: Westfield Road, Southam, Warwickshire, CV47 0RA
SCHOLASTIC and associated logos are trademarks and/or
registered trademarks of Scholastic Inc.

First published in the UK by Scholastic Ltd, 2012
This edition published 2019

ISBN 978 1407 19149 2

A CIP catalogue record for this book
is available from the British Library.

Printed by CPI Group (UK) Ltd, Croydon, CR0 4YY
Papers used by Scholastic Children's Books are made
from wood grown in sustainable forests.

1 3 5 7 9 10 8 6 4 2

This is a work of fiction. Names, characters, places, incidents
and dialogues are products of the author's imagination or are used
fictitiously. Any resemblance to actual people, living or dead,
events or locales is entirely coincidental.

www.scholastic.co.uk

F9

GOBLINS
VS DWARVES

For SAM REEVE

Far Penderglaze
The Autumn Isles
The Nibbled Coast
Porthstrewy
River Oeth
Lusuenn
CLOVENSTONE
Choun Head
Oeth Moor
STICKLEBRIDGE
Choon
Lyn Glas
Calchoen
River Ystwyth
River Ystrad
Porthquidden
CORIANDER
BOSKENNACK
BAY OF CORIANDER

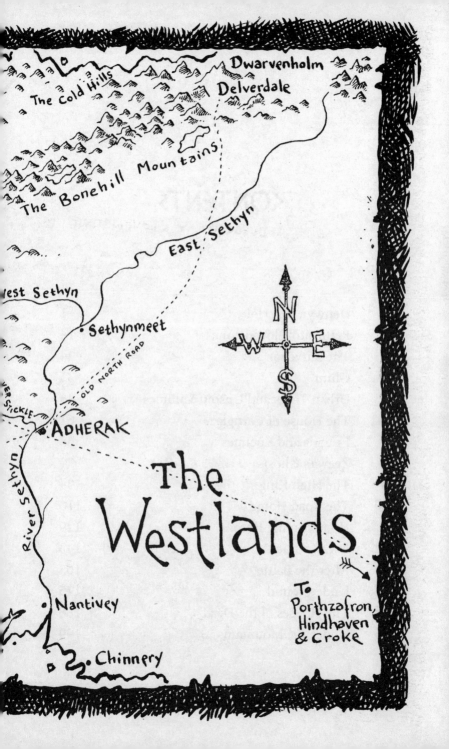

CONTENTS

HENWYN IN A HOLE

"Ghooooof!" said Henwyn.

It was an odd thing to say, but since the ground had just given way beneath his feet and he had gone plummeting down and landed in blackness at the bottom of a deep, dark hole, it summed up his feelings pretty well. "Ghooooof!" he said again, more thoughtfully, and rolled over on to his back. High above him he could see a raggedy-edged patch of daylight, which he guessed must be the opening through which he had fallen. Everything else was as black as midnight.

"Skarper?" he shouted.

Skarper was Henwyn's best friend. That was unusual, because Henwyn was a young human being, fair haired and honest-featured and really not bad looking if you liked that sort of thing, while Skarper was a goblin: a spindly, foxy-faced creature with yellow eyes, long ears and a ginger tuft on the end of his tail. Friendships between humans and goblins were a thing unknown. But all sorts of unusual and unknown things had been happening in the Westlands during the past year and a half. Most people put it down to the comet called the Lych Lord's star, which had come swooping back out of the depths of space to waken with its silver light the old magic which still lingered in the secret places of the land.

One of the most secret places of all was the great ruined fortress of Clovenstone, which had always been home to Skarper's goblin tribe, and where Henwyn lived now as well. It was from Clovenstone that the two friends had set out that morning, crossing the tumbledown Outer Wall and climbing up into the steep, stark valleys of the Bonehill Mountains. The cloud maidens who sometimes flew over Clovenstone had told Henwyn of smoke they'd seen, and fires by night, up in those uninhabited hills. It had sounded to Henwyn like mystery and adventure, and since he fancied himself as a bit of an adventurer, he had decided to investigate. He had persuaded Skarper to come with him. "Think what good practice it will be for next spring, when we set off on real adventures!" he had said.

And if adventures mainly consisted of getting bored

and footsore then it was good practice indeed, for that was all the pair had achieved by mid-afternoon, when they stopped for a rest at the top of an especially steep ridge.

"Well, there's nothing here," Skarper grumbled, rubbing his blistered paws. "Nothing but rocks and rain and those great, grey, slithery slopes of scree. Even the wind sounds bored. Listen to it, droning and moaning up in the crags there. Those potty cloud maidens must have been imagining things. Can we go home now?"

Henwyn wasn't listening. He was pointing down into the valley on the far side of the ridge. "What's that?" he asked.

"What's what?" said Skarper.

The valley looked just the same to him as all the other valleys they had seen that day: steep-walled and overhung by crags, with a milky river twisting along its floor, far below. But halfway down this valley a tall upright shape rose among the littered boulders.

"It's just an old tower," said Skarper.

"Not a tower," said Henwyn. "A chimney! Look! There's smoke coming out of the top of it!"

Skarper squinted. There were a few faint wisps billowing around the top of the tower or chimney or whatever it was, but he wasn't sure that they were wisps of smoke. He thought they might just as easily be scraps of the low cloud, which kept sinking down to brush the crags and drop cold rain on him.

"I'm going to take a closer look," decided Henwyn, and he jumped up and set off downhill in a clatter of dislodged stones.

"All right," said Skarper. "I'll stay here and guard our stuff." And he took the pack which Henwyn had been carrying, put it beneath his head for a pillow, and tried to pretend that he was back in his own snug little lair at Clovenstone.

In the darkness at the bottom of his hole, Henwyn sat up. There was a scent of wet earth, which you would expect at the bottom of a hole, and a faint smell of smoke, which you wouldn't. He heard a faint, far-off thudding sound. At first he could see nothing, but then he slowly began to make out wooden pillars and rafters reaching away from him into the dark, like ribs. It was not a hole that he was in; it was a tunnel. It stretched away in front of him for twenty paces or so, then turned a corner. From around that corner a dim, reddish-orange light was coming – and it was growing brighter.

The chimney had been very disappointing. Three or four times the height of a man, it stood all alone on the hillside. Sometimes one of those pale wisps of smoke emerged from its top. "Hello?" Henwyn had shouted. He had put his ear to the chimney, but he couldn't hear anything. He had walked all round it, wondering if there might be an opening; perhaps a little door for chimney sweeps to use. There was nothing.

Around the base of the chimney the thin mountain soil was scarred and churned. Many footprints showed there, and there were heaps of newly cut stones left over from the building work. Those, and the odd flutterings of smoke, were the only things which told him the chimney was not an abandoned ruin that had stood there for a hundred years.

Henwyn walked away, looking for more clues. He had gone about ten paces when, without any warning, the ground gave way under him. That was when he had plunged into the tunnel.

Up on the ridge, Skarper thought he heard something. A rattle and a sort of "Ghooooooof!" He opened his eyes and sat up. He could not see Henwyn. His friend was probably round the back of that stupid chimney, he thought. A pleasant smell reached him, coming from inside Henwyn's pack. He undid the straps and stuck his head inside it. He was so busy rummaging that he did not hear the little muffled cry of "Skarper!" drifting up the hill.

"Ooh!" he said. "Pies!"

The first thought that flitted across Henwyn's mind when he saw that fiery glow around the bend in the tunnel was *Dragons!* But no; that could not be right. Dragons did not build tunnels with pit-props and rafters. Anyway, this was not big enough to be a dragon's lair. The main thing was to stay calm, not to panic. "There are no monsters here, Henwyn," he told himself firmly.

Just as he said it, a monster came around the corner.

It was so large that, at first, Henwyn did not understand that it was a living creature. It looked more as if a small building with lighted windows was pushing its way through the tunnel towards him. Then he realized that the lighted windows were horn-paned lanterns, mounted on straps and harnesses which criss-crossed a blunt, furry head and powerful shoulders. By their light Henwyn saw the creature's huge, claw-fingered hands, its wet pink nose, its mouth opening to let out a gust of hot, foul breath and a terrible shrill cry: "Eeeeeeeeee!"

"Eeeee!" went Henwyn in return. When he was safe at home he always felt pretty brave, and found it easy to imagine himself fighting off monsters, but when actual monsters needed fighting he tended to feel much less certain of himself. He fumbled his sword out of its sheath, and the creature's tiny, half-blind eyes caught the flash of lantern light reflecting from the blade. It halted, a monstrous thing in mole-shape, snuffling at Henwyn's unfamiliar scent.

Henwyn glanced behind him to where the tunnel disappeared around another bend into shadow. He wanted to run from the terrible beast, but how could he know there was not something worse waiting for him in the darkness there? Besides, he did not want to stray too far from the hole he had dropped in through. What if that was the only exit from this horrid burrow, and he never found his way back to it?

Gruff voices were shouting. He looked back at where the monster mole crouched, and saw more lamps appearing, held by small figures who came scrambling over the creature's head or pushing past its flanks. Some had hold of chains attached to its harness and were tugging at them, trying to make it move forward again.

"What's afoot?" Henwyn heard one shout.

"Summat's frighted the diremole!"

"There's summat blockin' the way!"

"Roof fall?"

"Tunnel worm, maybe?"

"Nay, it's a person!"

The lantern bearers strode forward, through the vapour of their monster's hot breath. They were short and stocky and most had bushy beards. They wore close-fitting caps of iron or leather; dirty tunics; big boots; broad belts stuffed with tools. None of them was more than three feet tall.

Dwarves! thought Henwyn wonderingly. They were as common in the olden tales as goblins, but he'd never heard of anyone who'd met them in real life. Still, he'd never expected to meet goblins or trolls or giants in real life and he had run into all of those things since he arrived at Clovenstone, so he was not too astonished. And unlike goblins, trolls and giants, dwarves were not meant to be evil; in the stories they were always honest, sturdy creatures; swift to anger, maybe, but skilled smiths and miners.

Of course! That was it! He had fallen into a dwarf mine!

He lowered his sword and said with a smile, "Greetings, noble dwarves! I'm Henwyn of Adherak!"

The dwarves held up their lamps to shine on Henwyn's face. Their leader came closer. A candle was mounted on his leather skullcap and strands of wax had run down from it to hang like icicles from his bushy eyebrows and the rims of his big ears. He glowered up at Henwyn.

"This ain't a *person*," he growled. "It's a dirty *bigling*!"

The pie was very good. It was one of those meat pies with a whole egg baked into it – by magic, it seemed to Skarper (who didn't know much about cooking). He ate it and then looked at the other pie and wondered if that one had an egg in it too. He decided to take a few bites, just to find out.

It did, and he was just wiping the last of the crumbs from his mouth with the back of a paw when a word came into his mind. *Dwarves*. It was a long time since he'd read it, but he knew it had appeared in a few of the ancient scrolls he'd read in the bumwipe heaps at Clovenstone. The dwarves had been miners, dwellers in the deep places under the mountains. They had harnessed the great diremoles of the north to dig their tunnels for them, and they'd been fierce enemies of goblinkind, fighting terrible battles against them in the dark beneath the fells. And dwarf mines had chimneys, in order to let smithy-smoke out and fresh air in.

"Henwyn!" he shouted, leaping to his feet with a pie-y belch and scampering downhill. "Henwyn!"

*

"A bigling," growled the dwarf again. Behind him, his companions pulled out knives and hammers, and hefted pickaxes. "A sneaky bigling, come sneaking down here to spy on us. Where are your friends, bigling? Or did you come alone?"

"Quite alone," said Henwyn, sensing that these short strangers did not like him. "And I'm not a spy. Why would I want to spy on you? Whatever you're up to down here with your giant mole, it's your business, not mine. I'll be on my way. . ."

Just then it began to rain small stones and clots of soil. "Roof fall!" shouted some of the dwarves, scrambling backwards. But it was not the roof falling, only Skarper. With a shrill cry of "Bumcakes!", he dropped through the same hole that Henwyn had made and landed on top of the dwarf chief.

There was a moment of confusion: shouts of pain and anger; dwarves milling about; lanterns dropped. The giant mole went into a panic again and the dwarves who held it were almost dragged off their feet as they fought to control it. Shadows leaped madly up the tunnel walls. As Skarper scrambled off the dwarf chief, some of the other dwarves saw him and started to shout, "Goblin! Goblin!"

"He's all right," Henwyn tried explaining. "He's with me!"

That didn't seem to help.

"Run!" shouted Skarper.

Henwyn looked up helplessly at the little scrap of sky that showed above them, like a torn blue cloth stuck to the tunnel roof. There was nothing for it, though: Skarper was shoving him urgently along the tunnel into the dark, and behind Skarper all the dwarves who were not busy trying to control the skittish mole were surging forward, raising their picks and shovels menacingly.

So Henwyn did as he was told and ran, following Skarper along the twists and dips of the mysterious tunnel, through darkness so deep that it was like being blindfolded. Luckily for Henwyn he was young and sure-footed and his legs were long. As for Skarper, running away was what Skarper did best. They soon outpaced the stocky, panting dwarves.

The tunnel branched, and branched again. The sounds of pursuit grew faint, but they ran on, until they began to hear other sounds, and a red glow filled the tunnel ahead of them. They slowed, peeked cautiously around a corner, and looked out over an immense cavern, into which a dozen other tunnels opened. Scores of dwarves were at work there, attacking the rocky walls with picks and drills, climbing rickety wooden ladders to reach higher levels, loading shiny rocks into huge baskets. More of the gigantic moles were busy there too, some dragging the filled baskets away on sleds, some with heavy iron shovel blades lashed to their blunt heads, bulldozing heaps of spoil aside. The whole scene was lit by the glow of an enormous forge which had been built at the far end of the cavern. Dwarf children were feeding dried mole droppings into the furnace, while strong-armed dwarf smiths hammered out new pickaxe blades, drill bits and iron hats.

Luckily the dwarves were far too busy to glance up and see Henwyn and Skarper gaping at them, and the din of their work drowned out the two companions' voices.

"There are loads of them!" said Henwyn. "I thought dwarves lived in the far north. What are they doing under the Bonehills?"

"They must be on the move," said Skarper. "I 'spect it's all this new magic, mucking things up again. Come on, we'd better find our way out and get back to Clovenstone. Princess Ned should hear about these diggers. I'm not sure what they're up to but they're bad news, I think."

"Good idea," said Henwyn. "I shall be glad to see the sky again. And all this running about in burrows has given me an appetite. Once we're safe away from this mine we'll stop and eat those pies."

"Pies?" said Skarper guiltily. "Ah. . . There's bad news about those, too."

RETURN TO CLOVENSTONE

Clovenstone had changed. The long Outer Wall was still there, girdling the streets and buildings of the walled town, which rose steeply to the crag of Meneth Eskern in the centre. The Inner Wall stood too, its seven towers ringing the crag like a stony crown. But the old, dark heart of Clovenstone, the Keep that once rose from the crag's summit, was gone. Even its ruins had been cleared away, and in its place a garden was being made, with lawns and flower beds and stands of young trees. On the grassy parade grounds where, long ago, the Lych Lord's goblin armies had marched, young apple trees had been planted in rows. The goblins who lived in the towers of the Inner Wall spent slightly less time fighting and robbing each other now, and slightly more time cheese-making: Clovenstone cheese was becoming quite a well-known delicacy in the Softlands, the green country that lay to the south, beyond Oeth Moor.

On top of the tallest of those towers, the Blackspike, there rested an old ship. This was the home of Princess Eluned, "Ned" to her friends, who was the creator of the garden. She had become ruler of Clovenstone after all the biggest and most vicious goblins perished in the fall of the Keep, and after Henwyn, who was the true heir to the place, had decided that he wasn't cut out to be a Dark Lord.

Ned was not aboard her ship when Skarper and Henwyn returned to Clovenstone next day. They spent half the morning looking for her, and eventually found her round at the eastern side of the Inner Wall, gazing out across Natterdon Mire, the broad, misty marsh which had swallowed up the ruins there.

It was a place to which Ned often came. During the great adventures of the year before, she had encountered the boglins: savage, froggish creatures who dwelled among those mires and meres. She'd often wondered since what had become of them. Their king, Poldew, was dead, and his hall lay in ruins, but what of the boglins themselves? Were they still watching secretly from behind the mists and reed beds which screened their perilous pools and secret sinkholes? Or had they slunk away, across the Outer

Wall, into the still wider marshes which lay north of Clovenstone? And what of the monster they had woken, the dreadful, wet, dragonish dampdrake? Did it still slumber in the deep, dark mere at Bospoldew, waiting for more gifts of human blood?

Partly it was fear that kept the boglins in Ned's thoughts (for no queen likes to have a tribe of hostile savages living within a stone's throw of her realm). Mostly, though, it was just curiosity. As a girl, she had been taught that there were no such things as giants or goblins or twiglings. Since she came to Clovenstone she had made friends with all of them, and with the silly, flighty cloud maidens as well. Even the grumpy old troll who lurked under the bridge over the River Oeth was civil to her now. So it hurt her that the boglins would not even talk with her. Sometimes she took little gifts down to the margins of their marsh, to show them that she meant no harm to them. A basket of cheese; some windfall apples; a tray of fresh-baked scones. The gifts always vanished, but not while Ned was watching. She never saw a trace of boglins.

When Skarper and Henwyn found her that day, she was sitting quietly on a ruined wall, watching an apple and blackberry crumble which she had left on a tussock at the edge of the nearest lagoon. The marsh mist wove strange shapes around her, the mossy ruins came and went like ghosts, and when Skarper and Henwyn stepped out of the reeds she jumped up with a scream, thinking for a moment that they were boglins.

"Oh!" she said. "I did not expect you to come home from your adventures so soon! Did you find anything interesting among the Bonehills?"

"*Among* them, no," said Henwyn. "But *beneath* them; ah, that is another story!"

"Then you had best tell it to me," said Ned, glancing quickly at her crumble to make sure it was still there.

"The Dark Lady of Clovenstone" they called Eluned, down in the Softlands where news from the north came mixed with lots of rumours. In Coriander and Nantivey and places like that, they imagined her as a cold and terrible queen, presiding over a court of goblins. They would have been astonished to see the real Ned standing there, in her faded old russet dress with her apron still tied round it, a smudge of flour on her nose and her grey hair done up in untidy pigtails, listening to the tale of Henwyn and Skarper's adventure.

When they had finished, she sat down on her wall again, frowning thoughtfully. "Dwarves," she said. "I do not know much about them. I haven't heard of them for years, although when I was a little girl I remember hearing merchants from my father's harbour at Porthstrewy talk of how their grandfathers had done business with dwarf-holds further up the Nibbled Coast. A wild, rugged country lies there, between the Bonehills and the Winter Sea. Dwarvendom, they call it, and at its heart lies the great citadel of the dwarves, Dwarvenholm in the Delverdale. How nice they sound, those northern names! I wonder if these dwarves you saw could really have tunnelled all the way from there?"

"With those dreadful diremoles to dig their runs for them, I should think they could!" said Henwyn.

"They'll bring trouble with them," Skarper promised. "Dwarves is always trouble. Stubby little back-stabbing goblin-killers, that's all they are. Every goblin knows that."

Ned smiled. "And every human being knows that goblins are fearsome, red-eyed people-killers, Skarper dear. These dwarves are probably not nearly as bad as you think; you just made a bad impression by falling on their heads. And as long as they stay out in the Bonehills, beyond the walls of Clovenstone, I do not see that they are any business of ours. Let them do as they like up there. It does not concern us."

Henwyn shook his head. Ned's words were wise, but he was still troubled by the things he'd seen beneath the mountain. "I wish we knew more about these dwarves. What are they doing up there? And why?"

"You should ask Fentongoose," said Ned. "He is very learned, and he is bound to know something about dwarves. You could take him my blackberry and apple crumble, too. The boglins do not seem to want it."

But when she turned to pick the dish up, the tussock where it had stood was empty. While the three friends had been talking, the boglins had come and taken it, then vanished like ghosts back into the mazes of the marsh.

Fentongoose was one of the three self-styled sorcerers who had arrived in Clovenstone the previous year, believing themselves to be the heirs of the Lych Lord. They'd been wrong about that, and two of them, Prawl and Carnglaze, had gone back home to Coriander. Only Fentongoose had stayed on, acting as hatchling master to the young goblins. In his spare time he hunted for scraps of ancient knowledge among those mounds of valuable scrolls and ancient books which the goblins called "the bumwipe heaps".

Fentongoose made his home in a big, dilapidated guardhouse at the foot of Blackspike Tower. That was where Henwyn and Skarper went to visit him, after their talk with Princess Ned. A fire was glowing in the hearth there, and lined up in front of it were a dozen football-sized stone eggs. Fentongoose had fetched them a few days earlier from the slowsilver lake deep beneath Clovenstone. Soon they would crack open, and a dozen new goblin hatchlings would spill out and need to be taught that Hitting Other Goblins was Bad. That sort of lesson wasn't easy to drum into thick goblin skulls, so Fentongoose knew he had hard work ahead of him. In the meantime he was taking things easy in his favourite chair, his feet up on a padded stool, a plate of Princess Ned's biscuits on a table beside him and an old book open on his lap.

"Dwarves, eh?" he said, when Skarper and Henwyn told him what they'd seen. "Yes, I know a little about them. There was a scroll I found last month. Young Libnog was heading off to the pooing holes with it, but I thought it looked interesting and persuaded him to part with it. *On Dwarves and Their Ways*, it was called. It came from a time before the Lych Lord, when the dwarves were still one of the powers of the world. Honest, hard-working creatures, by all accounts."

"Hard-working, certainly," said Henwyn, thinking of the huge mine the dwarves had hollowed for themselves under the Bonehills. "But are they friendly?"

"Not really," admitted Fentongoose. "They like

to keep to themselves. When the first dwarves made contact with the first men they were shocked to discover that we are so much larger than them. 'Biglings', they call us, and I'm afraid they see us as clodhopping, overgrown, stupid and clumsy."

"But that's not true!" said Henwyn, and he thumped Fentongoose's table for emphasis, upset the plate, and catapulted the biscuits out of the window.

"Perhaps not," said Fentongoose. "But the dwarves believe it, and think that they are far superior to us. However, their scorn for us is as nothing compared with the scorn they feel towards goblins, whom they see as mere animals, interested only in food and violence."

"That's not true either!" shouted Skarper, over the noise from outside, where a whole bunch of goblins were fighting over the biscuits.

Fentongoose wasn't listening. There was a great deal of knowledge stored up in his head, and it wasn't often that anyone asked to hear some of it: he was not going to be distracted from his history lesson.

"Dwarves are mortal beings, much like men," he said. "They are born of dwarf mothers and grow up slowly, like ourselves. Once they lived under the open sky, although their love for minerals and metals soon led them underground. It's said that the old dwarf mines and tunnels run beneath every part of the Westlands. But when the first men arrived, the dwarves retreated into the hills. They withdrew to their great citadel, a hollowed-out mountain called Dwarvenholm, in the valley of Delverdale, in the far north. They shut its great burnished doors behind them and became creatures of the under-places. They are seldom seen in sunlight nowadays.

"But there was always trade between Dwarvenholm and the lands of men. The dwarves were great workers of metal. Slowsilver was the stuff they valued above all else. That's why they hated goblins, who guarded the natural pools of slowsilver where they hatched, down in the deep places beneath the hills. They fought the goblins, and drained the pools. The dwarf-smiths knew how to work magic into items forged from slowsilver. Even in the Lych Lord's time, most of the magical weapons and artefacts in the world came from the smithies of Dwarvenholm.

"But the magic faded, and the power of the dwarves declined. I am glad to hear that they are mining again. Perhaps we shall be able to trade with them. I wonder if they like cheese?"

"Oh, look!" said Henwyn, pointing to the hearth. Several of the stone eggs there had started to jiggle. As Skarper and Fentongoose turned to stare, a large black crack spread over one of them. They hurried across the hearthrug to bend over it as it shattered. A small, damp, speckled goblin blinked out at them.

"Hello, little fellow!" said Fentongoose kindly, all thought of dwarves forgotten. "Welcome to Clovenstone."

The hatchling snatched up a log from the hearth and belted him over the head with it. Around it, the other eggs were starting to hatch too, and the new goblins bared their teeth and clenched their tiny fists as they tumbled out into the ashes of the fire, as eager for mischief as every hatchling before them. How were they supposed to know that things had changed at Clovenstone?

THE SURVEYOR

Nobody gave very much thought to dwarves for the next few weeks. The new hatchlings turned out to be much too boisterous for Fentongoose to look after on his own, so Henwyn, Ned, Skarper, and even Skarper's batch-brothers Libnog and Yabber had to help him. Princess Ned was determined that this new batch of goblins would have a gentler start in life than the older goblins of Clovenstone, so everyone spent a lot of time prising makeshift weapons out of their paws, showing them how to use the pooing holes, and trying to teach them not to steal, or strangle one another, or throw one another out of high windows.

Summer was over and the long, golden days of early autumn were beginning. The first frost had come before Skarper and Henwyn had cause to think about the dwarves again.

They had gone out with Henwyn's bow, hunting rabbits along the shores of the wood, which reached almost to the foot of the Inner Wall round on the north-east side. Towards lunchtime a light rain began to fall. At least, they thought it was rain, until Henwyn looked up and saw that it was actually a big gang of goblins on the battlements of Growler Tower having a Who-Can-Pee-the-Furthest competition. Hurrying to escape the downpour, they ran away from the wall into a gully between some craggy outcroppings of rock. There, to their surprise, they found a trio of sturdy little figures hard at work.

One of the dwarves was busy with a hammer, chipping pieces off the rock. Another had set up a complicated-looking instrument on a spindly-legged tripod and was squinting through it, muttering to himself, and scratching notes on a slate which hung from a string around his neck. A third stood ready with a basket to collect up the chippings which the first was making. They all looked much the same as the dwarves Skarper and Henwyn had encountered in the mine, except that all three wore wide-brimmed leather hats and goggles of dark volcanic glass to protect their eyes from the daylight.

"Dwarves!" said Skarper.

"Goblins!" said the dwarf with the basket.

"No, one goblin, and one bigling!"

"What are you doing in Clovenstone?" demanded Henwyn.

"Hush!" snapped the dwarf with the tripod, not glancing up from the sheet of slate, where he was scratching some important-looking calculations.

The one with the basket came bustling over to confront the new arrivals. She was a girl dwarf, Henwyn realized; hairier than most human girls, with thick fair eyebrows which met in the middle and a faint, fair moustache, but she had no beard to speak of, just thick blonde braids which dangled almost to the ground. She whispered, "You must be quiet, bigling. My father is making important calculations."

"But how did you get in here?"

"We just walked," said the girl, pointing away north-westerly across the woods and ruins. "We came through the big wall where it has tumbled down and followed the 'croppings."

"The whats?"

"The outcroppings of rock. My father believes this whole crag is part of the same great batholith that forms the central Bonehills."

"Ah!" said Henwyn brightly, and looked at Skarper in the hope that Skarper might know what "batholith" meant.

Skarper didn't.

"A batholith is a large mass of igneous rock made from magma which formed deep beneath the earth's crust," explained the girl brightly, sensing their confusion.

"Etty," said the dwarf with the tripod, "hush! We dwarves do not waste our words on biglings, lass, nor on goblins neither."

The third dwarf, who had been hammering away all through this talk, suddenly turned, holding up a chunk of rock. "Look, Durgar!" he called. "Flecks of white pyrites!"

Durgar nodded, satisfied. "'Tis as I thought. White pyrites is a sure sign that there is slowsilver nearby. I suspect a vast reservoir of molten slowsilver lies beneath yonder crag." He pointed towards Meneth Eskern, the crag on which the Inner Wall and all its towers stood.

"Well of course there is!" said Skarper. "This is Clovenstone! The lava lake lies down below, where all us goblins hatch from. We could have told you that. Not that that's any business of yours."

The dwarves ignored him, except for the girl Etty, who gave him and Henwyn a quick smile. Her father was pointing now towards the Bonehill Mountains, saying, "We shall dig a new spur off the Milk Ghyll mine and strike into it from this side."

"What's he on about?" asked Skarper, turning helplessly to his friend.

Henwyn said, "Are you talking about digging up Clovenstone?"

Durgar glanced at him without interest. "Not digging up, bigling. Tunnelling under. Scooping out. That lake of slowsilver can't just be left there, serving no purpose, brewing up goblins. It needs to be extracted, processed, put to use."

"But it's ours!" cried Skarper.

"I can't help that," said Durgar. He had packed his measuring device away and was folding up his tripod.

"But it belongs to goblins!" said Skarper. "It's always been there!"

"'Belongs', does it?" said Durgar. "What lies beneath the earth belongs to dwarves, and to dwarves only: that's been the way of things since the world's beginnings. When the Lych Lord ruled this place, his spells and armies kept us out, but there's no Lych Lord any more."

"No!" agreed Henwyn. "There's Princess Ned, the Dark Lady of Clovenstone. She won't let you come undermining us!"

Durgar looked thoughtful. "I don't see as how she can stop us," he said.

Henwyn couldn't see how, either. The goblins who

lived in Clovenstone weren't big enough or brave enough or organized enough to be good warriors. He couldn't imagine them fighting the dwarves and their dreadful diremoles. Princess Ned did not really hold with fighting, anyway; she thought arguments were best solved by talking. "At least come and *talk* to her!" he said helplessly.

Durgar swung his pack up on to his back. "It's none of my concern, bigling. I'm just a surveyor. If this Dark Ned-Lady of yours has summat to say, then she should come and talk to Overseer Glunt: Overseer Glunt is the dwarf in charge of our operations here."

He strode off down the gully towards the shadows of the wood. The other dwarves followed, moving swiftly for folk with such short legs.

"Wait!" Henwyn shouted after them. "Where do we find this Overseer Glunt?"

Only the girl Etty bothered to look back. "At the mine in the mountains!" she called, then went hurrying after her father.

"Well," Henwyn shouted, "well, er, you shall certainly be hearing from Princess Ned about this!"

Skarper danced about with frustration at his side. "Don't just stand there shouting!" he urged. "Use your bow and arrows!" He'd have grabbed the bow and shot the dwarves himself, except he wasn't sure how to use it, and goblins were rubbish at shooting arrows. "You could get them all from here, if you're quick!" he said.

"What, shoot them in the back?" said Henwyn, appalled.

"You could shout first, so they turn round, then shoot them."

"It still wouldn't be very heroic. And one of them is a girl!"

"Is he?" (Skarper was still a bit vague about the difference between girls and boys.)

"Anyway," said Henwyn firmly, "it would make no difference. We saw scores of dwarves in that mine, and there were probably hundreds more that we didn't see. If we killed these three, their friends would come, armed and armoured and ready to fight. No, we must take news of this meeting to Princess Ned. When she hears what the little villains are planning – mining beneath Clovenstone – draining the lava lake – oh, she will have something to say about it, all right!"

GLUNT

Princess Ned certainly did have something to say about it. She loved Clovenstone, and she thought the goblins were coming along very well. She was not going to let all her hard work be undermined. The next day, along with Skarper and Henwyn, Fentongoose, and a small group of the less stupid goblins, she set out for the dwarf mines.

The valley where Henwyn had fallen through the dwarves' roof had undergone a startling change since he and Skarper had first seen it. Where one chimney had stood there were now dozens, dotted all over the valley floor and perched precariously on the steep scree slopes and crags on either side. Here and there metal pipes stuck out of the hillsides, and water gushed from these and went gurgling off down new stream beds to the river.

The chimneys were mostly for ventilation, Fentongoose said, but a thin haze of smoke still hung above most of them, and the mountain wind smelled faintly of burning diremole dung. Skarper put an ear to the ground and heard hammers beating faintly, far below.

Henwyn was planning to lead Ned to the chimney which he and Skarper had discovered, but Ned was tired after the long walk (there were no horses in Clovenstone, and she was not a young princess). She sat down on a stone, clutching her side and waving at everyone to be quiet until she had caught her breath. When she could speak again she said, "We shall meet the dwarf chief here. Come, Nurdle; blow your horn."

The goblin called Nurdle stepped forward: a little bandy-legged Chilli Hat from Redcap Tower, who carried a huge brass trumpet. He raised it to his snout and blew as hard as he could. A deep, tuneless fart went echoing up and down the valley, startling jackdaws from the crags. At Nurdle's side a goblin named Scratch unfurled the new banner of Clovenstone, a silver comet on a black field, stitched by Princess Ned herself. It flapped loudly in the wind, and Ned's long ash-grey hair blew out sideways like a second banner as she called, "O Dwarves! I bring you greeting from all the peoples of Clovenstone!"

There was no answer. Skarper put an ear to the ground again. The thud and rumble of the dwarves' work went on unchanging down below. "Perhaps they are too busy to talk to us," he said.

"Too busy to talk to the Lady of Clovenstone?" tutted Fentongoose. "How rude!"

"Perhaps they simply cannot hear us," said Princess Ned, who always liked to think the best of people.

But the dwarves had heard them. Their tunnels extended far beyond the mountains now, almost to the Outer Wall of Clovenstone itself. They were small trial tunnels, and the dwarves had not yet built tall chimneys to carry air down into them, but here and there, hidden among piles of stones and clumps of tussock grass, iron trumpets stuck up into the world above, and these trumpets served as both ventilation shafts and listening posts. The dwarves in the great burrow under the valley had known of the coming of the princess Ned and her friends for a long time.

Not far from where the visitors stood waiting, a concealed hatch in the hillside suddenly creaked open. A bearded, scowling dwarf stuck his head out and blinked at them through his black glass goggles. "What do you lot want?" he asked rudely.

"We would like to talk with your chief," Ned replied.

The dwarf stared at her for a moment. Then he grunted and drew his head back inside. The hatch shut with a bang, which sent loose rocks clattering and bounding down the screes above.

"They seem hostile!" said Fentongoose, in a worried voice. "I do wish we had brought Fraddon with us. They would not dare to harm us if we had a giant with us."

"We are not here to fight them, nor to frighten them," said Princess Ned. "We are here to talk."

"Can we fight them when we've *finished* talking?" asked Nurdle, who was a goblin of the old school.

"No," Ned told him firmly.

Just then the hatch opened again. This time three dwarves came out, one after the other. Their leader, Skarper noted with a sinking feeling, was the very one whose head he'd dropped on when he fell into the mine. The dwarf folded his arms and stared contemptuously at Ned and her followers through the black lenses of his goggles. "Well?" he asked. "I'm Glunt, overseer of this section. What do you mean by coming here, bigling?"

"Greetings, O Glunt," said Ned, and bowed low. "I am Eluned of Clovenstone, and these are my friends. We have come to introduce ourselves and to ask you what brings you so far from your homelands, and how we can be good neighbours to you."

Glunt snorted. "As for introductions, I've met that bigling beside you already, when he crashed through my roof, and I've no interest in meeting the other one, nor any of these maggot folk you call your friends. As for homelands, everything that lies beneath the earth is the homeland of the dwarves. And as for being good neighbours, the best way you can do that is by keeping out of our way and letting us work in peace. Now good day to you."

He turned away and was about to go back into the hill when Ned called out, "Master Glunt, what is it that you are digging for? Is it true that you mean to drain the lake of slowsilver which lies beneath Clovenstone?"

Glunt glanced back at her. "Aye," he said. "Slowsilver is no use to you biglings. Only we dwarves have the skill to process and to forge it, and work the smithy magic into things we make from it."

"But that lake is the heart of Clovenstone," said Ned. "It is where all goblins hatch from."

"All the more reason then to drain it," said Glunt. "Anyway, it ain't up to me. I have my orders from the Head."

"The Head? Is that your king?" asked Ned, but Glunt ignored her. Her polite smile was beginning to look strained. She said, "Master Glunt, the lake is within the walls of Clovenstone. It belongs to us."

Glunt gave another snort. "'*Belongs*', does it? Dwarves don't believe in things '*belonging*'. That's a word that only greedy goblins and gold-hungry biglings use. Dwarves hold all things in common, and the Head distributes them where they are needed. It is our right to mine and use everything that lies under the earth, stone or metal, fire or water. You want to talk of 'belonging', do you? Well then, this world belongs to the dwarves, bigling. You and your type are just pests who creep about upon its crust."

That was when Ned's temper finally broke. Nobody had ever called her a pest before. She clenched her fists at her sides and her voice trembled as she called out, "We shall stop you! We shall fight you if we have to!"

Glunt just shrugged. "You can try," he agreed. "You'll lose, though. And one way or another we shall drain that slowsilver and send it back to Delverdale for processing. Good day to you." And he went back into the hill with his two lieutenants following, and the door banged shut behind them.

The wind blew, the chimneys smoked, the banner with the silver comet fluttered on its staff. A few rocks, dislodged by the slamming of the door, came bounding down the hillside. One hit Henwyn on the shin.

"Ow!" he said.

"What are we going to do?" asked Skarper.

"I don't know," said Princess Ned. "You heard what Glunt said, and I don't believe he was bluffing or exaggerating. I don't think he has enough imagination to bluff or to exaggerate. The dwarves of old had mighty armies and cunning engines of war. The Lych Lord's armies could have held them off, but Clovenstone has no army now."

"Then we shall start one!" Henwyn cried, hopping about with his hands clasped to his bruised shin. "There are plenty of swords and shields in the old armouries! We must learn to use them! The twiglings will help us, and Fraddon, who has the strength of a hundred dwarves."

Fentongoose tugged thoughtfully at his beard. "I do not think the twiglings or Fraddon can fight under the earth," he said. "And that is where the attack will come. The walls of Clovenstone will be little help against an enemy who can tunnel beneath them. And dwarf warriors are ruthless, skilled and disciplined. Can our goblins really stand against such a foe?"

Everybody turned to look at Nurdle, who was picking his nose and staring thoughtfully at the bogies.

"I fear that Clovenstone is doomed," said Fentongoose sadly.

Henwyn turned away. "It's so unfair!" he said, and kicked a boulder. "Ow!"

In the days which followed, Henwyn looked everywhere for an army. The goblins would fight – fighting was still what goblins did best – but Fentongoose was right; it was doubtful they could defend Clovenstone against the dwarves for long.

So Henwyn went into the woods to ask the twiglings for their help. They might look like the heads of ragged witches' brooms with two beady eyes stuck on, but they could be fierce when they felt like it – he remembered how they'd captured him on his first day in Clovenstone, with their strange earth magic and sharp wooden spears.

But the twiglings just laughed at him and threw acorns down on his head before scampering off along their maze of mossy branches. They were creatures of the trees, and they mistrusted both men and goblins. Unless the dwarves threatened their woods they would not see any need to fight.

He walked down to Westerly Gate to ask Fraddon whether any of his relatives might be persuaded to help. But the old giant shook his head. "It is not the way of things, for giants to fight dwarves. Giants are stone-born, growing inside the mountains. Dwarves have always respected us. They leave young giants alone when they find them, and in return we split the hills open for them when we are born. If that were to change, if unfriendliness were to grow between giants and dwarves, that would be a very bad thing. And anyway, we giants are very few."

Walking home afterwards, Henwyn said to Skarper, "Is there no one who will help us?"

"Pity there aren't any heroes about, like in those old stories of yours," said Skarper, plucking a nice juicy toadstool and nibbling it thoughtfully as they climbed the steep way towards the Inner Wall.

"What?" said Henwyn.

"Heroes. You know, big fellows, all in mail-coats, riding great horses and waving dirty big swords about. If we had a few of them to help us we could send the dwarves packing, probably."

"Skarper!" shouted Henwyn. "You're a wonder!"

Skarper finished the toadstool and burped. "Am I?"

"A treasure! A genius!"

"Oh. Good."

"We shall bring heroes to Clovenstone! For there *are* still heroes in the world! The greatest warriors of all the Westlands are summoned to Coriander, where the High King lives. It is his job to keep peace between the different kingdoms, and stop them squabbling. The heroes dwell there in his castle of Boskennack. When any kingdom finds itself in peril, from brigands, say, or pirates, the High King sends his heroes forth to defeat wrongdoers and restore the peace. He has an army, too, to help them if need be. Of course! We shall go to Coriander, Skarper, and lay our case before the High King!"

"But he won't help goblins, will he?" asked Skarper.

"He will have to! It is the law of the Westlands that the High King must send aid to any realm that asks for it. And is not Clovenstone one of the realms of the Westlands?"

"Well, I suppose. . ."

"And is not Ned its queen? Ned is not a goblin."

"Yes. . ." said Skarper uncertainly. But he was remembering what Henwyn seemed to have forgotten: that things in real life were not always exactly as they were in old stories.

He had no better ideas, though, and Henwyn was already striding off towards Blackspike to find Princess Ned and tell her of his plan, so Skarper shrugged off his doubts and hurried after him. "Wait for me!" he called.

"Wait for me. . ." The wind took Skarper's words and wafted them away between the ruins and the twisty thorn trees until they fell into the mouth of an iron trumpet that had been thrust up between two flagstones there. Down the trumpet's long iron throat they went echoing, following the rest of Skarper and Henwyn's conversation, until they reached the ear of the dwarf girl Etty.

The dwarves had been more cautious about being seen above ground in Clovenstone since Princess Ned had paid her call on Overseer Glunt, but they had dug a couple of experimental tunnels underneath, joining up with sections of the old city's sewers and underground passages left over from the Lych Lord's time. There were all sorts of forgotten cellars and dungeons in that part of Clovenstone, and it was in one of these that Etty's father had stationed her, with orders to listen out for any activity among the biglings and their goblin friends up above.

It had been a dull job until now. Etty would much rather have been out surveying. But she was obedient, as a good dwarf should be, and she did not argue with her father. She had been whiling away the time embroidering a sampler with the motto of Dwarvendom: *The Head Knows All & The Head Knows Best*. She knew that she had to practise her needlework, for the days when she was married and expected to sew work clothes for her husband and children, but she was not a good needlewoman; she kept stabbing her fingers with the needle, she had lost her thimble, and the runic letters on the sampler looked distinctly wobbly. She was quite relieved when she heard the voices of Skarper and Henwyn come echoing tinnily down the listening pipe. Dropping her needlework, she snatched up a stylus and a fresh slate and began to copy down their words. It was hard to catch them all, for the long pipe distorted their voices, but she caught most of them, and her eyes widened as their meaning became clear.

"Oh dear!" she said, quickly reading back what she had written on the slate. She had been told to stay at her post until another dwarf was sent to relieve her, but this looked important. She dithered a moment, listened at the pipe again to check that Skarper and Henwyn had moved out of earshot, and then hurried away, finding her way as easily as a diremole through narrow passages, old oubliettes and new-dug dwarf-ways to the edge of Clovenstone, where her father was supervising the digging of broader tunnels.

She had been right to go. Durgar was as concerned as she had been when he saw what Skarper and Henwyn had been discussing. "Heroes, eh?" he said, frowning as he deciphered Etty's hastily scratched runes.

A few minutes later they were mounted on a diremole, being carried swiftly into the heart of the new workings under the Bonehills.

Etty did not like diremoles; they were so big, and so savage-seeming. But she did not want to let Durgar or the mole's driver see that she was afraid, so she concentrated on looking about her as the creature went lumbering along the miles and miles of new tunnel.

It was astonishing what dwarves had accomplished here in the space of a few short months! Wherever she looked she saw new galleries opening, new burrows being hollowed, and mined ore being loaded into wagons for transport back to Delverdale. Even she was surprised. For most of her life things had been quiet in Dwarvendom; work had gone on steadily, but never at this frantic pace. Since the Lych Lord's star returned, all that had changed. Diremoles, which had been rare when she was little, were breeding again in great numbers deep in the northern fells, allowing the dwarves to extend their mines into all sorts of new places. The smithy magic had begun to work again, too, just as it did in tales of olden times, and the spell-smiths cast their spells on picks and drill bits, which meant the miners could dig deeper and faster than they had before. The Head was sending out orders at a frantic rate, as if it, too, had been revived by all the new magic washing around the Westlands. How strange to think that a new star up there in the sky could affect the lives of dwarves here underground. . .

They came to a cavern where huge sections of pipe were being assembled. Overseer Glunt was looking on, striding up and down with a look of satisfaction on his usually angry face and his hands in the pockets of his moleskin coat. He greeted Etty and Durgar almost cheerfully when they scrambled down off their diremole and went over to join him. Even when Durgar showed him Etty's record of the conversation she had overheard his good mood did not vanish entirely, although a frown appeared between his bushy eyebrows.

"Asking help from the bigling king, are they? They don't realize what they're up against, the fools. They think a bunch of overgrown biglings can help them stop us? And yet. . ." He paused and looked thoughtful, tapping the edge of Etty's slate against his teeth. "We do not want any more biglings nosing around, not until our great work is complete."

"And what is this great work, Overseer?" asked Durgar. "All these tunnels and pipes; warriors and miners being ordered hither and yon. . ."

"You'll know when you need to know, Durgar,"

snapped Glunt. "It's the Head's orders. The Head Knows All and the Head Knows Best, you know."

"Oh, aye," agreed Durgar, "but. . ."

"I have an idea!" said Glunt, brightening again. He waved the slate under Durgar's nose. "Go asking favours of the king, would they? Well, why should they deserve his favours? Isn't Dwarvendom one of the kingdoms of the Westlands too? We shall send our own ambassadors to the High King!"

"But we don't have any ambassadors, overseer."

"We do now," snapped Glunt. "Gather your stuff, Durgar, and pick yourself a couple of companions. You'll be leaving for Coriander this very day."

URBAN TROLLS AND UNSOLD VOLUMES

It was almost a hundred miles from Clovenstone to Coriander: six days' hard walking across the wild uplands of Oeth Moor, past the clear waters of Lyn Glas and the frowning scarps of the Calchoen hills. A road had run that way back in the Lych Lord's time, but nowadays most of its stones were overgrown with grass, or had been dragged away by farmers to wall their fields. For most of the way Skarper and Henwyn trod a wet track paved only with puddles. At last they reached the green valley where the River Ystwyth ran, and as they struck south along its banks the track improved and the villages grew larger and more frequent, until the river widened at last into the great, grey, restless sea, and the road swung westerly and led them down to Coriander.

The city of the High Kings of the Westlands

lay upon the shore of a broad bay, whose waters were dotted with many-coloured sails as bright as petals. Along the waterfront were quays, shipyards, chandlers' shops, ropemakers' lofts and big, stone-built warehouses. Inland the houses were mostly built of wood, painted in red and blue and yellow, so that when Henwyn and Skarper first came in sight of it the city looked like a cheery patchwork counterpane spread over the hills. Just offshore, on a rocky island linked to the city by a causeway and a steady coming-and-going of ferry boats, stood Boskennack, the castle of the High King, with long banners rippling in the sea breeze and shining copper spires a-glitter in the afternoon sun.

"There!" said Henwyn, pointing proudly. (He'd never been within sixty miles of Coriander, but he'd heard so many stories of it that Boskennack seemed as familiar to him as his father's cheesery.) "That is where the High King lives, His Royal Majesty King Padstow the Twelfth, who is a direct descendant of King Kennack himself. And that lesser tower, lower down, is the Hall of Heroes. It's there that we shall find the brave warriors whose swords shall defend Clovenstone!"

Skarper did not feel so sure. Coriander did not look to him like a place for goblins. He had never seen a great city of men before, and he felt as out of place there as Henwyn had felt when first he came to

Clovenstone. As they neared the city walls the road grew busier and busier, and Skarper could feel the eyes of passers-by upon him, and hear their whispered comments.

"Look! 'Tis a goblin!"

"Nay, 'tis too small. It must be a gnome, or some rare type of dog. . ."

"Or a monkey from the Night-Forests of Musk!"

"I say 'tis a goblin for sure. Who'd have thought we'd see the day when goblins walked about in our fair city, bold as brass?"

A few did more than look; they also sniffed as the two travellers walked by, for the day was warm, and a strange smell was starting to emerge from Henwyn's pack. There had been a long debate back at Clovenstone about what sort of gift they should bring for King Padstow (for everyone knows that kings won't so much as give you the time of day unless you bring a gift with you when you come to see them). Henwyn had suggested a sword from the old armouries, Princess Ned had wondered about a statue for the royal gardens, and Fentongoose had thought of sending a rare and valuable old book from the bumwipe heaps. But they all agreed the High King must have more swords than he knew what to do with, and a statue would be far too heavy to carry all that way, while even Fentongoose had to admit that his books were mildewy, and rather worm-eaten. So, in the end, they had decided to take cheese: a wheel of Clovenstone Blue, which was not only delicious, but would prove that the goblins had given up fighting and raiding and had turned their paws to more peaceful occupations, e.g. cheese-making.

It was a decision that Henwyn had come to regret. Not only was the wheel of cheese heavier than he had expected, it was smellier too, and the smell had haunted him all through the journey south, getting into his head while he slept and giving him the oddest dreams. Still, the sight of Coriander in the sunshine was enough to make him feel proud of his role as cheesebearer again, and he straightened his pack and strode proudly towards the city gate, with Skarper scuttling beside him and a cheesy aroma wafting behind.

The guards at the gate sniffed at the strange smell too, and they looked long and hard at Skarper. But cheese was popular in Coriander, and as for goblins, well, there had been many strange arrivals since the old magic began working again, and they did not try to stop Skarper entering. Soon he and Henwyn were walking along the cobbled streets, gawping up at the tall buildings which loomed over them on either side. More than half of the houses were also shops, with carved and painted signs hung above their doors announcing what they sold: signs in the shapes of lamps, boots, swords, saddles. . .

"We must find our way to the Street of Antiquaries," called Henwyn over the low but constant thunder of cartwheels on the cobbles. "That is where Carnglaze has his house."

Carnglaze was their only friend in the city, but he was a good friend. He was one of the would-be sorcerers who had come to Clovenstone with Fentongoose. After the fall of the Keep he had returned home, for unlike Fentongoose he had a wife waiting for him in Coriander. Now he made his living as a merchant, selling genuine Clovenstone artefacts from a shop on the ground floor of his house on the Street of Antiquaries. Every few months he would take a train of packhorses to Clovenstone, and bring them back to Coriander laden with the treasures and curios which the goblins kept unearthing among the ruins. Henwyn and Skarper planned to stay with him, and hoped that he would be able to arrange an audience for them with the High King. But first they had to find him.

Skarper wanted to ask the way, but Henwyn was sure he knew it. "Fentongoose told me that Carnglaze lives on the southern heights," he explained. "The city is in two halves, you see, north and south, with the River Ystrad running through the middle. Come, here is a short cut. . ."

The short cut led down steep, shady alleys where the houses were narrower and meaner looking, and the shop signs were in the shape of knives, wine jars, and playing cards. Soon there were no shops at all, just dingy, half-abandoned-looking houses, the only signs of life the dogs that slept in the doorways and the lines of washing strung across the narrow spaces between the buildings. It seemed astonishing that in one city there could be streets so poor and others so busy and prosperous. The daylight was fading fast, and Skarper and Henwyn had to take care as they picked their way across open drains, and skirted fly-buzzing mounds of rubbish. The smells made Skarper think of home, but it still felt to him as if they'd taken a wrong turn.

"Are you sure this is the way to Carnglaze's house?"

"We'll come to the river in a moment," Henwyn promised.

Come to it they did, but it took more than a moment, and it was not much of a river: a sad, smelly, brownish stream flowing sluggishly between stone embankments. A narrow, litter-strewn path led along the riverside, and a few hundred yards downstream a footbridge spanned the grimy water, old and mossy

51

and sagging. Henwyn pointed to it. "Look! A bridge! Once we're across that we'll start climbing again, and we'll soon be at the southern heights."

What Henwyn couldn't know was that three trolls had made their home under that bridge. Big, gangling, blue-green trolls, who had been mossy boulders on the banks of the Ystrad till that spring, when the magic tingling in the water had awoken them. Instead of creeping into the lonely places of the hills, which were the usual abode of trolls, these three had scented the rich, exciting smells of the city, and come downstream to lurk beneath this ancient bridge. Their names were Torridge, Cribba and Kenn.

As Skarper and Henwyn walked towards the bridge, the knobbly head of Torridge broke the water like a half-submerged stone. His eyes gleamed watchfully, and when the two friends drew near he scrambled suddenly out on to the path in front of them. His brothers, who had crept a little way upstream beneath the dirty water, crawled out behind them, cutting off Henwyn and Skarper's retreat.

"Trolls!" cried Henwyn.

"I *think*. . ." he added. For these city trolls were not like any troll he'd ever met or heard of. The dirty water and poor diet had stunted them, and their skin was the pasty grey of lichen on a sooty roof. They all wore dripping man-clothes, and one even sported an old hat with a soggy feather in it. Each carried a cudgel of iron-bound wood, made from uprooted riverside bollards.

"Give us your MONEY," growled Torridge.

"And your CLOTHES!" roared Cribba.

"And your. . ." Kenn started, then stopped and frowned. "No, jus' your money and your clothes, that'll do."

"All right!" whimpered Skarper, dropping his pack and starting to take off his cloak. He was just glad the trolls didn't want to eat him, as less sophisticated trolls in country places would have done.

But Henwyn shouted, "Never!" He threw down his pack, and his sword came singing from its scabbard.

The trolls reeled back, surprised. Coriander folk weren't used to trolls, and the few who'd met Torridge, Cribba and Kenn had all been glad enough to hand over their purses and their clothes as soon as they were told to. No one had ever pulled a sword on them before. Kenn, the most cowardly of the three, slithered quietly back into the river. Cribba swung his cudgel at Henwyn, but Henwyn ducked under it. Skarper, who had seen which way things were going by that time, quickly drew his own little sword and stabbed it into Cribba's shin. The troll howled, dropped his cudgel and tumbled backwards into the water, throwing up a greenish splash full of old vegetable peelings.

Henwyn whirled to confront Torridge. The troll bared yellow fangs at him and snarled. *Swish, swish* went his huge cudgel, flailing at Henwyn's head, but he was too slow, and Henwyn avoided the blows with ease. When Henwyn raised his sword, Torridge squealed and retreated up one of the shadowy alleyways which opened off the riverside, flinging his cudgel away as he went.

Most people would have given up at that point, decided they'd won, and hurried away to better bits of town. Not Henwyn. He still fancied himself as a bit of a hero. He ran after the troll. "Begone, foul troll!" he shouted importantly. "I shall drive you back into the wild hills whence you came, and the good people of Coriander shall sleep sounder knowing you are gone!" But as he advanced on the cowering troll his raised sword snagged a washing line, and a load of damp sheets came down on his head. Blinded, struggling to free himself, he backed out on to the riverside path. Kenn, who had recovered his courage, was just climbing out of the river again to lend his brother a hand, but when that thrashing, sheeted shape appeared he screeched, "A ghost!" and dived back in.

Torridge wasn't scared of ghosts. Following Henwyn

out of the alley, he stuck out a stinking, trollish toe to trip him, and snatching up his fallen cudgel, he raised it high above the fallen hero's head, shouting, "I'll bash you flat, I will!"

Skarper was just wondering if a desperate sword-thrust at the troll's backside would save the day or only make things worse, when the day was saved for him. Something small and squarish went fluttering over his head like a bird with corners. It struck Torridge hard between his dim eyes and made them go dimmer still. The stunned troll staggered backwards, missed his footing at the embankment's edge and plunged into the river. There was another mighty splash, spattering the path with water, algae and an old boot. Then silence.

Henwyn finally fought his way out of the sheet. He ran, sword in hand, to peer down into the murky water, but the three trolls seemed to have had enough. Only a few bubbles marked their track as they slunk back beneath the rotting piles of the bridge to lick their wounds.

Skarper, meanwhile, had picked up the missile that had struck Torridge down, and turned to look for the helpful person who had thrown it.

The missile was a book, thick and heavy, with hundreds of printed pages bound between hand-tooled leather covers. The thrower was a gaunt, elderly man wearing robes which might have been costly once, but which now hung in grimy tatters. "Ridiculous creatures," he said, looking at Skarper, but probably referring to the trolls.

Skarper went over to him, holding out the book. Books like that were valuable objects in the Westlands, where printing presses had not long been invented. The man just shrugged and said, "Keep it. You are a goblin, I suppose?"

Skarper agreed that he was.

"The streets of Coriander are filling with creatures out of children's tales," the man sighed, shaking his head grumpily. Henwyn ran over to shake his hand and thank him, which seemed to improve his mood a little, but he became gloomy again when Henwyn asked if he knew the way to the house of Carnglaze. "That fake sorcerer? That seller of trinkets from the Lych Lord's tower? Friends of his, are you?" He looked them both up and down and muttered again, "Creatures out of children's tales."

"But do you know Carnglaze's house?" asked Henwyn, a bit confused.

"It happens that I do," the ragged stranger admitted. "A very fine house it is, too. It is in the southern heights, a far superior part of town. A long walk from here, mind. Come to my home and let me bind that wound before you set forth."

Henwyn had not noticed until then that he was wounded. His head must have hit the alley wall while he was struggling in the sheet, and blood was trickling down his face. He felt quite faint when he touched the place and his fingers came away wet and red. He followed meekly as the stranger led the way up one of the nearby alleys.

Skarper trotted after them. It was almost dark now, but candles had been lit in some of the windows that they passed, and by their light he picked out the name of the book he held, embossed in golden letters on its spine. *Why Magic Doth Not Exist*, by Doctor Quesney Prong.

"Are you sure you don't want your book back?" he asked. Growing up among the bumwipe heaps had taught him to prize books; he couldn't imagine someone throwing one away.

The man just gave a hollow laugh. "Keep it, goblin. It is yours. I have plenty more. See!"

They had come to the alley's end. Beyond it lay a patch of waste ground, covered in weeds and litter, where a sort of small, lumpy shack had been built. At first Skarper thought that it was made from squared stones, but as he and Henwyn went closer he saw that it was actually built from hundreds and hundreds of books. More books, left over from the building, lay in a heap outside the doorway. The man picked one up and flung it on to the glowing embers of a small fire, where it burst into flame. In the sudden wash of light, golden letters gleamed in the book hut's walls. All the books were identical copies of *Why Magic Doth Not Exist*.

"I have five thousand of them," said their host, adding a few more books to his fire and setting a pot of water to heat over the flames. "I am the unhappy Dr Quesney Prong, you see, and I had them printed at my own expense. I expected them to sell, for there had been great interest in my lectures from learned people, not just here in Coriander but in Porthquidden, Nantivey, why, even in Barragan! 'Dr Quesney Prong is the voice of reason!' That's what they said of me. 'He is rescuing us from a belief in all the superstitious nonsense of the past: he offers proof positive that there are no such things as goblins, trolls and fairies.'

"And then what happens? Why, on the very day that I take delivery of my five thousand bound copies, the Lych Lord's star rises again, and the world begins to fill with goblins, trolls and fairies once more. Mermaids singing on the beach all night! Ghosts and ghouls creeping out of the burial grounds! A fairy even flew into the very hall where

I was lecturing and punched me on the nose, the little beast! And of course, no one wanted to buy my well-argued explanation of Why Magick Doth Not Exist when they only had to look about them to see that it plainly *doth*. So I was ruined, and now these worthless books are all that I have left."

It was a sad tale, and he told it with great bitterness as he carefully sponged the graze on Henwyn's brow with water from the pot. When he was finished he used the rest of the water to make three cups of tea, which his guests drank politely, even though Henwyn wasn't thirsty and goblins don't like tea. They both understood how generous it was of Quesney Prong to share some of his dwindling stock of best Muskish tea leaves with strangers. It was tricky to make conversation, though, because every time they mentioned Clovenstone, or goblins, or trolls, or dwarves, Dr Prong would scoff and shake his head and say, "Children's tales!"

At last, draining his cup, Henwyn said, "So, can you tell us the way to the house of Carnglaze?"

Dr Prong looked wearily at him. "Of course I can. It is my house. At least, it was. I sold it to Carnglaze when he returned from Clovenstone, bringing all those treasures. He gave me a good price for it too; I'll not deny that. Enough to pay off my debts, but not, alas, enough to live on."

He rose, brushing the dust from his shabby clothes. "Come. I'll take you there."

THE HOUSE OF
CARNGLAZE

Coriander was not as large a city as Clovenstone, but it was alive and full of people whereas Clovenstone was dead and all but deserted. It was so alive and so busy, in fact, that Skarper grew quite weary from all the new sights he saw on the way to the House of Carnglaze. Dr Prong led the travellers back down to the River Ystrad and across another, much bigger, better bridge where no trolls lurked. Soon they were in parts of town where lanterns hung from metal trees to light the wide, paved streets; where carriages clattered by and people in bright clothes promenaded, enjoying the warmth of the autumn evening. They passed the shops of clocksmiths and locksmiths, map-makers and book-binders; they passed shops so high-class and select that Skarper simply couldn't work out what they sold. They passed parks and public gardens where fountains played, and a place where a big purple tent was being erected, the signs outside advertising *Your Fortune Told! Your Future Foreseen! See Visions of Things To Come in Madam Maura's Oracular Bathtub!* They climbed long stairways, and emerged on to quieter streets which looked out across the bay to where the lights of Boskennack twinkled.

In one such street Dr Prong led them to a tall, narrow building which looked almost as stern and lonely as he did himself. In an effort to make it cheerier someone had planted bay trees in tubs outside the door, and put up a knocker in the shape of a winged head – a trophy which Henwyn and Skarper recognized, for it had been the symbol of the Lych Lord and the ruins of Clovenstone were full of such things. It seemed to be the only sign that Carnglaze needed.

"The knocker is new, since my time," said Dr Prong, lifting it, and rapping briskly on the door. After a short time there came a sound of bolts and deadlocks being undone. The door creaked open just a crack, and a hideous face peered out.

"Woddyer want?" it growled.

Skarper let out a frightened yelp and darted behind Henwyn. He couldn't help himself. The face belonged to Knobbler, who had once been King Knobbler, the biggest, toughest and most ruthless of all the goblins of Blackspike Tower. The other goblins had lost all respect for him when they found out that he wore pink fluffy knickers under his armour, and he'd had to give up the whole kinging thing and come to work as servant and bodyguard to Carnglaze, but he was still a terrifying figure to poor Skarper, who had sometimes seen him bite the heads off smaller goblins just for "looking at him in a funny way".

"I know you," said Knobbler, glaring at Henwyn. "You're that softling, Hedwig."

"Henwyn," said Henwyn.

"Hmp," said Knobbler. Then his gaze fell on Skarper, peeking out from behind his friend's cloak. "And I know you too! You're that troublemaker, Skratcher. . ."

"Skarper," said Skarper.

Knobbler's yellow eyes narrowed suspiciously. "Are you looking at me in a funny way?" he growled.

"Oh no! No! Not a bit!" said Henwyn and Skarper at once. But they were, and so was Dr Prong, because while they had been talking Knobbler had opened the door a little further, and they had seen that the former king of Blackspike was wearing a flowery, full-skirted dress with a frilly white apron over it.

"Master Carnglaze," said Knobbler, slightly

defensively, "says that 'goblins are neither male nor female'. That means that if I find it more comfy to wear a dress, I can. And I *do* find it more comfy to wear a dress." He leaned towards the visitors slightly, clenching his massive fists. "Have you got a *problem* with that?"

"Oh no! No! Not at all!" they all said, and Henwyn added, "It is very fetching, really. But we are actually here to talk with Carnglaze."

Knobbler grunted and shoved the door shut. Henwyn and Skarper exchanged a quick, bewildered look as they stood waiting on the step. Behind them, Dr Prong shook his head and muttered softly, "Children's tales. . ."

The door opened again. This time Carnglaze himself stood there, smiling at his visitors. "Henwyn! Skarper! Welcome! This is a surprise! I was not expecting you! What brings you here? Do you have any more treasures from Clovenstone for me? The stuff I brought back after my last visit is selling fast; I shall soon need more. Come in! Come in! Oh, and you too, Dr Prong!" he added, calling out to the philosopher, who had turned and was walking sadly away from the house which had once been his.

They all went inside; through a big room where objects and artefacts from the Lych Lord's time were arranged on shelves and tables like a museum with price tags, and then upstairs into a cosy, curtained parlour where Carnglaze's wife came bustling to meet them. Henwyn and Skarper knew her: a plump, cheerful woman, she'd come with Carnglaze that summer when he brought his string of packhorses over the hills to Clovenstone to fetch away more treasures. But behind her stood someone they did not know; a young woman who rose nervously from the chair she had been sitting in and backed away, as if she wanted to hide herself from the visitors.

"This is Zeewa, my niece," Carnglaze explained. "She has come all the way from Musk to visit me."

Henwyn bowed, and Zeewa nodded back. She was a tall, big-boned young woman, as dark skinned as her uncle, her hair done up in tight rows of tiny plaits. She wore a fine dress of some Muskish fabric and silver rings glittered in her ears, but she seemed nervy and ill at ease. Around her the air shimmered, and something about that shimmer made all Skarper's hair stand on end, and his tail begin to tingle. His sharp goblin ears detected sounds that the humans around him could not hear: thin whisperings and a faint, high-pitched drone.

"If you will excuse me, my uncle. . ." said the girl, and she turned and went hastily from the room.

Carnglaze tutted sadly. "A fine young woman,

but troubled. She came here in the belief that I was a sorcerer and could help her with certain . . . difficulties that she is having. But of course I am not a sorcerer, just a humble merchant." He looked hopefully at Henwyn's pack. "What have you brought from Clovenstone? Some new treasure from the deep storehouses?"

"Only cheese," said Henwyn, setting the pack down.

"Ah, that explains the smell," said Mistress Carnglaze. "I'll take it to the cold store."

"It is a gift for the High King," Henwyn explained. "Ned said he must have all sorts of treasure and things at Boskennack already, so we thought cheese instead."

"Very sensible, I'm sure," said Carnglaze, wafting the smell of Clovenstone Blue away as his wife went out with the cheese. "But why do you wish to see the High King?"

They explained, while Knobbler served spiced wine in pewter cups, and the Carnglazes and Dr Prong all listened carefully. "So that is why we must see his majesty," Henwyn finished. "When he hears of the dwarves' intentions he is sure to send a few heroes and a band of men-at-arms to defend us."

But Carnglaze looked doubtful. "Oh dear! Oh, I wish I could be so sure. You see, dwarves have arrived in Coriander too! Not mining or anything, just a small embassy, come to see the High King for themselves. They are led by someone called Chief Surveyor Durgar. He and his friends are staying at a tavern called The Sleepy Mermaid while they wait for an appointment with the High King. I have not heard why they are here, but I suspect they hope that the High King will give his blessing to *their* plans for Clovenstone!"

"The rotters!" shouted Henwyn, leaping up. "Of all the sneaky. . ."

"It seems to me," said Dr Prong, "that you must make sure the High King hears your plea before the dwarves can tell him theirs."

"Prong's right!" agreed Carnglaze. "And I think it can be arranged. I have the ear of the High King."

"Eww!" said Skarper.

"That is to say," Carnglaze went on, "his majesty will listen to me. He has bought several statues from me for the gardens of Boskennack. I shall send Knobbler with a message first thing tomorrow. I am sure that the High King will see you as soon as he can."

FRIENDS AND ENEMIES

Carnglaze was as good as his word. At low tide the next morning Knobbler went hurrying along the causeway to the High King's castle, wearing his fanciest frock and bearing a letter that explained the urgency of Henwyn and Skarper's mission. But kings like to do things in their own good time. Three days passed, and still the two friends were lodging at the house of Carnglaze, awaiting their summons to Boskennack.

At least they knew their dwarvish rivals were waiting too. Each morning Skarper left the house on the Street of Antiquaries and went scampering goblin-fashion over the city's rooftops and chimney pots until he reached the tavern called The Sleepy Mermaid. By listening to the potboys and ostlers who lounged about in its courtyard on their breaks, he soon learned that the dwarves had rented rooms down in the cellar. (It was obvious, when you thought about it, that dwarves would feel more at home underground.)

For someone who had grown up slinking and sneaking around in the goblin mazes of Blackspike Tower, it was easy to creep unnoticed down the steps into the gloomy, paved area outside the cellar entrance. The cellar had a door and a window, and the dwarves kept the door bolted and the windows shuttered, but Skarper's sharp goblin ears had no trouble hearing their gruff voices as they talked together inside. There were four of them: Surveyor Durgar, his daughter Etty, and two lesser dwarves, Langstone and Walna, who seemed to have come along mainly to carry things and be scolded by Durgar. Each morning Skarper heard Durgar tell the others, "We must send word to Boskennack again. We have to see that bigling king at once, so we can give our side of the story before these goblins and their friends can ask his help."

"The bigling king would not help goblins, would he, Dad?" asked Etty, the first morning.

"Who knows, with biglings?" Durgar had replied gloomily.

It was all welcome news to Skarper. The dwarves were no closer to a meeting with the High King than he and Henwyn were, and they did not have

Carnglaze to speed things along for them. The more gloomy Durgar got, the better, as far as Skarper could see.

Then, on the third morning, Skarper was caught. He was hanging from a water pipe that ran down the wall beside the cellar window, listening to Durgar grumble inside, when suddenly someone took hold of his tail by the ginger tuft on the end and tugged it as if it were a bell pull.

"Bumcakes!" said Skarper, losing his grip and landing with a thud on the cobbles below.

The dwarf girl, Etty, was looking down at him. She must have come outside very quietly while he was busy listening to the others. Usually the scent of her would have warned him, but Mistress Carnglaze had made him wash that morning, and the clean ungobliny odour of the soap still clung to him, spoiling his sense of smell. Not only that, but Etty had been using the same soap – it was a Coriander speciality, made from kelp and sold in big cakes at the Soapmarket – so she smelled just the same, and not like a dwarf at all.

"Ugly gargoyle!" she said angrily. "What are you doing? Spying, I'll be bound!"

There was no point in denying it. "I have to have some way to pass the time," Skarper said. "We're waiting to see the High King, just like you."

The girl's anger faded. After being cooped up in a cellar with only three grumpy dwarves for company, she was glad of somebody new to talk to, even if he was only a goblin. "Oh, isn't it *boring*?" she said. "We've been waiting for days and days. And my father won't even let us leave our rooms, for fear we'll be jeered and pointed at by biglings, or trampled by their great big horses, or run over by their mighty wagons."

"How did you get here?" asked Skarper, thinking that the dwarves should have got used to being pointed at and trampled if they'd come along the main road like Henwyn and himself.

"Through the tunnels, mostly," Etty said. "Dwarves mined all this country long before biglings came, and a lot of the tunnels are still open. They are quicker than your roads, and we travel easier in the dark. But oh, I would dearly love to see something of this city of men! Is it very splendid?"

"Why not come with me now and take a look?" asked Skarper.

"Because you are a foul goblin!" said the girl, shocked. "Because you're a sneaking, thieving maggot man who'll murder me most probably!"

"No I wouldn't!" said Skarper (although actually he did have a vague, goblinish plan to kidnap her and send notes to her father saying things like *Leave Coriander NOW or you'll never see your girl again*).

Etty looked hard at him. "No," she said, "I don't believe you would."

"Well, come on then," said Skarper. "It can't do any harm, unless your father finds out."

Etty shrugged. "We dwarves mostly sleep by day. They're all off to their beds now, and they think I was in mine ten minutes ago."

"Come on, then," Skarper said.

The girl pulled her black glass goggles out of a pouch on her belt and put them on as she followed Skarper up the steps, out of the basement shadows. Skarper wondered whether he should kidnap her straight away or wait a bit. He decided to wait: she was a sturdy little person, and seemed more than able to look after herself. In fact, he realized, kidnapping her would probably be impossible unless he could find Henwyn and persuade him to help, and he was fairly sure that Henwyn did not approve of kidnapping.

So he abandoned the kidnap plan and came up with an easier one. He'd just learn all he could from Etty about the dwarves and their designs on Clovenstone. As he followed her through the streets he began thinking up cunning questions which would make her reveal all sorts of secrets about the dwarves and their schemes.

But Etty had questions of her own.

"Why such big houses?" she asked. "And why so many?"

"Softlings – biglings as you call them – are big folk," said Skarper. "And they have a home for each family, if they can."

Behind her tinted goggles Etty's eyes were two O's of amazement. She turned around, staring up at the tall fronts of the houses. "Just one family in each of these great places? Oh, what wanton waste!"

"Don't dwarves have houses, down underground?" asked Skarper, pulling her out of the path of a passing cart.

"Oh no!" said Etty, and began to tell him in great detail about how dwarves lived. In their great dark burrows each family was allowed one small cell. They did not need much space because they had no possessions; they just signed out the clothes and tools and lanterns that they needed from communal stores, and returned them when they needed them no longer. It sounded horrible to Skarper, but he kept listening politely, and went "Oh!" and "Mmm," and "Really?" whenever he felt that Etty expected it of him. By the time they reached the flower market he had learned far more than he could hope to remember about the ways of the dwarves, and each new thing she saw set Etty off on a new tale of Life Underground.

"Oh, so these are flowers! They are pretty! All we see of flowers usually is their roots, dangling down through the ceiling where a burrow goes too close to the surface. I've often wondered what the top parts look like!" Then the sight of all the people milling about among the market stalls caught her attention, and before Skarper could think of anything useful to say about flowers she was off in another direction. "Aren't there a lot of different jobs for biglings? With us there are only a few. You are a miner or a smith or a surveyor, or a farmer or a warrior or a dwarfwife. I should have liked to be a surveyor like my pa, but the Head says I'm to be a dwarfwife, so that's that. In two summers' time, when I am old enough, I shall be wed to Langstone, Father's deputy."

Skarper had seen Langstone at The Sleepy Mermaid. He was a rather pompous young dwarf, with a splendid, gingery, forked beard, which he kept combing the tangles out of with a little bone comb. Hurrying to keep up with Etty as she strode on through the market and out into the streets beyond, Skarper wondered who had the right to tell her she had to get wed at all, especially to someone like Langstone. "Who is this

74

'head'?" he asked breathlessly. "I remember old Glunt mentioning him. . ."

Etty stopped and stared at him. "Of course! You don't know about the Head! Poor you! Imagine having to live without the Head to guide you and tell you what you must do!"

Skarper recalled the shining head he'd seen upon the shields and banners of the dwarves. "Who is he, then?" he asked again. "Some super-dwarf? A king?"

Etty laughed. "Dwarves do not have kings! Kings are just people, and might have silly ideas, or make bad decisions based on nothing but how they happen to be feeling that day. That is why all the wisest of the dwarves got together, long ago, and made the Brazen Head."

"So it's a statue?"

"Yes, I suppose so. And it tells us what to do."

"You mean it talks?"

"Not in words; not speaking, like. But the overseers write questions for it on stones, and it answers on other stones. It is magic, I suppose. Dwarf magic. Smithy magic. It tells us what to mine and where, and it decides whether young dwarves should become miners or surveyors or farmers or whatever."

"But what if they want to decide that for themselves?" asked Skarper, who would have hated having some bossy Brazen Head telling him what to do. "Like you: you want to be a surveyor, so why can't you? Why can't you do what you want?"

"Oh, that wouldn't work!" said Etty. "What if everybody wanted to be surveyors and nobody wanted to be a miner? What if everyone decided to be farmers? 'The Head Knows All, and the Head Knows Best', as we say in Dwarvenholm. Like at the moment, it must have *known* we were going to have a war with you goblins because it has been telling the overseers that we need more warriors. And more dwarfwives, of course, to have babies to replace the dwarves who fall in battle."

"But why have a war at all?" said Skarper. "Why come pinching our slowsilver when you could go and mine something else, in some other place. It's not like the north is a busy place. It's not like it's *crowded*."

Etty shook her head firmly. "The Head has told us to mine slowsilver," she said. "For years it has been asking us for iron and tin and bronze, but now it wants slowsilver, and the only fresh slowsilver we know of is at Clovenstone."

Skarper decided that he definitely didn't like this Head.

They came to Coriander's waterfront. The tide was right out now. People were walking and riding across the causeway which separated the city from Boskennack. Up in the High King's citadel, trumpets sounded, announcing the start of the new day.

"Oh!" said Etty, delighted with it all. "How I wish I could go surveying, and see something of this big old world!"

"If you'd stop listening to that old Head of yours, you could," said Skarper. "You could stop pestering other people and trying to take what's theirs, too."

"'The Head Knows All, and the Head Knows Best'," Etty repeated sternly. Then, as if sensing that she'd hurt Skarper's feelings, she rummaged in her pouch again and pulled out a strange object. "Here," she said. "Breakfast for you. Supper for me. We'll share."

"What is it?" asked Skarper. It looked like a fat envelope made of concrete.

"'Tis a pasty, of course!" said Etty. "Proper dwarven food. Meat and vegetables in one end, fruit in the other. Which will you have?"

"Bit of both, please," said Skarper.

So Etty broke bits off for him and they sat together on the sea wall eating it, waving their arms occasionally to ward off hungry gulls. It was, to Skarper's surprise, Quite Tasty. And when it was finished, Etty said that she must be getting back to her people, and Skarper agreed that he must be getting back to Henwyn, and so they parted, still not sure if they were friends or enemies.

ZEEWA'S GHOSTS

The House of Carnglaze was quiet that morning. The previous days of Henwyn's stay had begun busily, with Mistress Carnglaze serving breakfast, customers arriving to see Carnglaze's wares, and even visits from Dr Prong, who seemed glad to have someone to talk to, even if it was only a former sorcerer and his friends. But that morning Mistress Carnglaze had gone to market, leaving fresh bread and a jug of milk on the kitchen table, while Carnglaze had set out for Boskennack to deliver in person another message to the High King. Skarper, of course, had gone out to spy on the dwarves, and ended up talking to Etty. Henwyn was left all alone. Or so he thought, until he walked into the breakfast room, where a large lion pounced on him.

He did not even have time to scream. He flung

up his arms, as if that could ward off all that flying muscle and those dreadful teeth and claws. He knew it was a lion because he had seen pictures of lions, and he recognized that great ruff of tawny fur around its snarling face. It occurred to him, in the slow-motiony moment while he waited for the impact, that lions lived in Musk and Barragan, not in the cool, wet Westlands, but that didn't seem to help much.

Then, just as it reached him, the lion grew vague. Henwyn found that he could see the table and the window quite clearly through it. He had never heard of see-through lions before. He felt no jolt as it hit him, either, only a strange, faint chill.

The lion passed through him, through the panelled wall behind him, and was gone.

"Tau!" shouted the girl Zeewa, padding quickly into the room on her bare brown feet, and the lion came back through the wall and went sheepishly to her side like a big misty cat.

"But – but – but – blurgle!" said Henwyn. He stared at the girl, trying to control his hammering heart, which had jumped straight up his throat when he saw the lion and now seemed to be wedged somewhere in the neighbourhood of his tonsils.

He had not seen Carnglaze's niece since the night

of his arrival. She seemed shy, and kept out of the way of her uncle's guests, taking all her meals in her room. Her bedchamber was above the one which Henwyn and Skarper were sharing, and sometimes in the nights he'd woken to hear her pacing restlessly about up there. There had been other noises too, odd moans and whisperings, but nights in Coriander were full of strange noises, and he soon went back to sleep. Other than that, he had scarcely thought of Zeewa.

Now he pointed at the lion which was nuzzling her hand, but he could still find no words to say except, "But—!"

"Tau cannot harm you," said the girl. She would not look at Henwyn. Her hand stroked the lion's mane, but he did not think she was actually touching it: her fingers passed through it as if it were smoke. All around her the air was twisting and shifting, like the air above a hot roof on a sunny afternoon.

"But he's a g – a gh – a ghgh. . ." Henwyn managed to splutter.

Zeewa looked up at him for the first time, defiance in her dark eyes. "He is a ghost," she agreed.

And now Henwyn saw that the movements all around her were other ghosts: animals and birds which took shape and grew solid for an instant, then faded again.

Zeewa darted forward, grabbed some slices of bread, and made to leave again.

"No!" said Henwyn. "Don't go! I don't understand! Where have all these spectres come from? Is this house haunted?"

"The house is not haunted," replied the girl. "I am."

She came from the Tall Grass Country, west of Leopard Mountain. She was a huntress and a daughter of warriors. Her father was King Ushagi, lord of ten thousand buffalo, and she had been proud and queenly and certain of herself for all her life, right up until the day she let her shadow fall across the wizard G'angooli as he sat in the evening sun outside his hut.

Why G'angooli should have been so offended, Zeewa did not know. Maybe because he was old, and he relished the sun's warmth so much that he resented even that little flick of shade as she walked past him. Maybe because he was thinking deep thoughts, and her passing shadow had distracted him. Or maybe it was just because he was a mean old man who had grown used to terrifying people with his conjuring tricks and mumbled spells. Maybe the dreadful curse he had shouted after her was only meant as bluster.

(The truth was, old G'angooli was no more a sorcerer than Fentongoose or Carnglaze. He had never expected his curse to work. But the light of the slowsilver star had fallen on Leopard Mountain and the Tall Grass Country just as brightly as on Clovenstone, and things had woken in Musk as they had in the Westlands. The dark powers that G'angooli called on were actually listening, for once.)

What he shouted after Zeewa was this:

"Insolent girl! May the spirits of all you've ever killed come back to haunt you!"

And they had!

Zeewa had not noticed them at first, out in the bright sunlight. It was when she was back in the darkness of her father's hall that she began to hear them. The whisperings and the flutterings. The buzzing. The ghosts of everything she'd ever killed had risen, and found their way to her.

Zeewa was fifteen, and a girl can kill quite a lot of things in fifteen years, especially if she's a huntress and a daughter of warriors, living in the Tall Grass Country west of Leopard Mountain. Most of her ghosts were insects: a cloud of swatted wasps and mosquitoes that whirled about her head, a smoky tide of stomped spiders and squashed scorpions that washed around her feet. Through the fluttering storm of the wings of ghost flies she glimpsed the larger spirits: ghost antelopes, ghost birds, a ghost hyena or two, and the big old lion she'd speared at Two Rivers Meet the summer before.

Last of all, as if his shade was the hardest to summon from the afterworld, there came a man; the young enemy warrior she'd killed that winter when he and his companions had raided her father's cattle pens. He still looked just as surprised as he had at the moment when she stuck her spear through him.

"I could not stay in my father's house," Zeewa told Henwyn, sitting by the window in Carnglaze's breakfast room while the ghosts swirled whitely round her. "Everyone was scared I'd bring bad luck. The animals took fright and ran from me. The buzzing of the ghosts kept everyone awake. The children were afraid."

"It's no fun for us, either," said a tall young warrior, appearing at her side and making Henwyn jump. He carried a leaf-shaped oxhide shield and a broad-bladed sword, and there was a hole in his middle where Zeewa had speared him: Henwyn could see clear through it to where seagulls twirled in the sky outside the window.

"There we were," the ghost complained, "minding our own business in the afterlife, and suddenly we were dragged back here and made to follow you around!"

"Be quiet!" shouted Zeewa angrily, rounding on

him and slapping at him with a hand that went straight through him. "Leave me alone!"

The ghost shrugged, dissolving away into smoke and shadows. "That's the point! We can't leave you alone! We must follow you everywhere, Zeewa, until this curse is lifted."

Henwyn scratched his head, feeling sorry for Zeewa and her ghosts. "How awkward!" he said.

"Awkward," agreed the girl.

"Could you not go back to this G'angooli fellow and get him to lift the curse? Perhaps if you asked really nicely. . ."

"That was the first thing I did," said Zeewa. "Unfortunately, when G'angooli saw the cloud of ghosts that he'd raised, he was so frightened that he dropped down dead. I was afraid his spirit would come haunting me too, but wherever he fled to, he is not among my ghosts.

"For a long time after that, I wandered alone. I thought that perhaps if I walked for many miles I might leave the ghosts behind, but they always kept up with me. I tried running through brakes of thorn trees, in the hope that the ghosts would get caught on the thorns and I could leave them there, but although I scratched myself half to pieces, they were still with me when I stumbled out all bloody on the far side.

"It was then that I remembered my uncle Carnglaze. I had never seen him, but I had heard it said he was a powerful sorcerer in the far-off, outlandish place called Westlands. 'Perhaps he can find a cure,' I said. I walked to the coast, and tricked my way aboard a ship. The ghosts do not show up so much in bright sunlight, so the sailors did not notice them when I went aboard. When they found out about my haunting we were already in the middle of the sea. They set me adrift in a small boat, but luckily Kosi knows something of the stars, and helped me steer my way to Coriander."

"Kosi?" asked Henwyn.

"That's me," said the warrior ghost, reappearing.

"Oh! Pleased to meet you," said Henwyn.

Zeewa shook her head sadly. "But my journey has been in vain. Uncle Carnglaze knows no magic, and nor does anyone in these Westlands, it would seem. My curse cannot be lifted. I am doomed."

"Oh, don't say that!" said Henwyn, wondering what on earth he could do to help. "I know! There is a new sorceress in town! *Madam Maura and her Oracular Bathtub: Fortunes Told! Genuine Magick Work'd!* Skarper and I saw her setting up her tent the night we arrived. Have you tried consulting her?"

Zeewa shook her head again. "They are all frauds, these Westlands wizards. They know nothing."

"Madam Maura might be different,"
Henwyn said. "You never know. Things
have changed since the star came. And look, the
sun is shining as brightly as anything outside! We can
go and consult Madam Maura and nobody will notice
all your see-through companions."

Zeewa was about to say no, but she looked at him
and changed her mind. Henwyn had that effect on
people. He was so optimistic and so eager to be helpful
that you didn't like to disappoint him. So Zeewa
fetched her cloak, and, still barefoot, ventured out with
him into the streets of Coriander.

It was true; in the bright sunlight her ghosts were
almost invisible, and the noises of the busy city
masked the buzzing of the phantom flies. But a strange
chill went before her where she walked. Dogs sensed
the presence of the ghosts at once and fled, yelping.
Horses reared and whinnied as Zeewa passed, and
people shivered and moved out of her path without
knowing why.

They soon came to the place where Madam Maura's
tent was pitched, on a patch of greensward above
the harbour. Seen by daylight it was a shabby thing.
Madam Maura was standing outside it, telling a small
audience of onlookers the things she had foreseen. All
sorts of visions of the future had come to her since the

Lych Lord's star rose, but they were so strange that it was difficult to make anyone believe her.

"Men and women will fly across the sky in birds made of metal which soar high above the clouds!" she prophesied, as Henwyn and Zeewa approached.

The onlookers shook their heads and grumbled. It sounded a bit unlikely to them.

"People will talk to each other across great distances, by means of magic boxes which they shall carry in their pockets!" Madam Maura added. "And lo! These magic boxes shall have Personalized Ringtones!"

The audience sighed, unimpressed. "She's just making it up!" someone said.

"A popular celebrity chef will be arrested for stealing cheesy pancakes from the freezer section of Morrisons in Cleckheaton!" Madam Maura foretold. But her audience had never heard of such a place, and couldn't imagine what a celebrity chef might be. Besides, many of them had started to sense a strange, unearthly chill. They started to drift away, and soon the sorceress was left alone with Henwyn and Zeewa.

"Hello, dears," she said, sitting down on a barrel and mopping her large face with a spotted handkerchief. "Oh, it takes it out of a body, this here prophesying. It used to be much easier in the old days when I was just making it up. Now I gets these visions all the time, and they shows me the strangest things. Talking boxes and moving pictures. Boats that move with no sails and lamps that shine with no flame."

"Does the future really hold such things?" asked Henwyn.

"Who knows, dearie? I just tell what I see. Maybe the visions are showing me the future of some other world. Anyway, what can I do for you? I suppose it's about these here ghosts, is it?"

Until then, Henwyn and Zeewa had both suspected her of faking her strange powers, but now she looked straight at Kosi, Tau and the rest of Zeewa's spectral retinue, and it was clear that she could see them.

"Can you get rid of them?" asked Henwyn. "I mean, exorcize them? I mean, lay them to rest?" (He did not want to offend the poor ghosts.)

Madam Maura sadly shook her head. "I'm sorry, dearie. Not up my street, that sort of thing. I do prophesies mostly, and a few love potions and things like that. But. . . Ooh yes! Oh, dearie me! Yes, I do see something. . ." She stood up and beckoned them to follow her into the purple tent. "Come in, dears; come quickly!"

They followed her in through the heavy canvas flap, into darkness and swirls of smoke from an incense burner which hung from the ridge-pole. The ghosts became visible as they stepped in out of the sun: frail antelope with soaring horns; spotted hyenas; the big lion padding; Kosi looking as wary and intrigued as Henwyn and Zeewa.

Beneath the incense burner stood a bathtub; an ordinary copper bathtub of the sort that you could find in any merchant's house in Coriander or Adherak. It had been filled with clear water, and the water's surface reflected the swirlings of the smoke above it. Madam Maura waved her plump hands above the tub, and suddenly the reflections grew brighter, forming dim and shifting pictures. A greenish landscape, misty and uncertain; ruined buildings; towers. . .

"That's Clovenstone!" said Henwyn.

"Far to the north must you go, Zeewa of the Tall Grass Country!" said Madam Maura. Her voice was deeper and clearer than before. In the light from the glowing water they saw that her face was slack, like a sleepwalker's, and her eyes had rolled upwards so that only the whites showed. She spoke again. "There, among the Houses of the Dead, shall you find the freedom that you seek. But great dangers loom! 'Loom! Loom!' they go. You must depart soon, or all will be in vain!"

The images in the water trembled and changed. Henwyn saw fire; the fall of great buildings; the vague shapes of battling warriors. For a moment he thought the enchanted bathtub was showing him visions out of Clovenstone's past; the last, dreadful clash of men and goblins when King Kennack's armies defeated the Lych Lord's hordes. Then he saw that it was not against men but dwarves these goblins battled: massed ranks of dwarven warriors, masked and armoured. Great diremoles moved among them, with more dwarves riding on their backs, shooting crossbows and raining down fire from dreadful weapons.

Then the image changed again. For a moment all was drifting smoke. Then the smoke cleared, and Henwyn saw Princess Ned. She was lying on a lawn of soft green grass, and he knew at once that she was dead.

"No!" he cried, and reached forward to touch her. But as his hand brushed the surface the image broke apart, and there was only the water lapping at the bath's sides, and a yellow toy duck which his lunge had dislodged from the soap rack, bobbing out into the middle.

"Well, dearies," said Madam Maura, her face and voice returning to normal. "Was that any help at all?"

"What did it mean?" asked Zeewa. "What are the Houses of the Dead?"

"Was that the future?" demanded Henwyn. "Was it

the real future? Or was it just a vision of the future as it might be?"

"Search me, love," the sorceress said. "That one didn't stick in my mind for some reason. They don't always. It's just a blur to me. Did you see anything you thought you recognized?"

"Yes!" said Henwyn. He was so upset that all the ghostly insects caught his mood and swirled in a buzzing whirlwind of wings under the tent's roof. "Yes! I saw Clovenstone burning, and Princess Ned. . . Oh, I must go back to Clovenstone at once!"

"And I must come with you, I think," said Zeewa. "At least, that is what I think the vision said. I must go far to the north, and seek the Houses of the Dead."

They said their goodbyes to Madam Maura. Henwyn's hands were trembling as he crossed her palm with silver. All he could think of was getting home to Clovenstone. He had waited too long in Coriander. For all he knew, the dreadful things that he had seen might be happening already! In silence he made his way back to the Street of Antiquaries, while Zeewa and her pale ghosts followed. I shall start for Clovenstone this very day, he thought. It is useless, waiting here. The High King will not even see me, let alone lend me his warriors to fight against the dwarves!

But when they reached the Street of Antiquaries,

Carnglaze met them on the steps of his house. He was wearing his best embroidered robes, and looking harried. "Henwyn!" he cried. "Where have you been! We've been looking everywhere! The High King has agreed to meet with you and hear your plea, this afternoon!"

THE HIGH KING

One of the treasures which Carnglaze had brought back from Clovenstone was the Rolls-Royce Silver Shadow, a strange carriage which the Lych Lord had fetched by magic from another world. It was supposed to run without horses, but Carnglaze had never mastered the sorcery that made it go. Now it lived in a stable near his home and was pulled through the streets of Coriander by a team of white horses whenever he wanted to look important.

If Madam Maura had seen this remarkable carriage she would have been most intrigued. The Rolls-Royce Silver Shadow was exactly the sort of vehicle which rolled through the streets of that strange otherworld she saw so often in her visions. But Madam Maura was exhausted by conjuring up those pictures of Clovenstone in her enchanted bathtub, and she was fast asleep and snoring when the Silver Shadow went past her tent, carrying Henwyn, Skarper and Carnglaze to their meeting with the High King.

Usually it was Carnglaze himself who sat on the Silver Shadow's roof, controlling the horses. Today, however, he wished to look particularly important, so he had persuaded Dr Prong to act as his coachman. (This wasn't difficult; Dr Prong would have acted as almost anything in exchange for a bath and a hot meal.) Carnglaze sat inside with his guests on the soft red leather seats. King Knobbler, who had swapped his frock for footman's livery, stood ready on the running board with a whip to lash any impertinent urchins who tried to hitch a lift on the back bumper.

Down the steep streets to the waterfront they went, and out across the causeway which led to Boskennack. In the back seat Skarper and Henwyn sat side by side in silence. Skarper was wondering whether he should tell Henwyn about his talk that morning with the dwarven girl. He decided not to. Henwyn might think it odd that Skarper had sat eating pasty with one of their sworn enemies. Not only that, he had a feeling that there was something embarrassing about going around with a girl; Henwyn might well tease him about it.

He had not seen Henwyn come home with Zeewa,

for the haunted girl had run straight up to her room. Nor had Henwyn mentioned it. If he had told Skarper about Zeewa he would have had to explain where they had been, and describe his dreadful vision in Madam Maura's tent. Just *thinking* about that seemed to make it more real; he certainly did not want to speak about it. (Besides, there was something embarrassing about going around with a girl; Skarper might well tease him about it.)

Henwyn's instincts were still telling him to go back to Clovenstone as soon and as fast as he could, to try to stop the terrible events which the magic bathtub had shown him. But now, at least, he had a chance of winning the help of the High King before he left. As the Silver Shadow rolled smoothly up the steep spiral road from the causeway to the castle gate, he leaned forward in his seat, eagerly rehearsing in his mind the things that he would say when he finally stood before his majesty.

In the yard of the castle, guards in coats of shining mail greeted Henwyn, Skarper and Carnglaze as they stepped out of the Silver Shadow, and led them through courts and colonnades into an audience chamber whose windows overlooked the wide blue sea. There stood the High King, a mild-looking little man who seemed more like a grocer than a descendant of King Kennack. Behind him waited the champions from the Hall of Heroes. Henwyn, kneeling before the king with his head bowed, sneaked a look at them through his fringe, and was surprised to see that they were mostly stout, red-faced men of middle years. Of course, it was a long time since peril had threatened the Westlands: there was not much call for heroes nowadays, and perhaps they did not get much exercise. There was only one of them who looked lean and craggy and wolfish as a good hero should, but he seemed to be asleep.

"That is Garvon Hael," whispered Carnglaze, who was kneeling beside Henwyn and had seen where he was looking. "He is a terrible drunkard, a disgrace to the Hall of Heroes. His sword once saved the island of Far Penderglaze from an attack by pirates, but after that he crawled into a wine jug, and he has never come out again."

"So," said the High King, in a fatherly tone. "What can we do for you, gentlemen and, er, goblin?"

"Greetings, my king," said Henwyn, and went forward humbly, bearing the wheel of cheese which he had brought with him all the way from Clovenstone. He knelt with it before the king, and the smell that rose from it tickled the royal nostrils.

"What *is* that awful reek?" the High King asked.

"It is Clovenstone Blue, your majesty," said Henwyn. "It is a sort of cheese; the produce of the new cheesery at Clovenstone. It is our gift to you."

"Oh! Ah. . . Jolly good," said the king, motioning for a servant, who came hurrying to take the cheese away. "Now then, young fellow, what's all this about? Good Carnglaze here says it's all dreadfully urgent; somethin' about dwarves and goblins and suchlike?"

Henwyn explained about the dwarf problem. He was a little nervous, talking in such a grand hall, with all these noble and heroic men listening, but whenever he stumbled or hesitated or missed something out Skarper would step in, and between them they quickly told the whole story.

"So, your majesty," Henwyn said, when they were done, "Princess Ned sent us here to bring the news to you, and to ask if you would send help to our little kingdom in its hour of need."

The High King rubbed his nose thoughtfully. "Well, I must say, this all sounds most unusual. Most undwarflike, wouldn't you say? I've only come across the dwarves in tales and songs, but aren't they meant to be bluff, honest, jolly fellows? Red noses and pointy red hats. Sit about in gardens, fishin', or perchin' on toadstools."

"I think that's gnomes you're thinking of, your

majesty," said Carnglaze.

"Is it? Is it? Well, maybe. But even so, dwarves are good sorts, I've always been led to believe. Whereas Clovenstone is well known to be the citadel of all evil."

"Oh, not any more, your majesty!" said Henwyn. "The Keep has fallen; there is no Lych Lord any more."

"No, Carnglaze told me all about that: a murky-soundin' business it was too. But they tell me that a wicked Dark Queen has taken the place of the Lych Lord."

"That's just silly!" said Henwyn. "Princess Ned is not wicked, and she is not a queen; she does not think of herself as ruler of Clovenstone at all. It's just that she is by far the most sensible person there, so the rest of us usually look to her for guidance."

"The rest of you?" the king said. "How many people live at Clovenstone?"

"Oh, hundreds," said Henwyn, who had never counted.

"Thousands," said Skarper, "if you count the twiglings and the troll and the boglins in the marshes."

"But I *don't* count them," said the High King. "And I don't count goblins, neither. How many *actual human people* live at Clovenstone?"

"Well," said Henwyn. "Well, there are just the three

of us. Princess Ned and Fentongoose and myself."

"I see."

"My family visit from Adherak sometimes. It was they who helped us to set up the cheesery."

"And you three are asking me to send you soldiers and champions to defend you against these dwarves?" the High King mused.

Carnglaze said, "Your majesty, the law of the Westlands states that the High King shall send help to any kingdom which is in peril. It does not matter how many people live there, nor what sort of people they are."

"Hmm," said the High King, glaring at him. He turned and clapped his hands, attracting the attention of his heroes and champions, who had been fidgeting and staring listlessly out of the windows while all this was going on. "Well, my warriors? What say you?"

The heroes and champions looked at one another, as if none wanted to be the first to speak.

The High King pointed to one of them, a tall, sandy-haired man wearing a gorgeous sea-green cloak. "Merion of Porthkindlass, what say you? Shall you ride north to defend these cheese-making goblins against the onslaught of the dwarves?"

"Dwarves?" said Merion. "Oh, it is very difficult

to fight dwarves. They live underground, you see. We can't ride our horses underground, and only common people fight on foot."

"How do we know the dwarves are in the wrong, anyway?" asked another man. "These goblins and their human friends may just be trying to win our sympathy so that we'll help them do away with some perfectly decent, hard-working dwarves."

"It's all a trick!" agreed a third man, and a fourth said, "I never heard a story yet where the dwarves were the villains and the goblins were good."

Then another voice, harsher and flatter than the rest, cut across their babble.

"They are scared," it said.

Garvon Hael, who had not moved from his seat in all this time, and who had appeared to be fast asleep, opened one wolf-grey eye.

"They are scared," he said again, "and that is the truth of it. They call themselves heroes and champions, but how did they earn their place in Boskennack? By running their swords through brigands armed with nought but cudgels, like Merion here. Or by riding their horses over rebellious peasants, like fat Kerwen of Bryngallow over there. Or just by play-fighting; winning honour wreaths for riding or swordsmanship at the summer games (yes, I'm looking at you, Lord

Ponsadane). You, young Henwyn of Clovenstone, you're asking them to fight real battles, against real warriors, and that thought makes their blood run cold."

The heroes reddened, or grew pale with anger. Several muttered that it was a disgrace and shouldn't be allowed. "The man is drunk!" said Kerwen of Bryngallow, his chins wobbling with indignation. "Drunk, as always! Throw him out, your majesty!"

"Aye, banish him!" roared Ponsadane.

But before the High King could say any more, or Garvon Hael defend himself, there came a blare of brazen trumpets from outside the hall and a servant at the door said, "Your majesty! The dwarves are here!"

That brought silence. Everyone turned and stared as in through the arched entryway the dwarves came stumping. Chief Surveyor Durgar wore the same work-worn clothes that he had been wearing when Skarper and Henwyn first met him, and the two dwarves who walked behind him had not even bothered to clean the half-melted candles from the tops of their helmets. Only Etty had made an effort, plaiting blue ribbons into her hair. She walked a little way in front of her father, carrying a plain slate box with iron hinges.

"What are they doing here?" said Henwyn.

"I summoned them here myself, young man," said the High King, sounding rather pleased with himself. "I thought that we should hear both sides of this fishy-soundin' story before we made any decision."

Etty glanced sideways as she passed Skarper, and he thought that she winked at him, though it was hard to tell behind those black glass goggles. She marched straight up to the High King and did not bow or curtsey, just shoved the box at him. A servant ran forward to take it from her, and held it while the High King opened the lid.

"A gift from the dwarves, your majesty," said Durgar. "We are a plain people, and we don't know much about court etiquette and the way to deal with kings, but we give you this as a token of friendship between men and dwarves."

"Ooh!" said the High King, lifting it from the box. It was a magnificent crown, wrought from many different metals: copper and bronze and gold and slowsilver. Diamonds glittered and winked on its prongs. The sunlight reflecting from it seemed to make the whole hall brighter as the High King lifted it and tried it on.

"If it's too big, we can always adjust it," said Durgar.

"Oh no!" the High King breathed. "It's perfect! My thanks to you, O dwarves!"

Henwyn, Skarper and Carnglaze exchanged a look

which meant *We wish we'd brought him something more valuable than cheese.*

Garvon Hael spoke again, watching all this with a wry smile. "So I suppose you've come to ask our help against the goblins, have you?" he asked Durgar.

Durgar shot a a quick, questioning look from beneath his wire-wool brows. "No. Dwarves have never asked the help of men, and don't now. All we ask is that we be allowed to go about our work without interference. There is much precious metal to be had beneath Clovenstone. Let us mine it, and do not aid the goblins if they try to stop us. Some of what we mine will go back north to Delverdale, but much will find its way into the markets of the south."

"O king!" said Skarper, butting in. "The metal that he means is slowsilver. There is a lake of it under Clovenstone, and that is where goblin eggs come from. If Durgar and his dwarves drain it, then there will be no more eggs, and no more goblins!"

"I was about to point that out, O king," said Durgar. "Goblins may be no threat to you now, but do you really want a whole kingdom of them, only a hundred miles from Coriander? They are wicked by nature. Who knows when a new dark lord may rise to lead them? Let us dig our tunnels, as dwarves always have. Let us drain that lake of slowsilver, and cool it into forms that can be worked with, and forge it into rare and wonderful shapes. And if by so doing, we rid the Westlands for ever of these pestilential goblins, why, is that such a high price to pay?"

The High King looked at Skarper, and it was pretty clear that he was thinking no, it wasn't. The world would be a better place with a few less things like Skarper in it, seemed to be his view.

"Your majesty!" blurted Henwyn. "Don't listen to him! Goblins are not wicked by nature. They like a fight, it's true, and steal things sometimes – well, quite often – and they don't like washing, or wiping their bottoms, or tidying up after themselves. And their table manners are atrocious. But they are good and bad and in between and often all three at different times, just as other people are. Clovenstone needs your help! You must not let these devious dwarves tell you what to do!"

"Oh, but I should let you tell me, should I?" snapped the king, losing patience with Henwyn. "My decision is made, young fellow. The dwarves should be allowed to go about their business undisturbed. We shall neither aid nor hinder them."

"But. . ." Henwyn began.

"Throw this impertinent scoundrel out!" ordered the High King, turning to his heroes. "His friends too.

Let them go back to their nasty little kingdom. I've heard enough of them."

The heroes were eager to show how brave and strong they were after Garvon Hael's mockery. Merion of Porthkindlass picked Skarper up by his tail, Kerwen and Ponsadane took hold of Henwyn, and two others seized Carnglaze. Roughly and speedily the three friends were marched out of the great hall, back through the colonnades and courts, and flung out on to the paving in front of the castle, where Knobbler and Dr Prong were waiting beside the Rolls-Royce Silver Shadow.

"How did it go then?" asked Dr Prong, as they picked themselves up and dusted themselves off.

They did not bother to reply.

"If the High King will not help us," vowed Carnglaze, "we must help ourselves. I will raise an army of mercenaries! There are many old warriors in Barragan and Musk who would be glad of employment now the wars there are ended!"

Henwyn shook his head. "That may take too long. The dwarves' tunnels must already reach almost to the Inner Wall. But you are right, we must help ourselves. Skarper and I have wasted too many days here already. We shall start for Clovenstone this very afternoon!"

They drove back down the corkscrew road, but

when they reached the waterside they found the tide had risen, and the waves now rolled over the causeway. Worse, the people who plied the little ferry boats that went to and fro between Boskennack and the shore had all heard that Henwyn and his friends had earned the High King's displeasure. None of them would take the companions back across the bay to Coriander.

"We shall have to wait here until the tide subsides this evening," said Carnglaze angrily.

"I mean to be on the road to Clovenstone by then!" said Henwyn, and he scooped up Skarper, set him on his shoulders, and waded into the sea.

He had not gone ten paces before he started to regret it. The cold waves came up to his knees, his thighs, his waist, and he had a nasty feeling he'd be swimming by the time he reached the middle of the causeway. But behind him he could hear all the ferrymen jeering, and he did not want to give them the satisfaction of watching him turn back, so he kept going.

"What can we do when we get back to Clovenstone?" asked Skarper.

"I don't know. We'll think of something. Perhaps between us, if Fraddon lends a hand. . ."

"Fraddon wouldn't even fit down those little dwarf tunnels," said Skarper.

The waves were lapping around Henwyn's chest by then. He heard the creak and splash of oars behind him, and guessed that one of the ferrymen had rowed after him to do a bit more jeering. "Don't look round!" he said to Skarper. "Don't give him the satisfaction. . ."

The boat came alongside. It was a shabby little tar-stained lobster boat, and the oarsman was Garvon Hael.

"So you are going home alone?" the grey man asked, resting on his oars and watching Henwyn push through the waves.

"What other choice do we have?" asked Henwyn.

Garvon Hael snorted. "It seems to me that you came to Coriander looking for warriors, and found only a gaggle of fat and pompous old windbags. It seems to me that if it is warriors you need, you must find them for yourself, not look to the High King to provide them."

"And where would I find warriors?" demanded Henwyn. "Carnglaze said he would find some in Barragan or Musk, but that will take weeks, and we may have only days!" He was about to add something more but a wave chose that moment to break right in his face and so he just said, "Glup!"

"Well, here is one, for a start," said Garvon Hael, when Henwyn had shaken the seawater out of his ears.

"I'm tired of being a decoration at Boskennack. My sword is at your service, if you want it."

THE ROAD HOME

The evening sun was warm, but Henwyn and Skarper were still soggy by the time they returned to the house on the Street of Antiquaries. Mistress Carnglaze persuaded them that it would be silly to set off in wet things, with darkness drawing on, and so they had one more night in comfort, eating fish pie in the Carnglazes' kitchen while their damp clothes dried on racks beside the fire.

"But we must leave early tomorrow!" said Henwyn. "Those dwarves will already be on their way home, I expect; off to tell their king that Clovenstone is defenceless."

"They don't have a king," said Skarper. "They have this brass head thingy that tells them what to do."

"How do you know that?" asked Carnglaze, and Henwyn looked surprised as well. Skarper kicked himself. He had not told anyone about his talk with Etty, and it seemed too late to do so now. "I, er, read it somewhere," he said.

"Well, brass head or not," declared Henwyn, "he shall soon know that the High King refused to help us. We must leave for the north at dawn!"

He regretted saying that, for Mistress Carnglaze took him seriously, and he and Skarper barely seemed to have closed their eyes that night before she was in their room and shaking them awake. A dim grey light lay over the rooftops of Coriander. They stumbled about bleary-eyed, getting dressed. Downstairs in the kitchen bowls of hot porridge waited for them, and so did Zeewa. Her ghosts roiled around her, clearly visible at this twilight hour. She had swapped her bright dress for a linen tunic, and she carried a square oxhide shield and a quiver of spears on her back. Her hair, undone from its plaits, stood out in a crackly black cloud around her dark face.

Skarper yelped as a ghost hyena came sniffing at him.

"Oh, Zeewa will be coming with us, too," said Henwyn, who had somehow not found time to mention her to Skarper before.

"And all her phantom friends as well?" asked Skarper nervously.

"They may be useful," said Henwyn. "Perhaps dwarves are scared of ghosts."

"They will be scared of Zeewa's spear!" said the ghost warrior Kosi. "I wish I were flesh and blood again, so that I, too, could wash my blade in the blood of your enemies, Henwyn of Clovenstone!"

"You?" sniffed Zeewa. "You only fought one battle, and look what happened to you!"

"That was an accident," said Kosi, looking hurt. "If I hadn't tripped and landed on your spear. . ."

The girl and the ghost were still quietly bickering ten minutes later, when they all went outside into the grey and silent street. Mistress Carnglaze wept and hugged them and handed them bags full of fresh rolls and cold meat; her husband said, "Farewell, but not for long. I'll be at Clovenstone as soon as I can, with the best army money can buy!" King Knobbler slapped Skarper so hard on the back he nearly sent him face first on the cobbles, and growled, "You sort them dwarves out, young Scuffler."

And then they were off, stomping through the cold silence of the streets, with the cats of Coriander fleeing from the ghosts which trailed behind them. They had expected to find the city gate closed, but the guards had opened it, and there beneath the archway waited Garvon Hael, seated on a huge, shaggy war horse as grey as the morning. Beside him stood a familiar, shabby figure.

"I thought I might come too," said Quesney Prong hesitantly. "I should like to take a look at this Clovenstone place, and there is nothing left for me in Coriander. The autumn rains will be here soon, and they will turn my book-house to papier mâché. Anyway, I did a little sword-fighting in my younger days, at university. I may be of some use."

"How?" asked Skarper, rather rudely, but Henwyn gripped the old man's hands in his and said, "All are welcome! The dwarves will flee before us!"

Which was nonsense, of course, but even Skarper hadn't the heart to point that out. Only Garvon Hael, high on his great horse, gave a wry smile: he remembered when he himself had been as young and as foolhardy as Henwyn.

Introductions were made: Garvon Hael dismounted and shook Zeewa's hand, while his horse sniffed uncertainly at Tau the ghost lion. Kosi materialized in front of Dr Prong, who said, "I do not believe in ghosts, young man, but I suppose in your case I could make an exception." The gate guards looked on curiously, and the flames in the brazier outside their guardhouse fluttered as ghost flies and ghost moths swarmed around it.

Skarper looked at his companions. A haunted girl; a penniless old philosopher; a drunkard; a shower of ghosts; and Henwyn. It wasn't much of an army to fling against the whole dwarven nation. For a moment he thought about turning and running back into the city, finding himself a nice cosy nook somewhere, like those three trolls under their bridge, and forgetting all about Clovenstone. That would have been the gobliny thing to do, and he knew it. But he'd changed, just as Clovenstone itself had, and he didn't always do the gobliny thing any more. With a last reluctant look over his shoulder at the waking city, he pulled his cloak tight against the chilly air and set off after his friends, along the pale road that led into the hills.

In fact, the three trolls were no longer living under the old bridge. Demoralized by the ease with which Skarper and Henwyn had defeated them, they had decided that city life was not for them. "These townspeople are too sharp for us, brothers," Torridge had decided, as they all nursed their wounds on the night after the fight. "We're hill trolls, we are, and the hills is where we should have stayed. Let's go and find a nice bridge up on the moor's edge: the sort that farmers drive fat flocks of sheep to market over."

"Sheep!" said his brothers, and their eyes shone dimly like wet pebbles. They'd been living on old bones and midden scraps since they'd come to the big city. Just the thought of a nice plump sheep was enough to set their mouths watering.

So, while Henwyn and Skarper were waiting for an audience at Boskennack, the trolls had set off up the River Ystrad to the marshes, and across the marshes to the Ystwyth, and up the Ystwyth and its smaller, tributary rivers, until they reached places where men were few and the plump green downs of the Softlands lapped against the stony, brindled slopes of Oeth Moor. There, in a hollow among some ferns, beneath an old stone packhorse bridge, they made their new lair, and they waited.

On the first day nothing crossed the bridge except a stray cow. It had pointy horns, and looked far too fearsome for the nervous trolls to tackle.

On the second day a farmer rode across the bridge on his horse, but he had a sword slung from his saddle; the trolls thought better of it, and ducked back under the bridge before he noticed them.

On the third day, nothing crossed the bridge at all.

Then, as darkness fell, Torridge, who had gone out for a sulky walk to get away from the rumblings of his brothers' empty bellies, came haring back to their holt in high excitement. "There's a fire! A fire!" he panted.

"So what?" asked Kenn.

"We can live underwater, Torridge," whined Cribba. "Fires don't frighten us."

"Not a *wild*fire! A campfire!" Torridge urged, waiting for understanding to dawn on their broad, stupid faces. It showed no sign of doing so, so he pressed on. "That means campers. Travellers! All alone in the wilderness! At our mercy!"

Like boulders on the move, the three trolls crept out of their lair and along the riverbank towards the orange eye of the fire.

The companions had made their camp that night on a little knoll where oak trees grew, surrounded on three sides by the river but high enough above the water that it would not flood. Garvon Hael's grey horse cropped the grass under the trees, and Zeewa's ghosts swirled like river mist just outside the circle of firelight. Within the circle, Henwyn was trying to help everyone get to know one another. He thought that, since they were travelling companions, and might soon be comrades in a dreadful battle, they should know one another's stories. He tried to persuade Zeewa to tell them something about her homeland, but all she would say was, "It is much like this place, except warmer, and not so wet."

Next he turned to Garvon Hael, who was sharpening his sword, his back resting against an oak as weathered and as grey as he was. "Come, Garvon Hael," said Henwyn, "you have fought real battles. Tell us about them!"

"Only one," said Garvon Hael, looking up at him, and the red reflections of his firelit sword were in his eyes.

"That was the fight at Far Penderglaze?" asked Henwyn eagerly. "Carnglaze told me something of it: how you drove the pirates back into the sea, and killed their chief in single combat in the shallows, and burned their ships! It was a glorious victory!"

"Glorious?" said Garvon Hael. "I'd not call it that. A battle is a dreadful thing, Henwyn of Adherak, even when you win. I do not choose to talk of it."

"Oh," said Henwyn. Then, "Skarper, perhaps you'll tell us something of Clovenstone, for you know it better than I."

But Skarper was tired out by the long walk, and had fallen fast asleep, wrapped in his tatty cloak.

"Very well," decided Henwyn. "I shall sing you the Lay of Eluned, which is the story of how Princess

Eluned came to live at Clovenstone. This happened long ago, you understand: she had no idea then that she would one day be queen of the place."

He stood up, stuck one finger in his ear, and began to sing in a high, nasal voice quite unlike the voice he spoke with.

> 'Twas on a summer's morning
> A Tuesday they do tell
> The princess of Lusuenn sailed
> Upon the grey sea's swell,
> And there upon the ocean deep
> A dreadful thing befell. . .

The ghosts whispered in the darkness; Skarper stirred uneasily in his sleep; Garvon Hael's war horse threw up its head and whinnied nervously, and its master exchanged a worried look with Zeewa. Some of these folk songs went on for twenty or thirty verses, and Henwyn hadn't even reached the first chorus yet!

All in all, it was something of a relief for everyone when a large, wet rock came whirling out of the shadows and hit Henwyn a glancing blow on the head.

He collapsed in mid-song, luckily falling away from the fire, but unluckily landing on top of Skarper, who awoke with a strangled cry. But everyone was crying out by then; Zeewa screeching some Muskish war cry as she snatched up her spears, the horse rearing, Garvon Hael leaping up with a yell, reflections of the firelight darting as he swung his sword at the big shapes lunging out of the dark.

The trolls had scrambled up the riverward side of the knoll, from which Henwyn and the others had not imagined any attack would come. The voice of the river, tumbling in the darkness down below, had masked the sound of their approach. For a moment, as they leapt out upon the startled camp, the travellers were taken completely by surprise. As Zeewa straightened up, her short stabbing spear in her hand, Torridge swung a branch at her. Although it was soft and rotten, and broke on her shield with a wet thump, the blow was still enough to knock her down. But as the troll reached for her, the storm of ghosts came swooping and swirling around him, Kosi brandishing a ghostly spear, Tau the lion baring teeth and claws.

Meanwhile, Cribba's attack on Garvon Hael had gone all wrong too: his tree branch was stronger, but the grey warrior parried it expertly, kicked his legs from under him and set his sword's point against the troll's throat. Kenn ran to help, but Dr Prong jumped on him from behind, and although the old man could not have weighed a quarter as much as the young troll, Kenn overbalanced and went sprawling in the cinders at the edge of the fire. He started to scramble up, but came face to face with the glowing, ghostly lion, so he gave up, put his big hands over his head, and crouched there, whimpering.

Torridge stumbled backwards against a tree, clutching at his chest, from which jutted the shaft of Kosi's ghostly spear. It dissolved into smoke and nothingness before his boggling eyes, and when he tore open his clothes there was no blood, no wound, only his bald, pale, speckled chest.

Zeewa, recovered, approached him with her own spear raised. "What are these creatures?" she asked, never taking her eyes from Torridge.

"Urban trolls," said Dr Prong, who was still sitting on the one he'd felled. "The same trio who used to haunt the riverside in Coriander, if I'm not much mistaken. They're completely imaginary, of course."

"Do we kill them?" asked the girl.

In a high, piteous voice, Cribba said, "Oh, please, your worships, don't harm my poor brothers and me. We didn't mean no harm. Well, we did, but not to you. It was all a case of mistaken identity, see: we mistook you for people who wouldn't fight back. Oh, spare our lives, we'll trouble you no more."

Garvon Hael kept his sword point at Cribba's throat but called over his own shoulder to Dr Prong. "How is the boy?"

The philosopher scurried round the fire to stoop over Henwyn. Garvon Hael glared down at Cribba and softly growled, "If you have killed him, troll. . ."

But Henwyn stirred and groaned as Dr Prong shook him. "Princess Ned!" he cried, and sat up, allowing a rather bruised and crumpled Skarper to emerge from underneath.

"It's *them*!" wailed Kenn, peeking out between his fingers. "It's those two from Coriander! They've followed us here!"

"Troll hunters!" wailed Cribba, quailing. "We'll all be murdered in our riverbeds!"

The oak-grove filled with the stony clatter of the trolls' knees knocking.

"What shall we do with them?" asked Zeewa.

"We must not kill them," said Henwyn, dabbing at the blood that was trickling down the side of his face. "It would not be heroic at all."

"Well, we can't let them go," grumbled Skarper. "They'll just sneak back and attack us again, and maybe they'll have better luck next time. And I wish you'd take a bit more notice of who you're collapsing on: look, my tail's all bent."

"Please spare us!" whined Cribba. "We'll do anything you want!"

"Anything?" asked Henwyn.

Garvon Hael glanced at him. "What are you thinking?"

Henwyn shrugged. "That they could come with us to Clovenstone. That they could fight with us against the dwarves."

"They fight badly," said Zeewa.

"I thought they did all right," said Henwyn, rubbing ruefully at the lump on his head. "And they are big, and strong. You could teach them, Garvon Hael."

Cribba was nodding eagerly. Kenn, down on the ground, said, "Oh yes! Take us with you! We'll kill dwarves for you, loads and loads of dwarves."

Torridge added, "Are dwarves like pixies? I hate pixies. They're chewy."

Garvon Hael stepped back, lowering his sword. After a moment, Zeewa did the same. The trolls relaxed a little, peering about meekly at their captors.

"They are quite young trolls," said Garvon Hael.

"We hatched last spring," said Torridge. "Three stones in the Ystwyth, that's all we was till then. Then we woke, and felt hungry, and we moved downriver to that big man-town, but it was hard for us there, only scraps and cats to live on. So we came upstream again, looking for a good lair, and sheep to eat."

"We're starving," whimpered Cribba.

"I think we have some rolls left," Henwyn said. "And we can buy more food in Sticklebridge tomorrow."

He fetched the last of Mistress Carnglaze's provisions from the packs and the trolls squatted down gratefully to eat. Henwyn said, "It sounds as if Clovenstone is the place for you. There are rivers and woods and crags there, and lairs aplenty, so long as you promise to eat no people or goblins, only the wild goats and deer."

The three trolls meekly munched their rolls. Garvon Hael had sheathed his sword, but his hand never strayed far from its hilt. Zeewa was looking at Henwyn as if she thought he was mad, though she was too polite to say so.

Skarper wasn't. "Are you mad?" he asked, pinching his nose shut against the wet, weedy smell of troll. "Did that rock on the noggin knock you silly? There's already one troll at Clovenstone, and one's enough."

But Henwyn didn't think he was mad. If the dwarves were to be stopped, then Clovenstone would need all the help it could get, no matter what form it came in, or what it smelled like. And the dwarves had to be stopped. While he'd been unconscious, while the others were busy subduing Torridge and his brothers,

Henwyn had drifted into a dream of the future. Once again, just as he had in Madam Maura's tent, he had found himself at Clovenstone, and had seen it wrecked and burning. Once again he had stood in Ned's garden, and seen her stretched out dead beneath the falling ash.

Henwyn knew that it had been no ordinary dream. It had been far more vivid; far more like the vision he had seen in the oracular bathtub. It had been the future that he'd seen, and it was a future that he was determined to change, even if changing it meant making friends with trolls.

Durgar and his dwarves were on their way homeward too. All the way, through old tunnels and new, Etty remembered the sights and sounds and smells of Coriander. Flowers and seagulls, painted houses and dresses made of printed Muskish silk: she had never realized that there was so much colour in the world.

She had been above the ground before, of course; in Clovenstone and the Bonehill Mountains, and in the dwarf farms at Delverdale, but those places were mostly the colours of stones and grass and trees; there was none of the brightness in them of the city she had seen. Why didn't dwarves have bright clothes? she wondered. Why didn't they paint the lovely houses that they carved, deep under the hills?

Most of all, she remembered Skarper. He had been a bigger surprise than all the colours. To meet a goblin, to sit talking with him, and to find that he was not so different from herself. It went against everything she'd ever been told.

She thought about it all through the long walk north, and when they were nearing the new workings she finally summoned up the courage to ask her father.

"Why are goblins our enemy?"

Durgar looked back at her and frowned. "Why? Because they're goblins, of course. Cruel, brutish creatures. Wreckers and wasters of good things; murderers of dwarves."

"But Skarper's not like that."

"Who?" asked Langstone, smoothing his beard.

"The goblin we met at Clovenstone, and again at Boskennack. Henwyn's friend."

"Aye, well, he may not seem so bad," said Durgar, "but they can be cunning creatures, some of them. This Skarper must be one of the cleverer ones; that'll be why Henwyn brought him to see the bigling king; to try and prove that goblins aren't as bad as folk believe. But we know they are, don't we?"

"Aye," agreed Langstone and Walna, nodding.

"But how do we know that?" asked Etty.

"Because the Head tells us so," her father replied. "The Head Knows All and the Head Knows Best."

"Even so," said Etty, "it seems mean to be stealing all their slowsilver away."

"Too late to be fretting about that, lass," said Durgar. "That plan is well advanced."

And so it seemed, for as they entered the new workings they passed great troops of dwarf warriors, newly arrived from Dwarvenholm, sharpening their swords in readiness for the coming war. The workings echoed to the fall of armourers' hammers, the shouts of mole drivers, and the hollow clangs as mysterious lengths of iron pipe were dragged into position.

Overseer Glunt was climbing up on to a diremole when they found him. "Can't talk now, Durgar," he shouted. "I must get back to Dwarvenholm to let the Head and the Council of Overseers know how things are going. General Cardle's in charge of things here while I'm gone."

The diremole started to lumber off, heading north-east up a broad underground road which the dwarves had recently finished widening. Durgar, rather flustered at not getting a chance to make his report, trotted alongside it. "The High King refused help to the goblins and their friends at Clovenstone," he called up.

"Good," said Glunt, not really listening.

"I was wondering, though, Overseer, if it might be worth talking again to their Princess Ned? Young Henwyn and the goblin who came with him did not seem bad sorts, really. Mightn't it be possible to reach some arrangement about the slowsilver without any need for fighting?"

Etty, listening to all this, smiled to herself. Her dad might seem gruff, but she knew he loved her, and he'd asked that question for her sake, she was sure. But Glunt glanced down at him with a sneer. "No need for fighting? Then why has the Head sent us all these warriors and war machines? Do you think you know better than the Head? Of course you don't: no one does. The Head has ordered an attack on Clovenstone, Durgar, so an attack there shall be. It is all part of the Head's great plan. Driver, won't this beast go any faster?"

The mole's driver reached behind him and stuck a pointed goad into the monster's haunches. With a squeal, it broke into a lumbering gallop, and was soon lost in the shadows of the tunnel, far ahead.

Durgar watched it go, then turned back to his companions, looking very dignified and trying to pretend the overseer had not just brushed him off like an irritating dwarf child. "Well, that's that," he said, careful not to meet Etty's eye. "Let's not stand here yammering. The Head has spoken. There's work to be done."

HOMECOMING HEROES

In the world above, Henwyn and his companions found that winter had come to Oeth Moor in the few days that they had been away. The thorn trees on the rocky hillsides stood bare and bleak, their leaves stripped away by a cold wind from the east. The travellers skirted Sticklebridge and headed north on the old faded road to Clovenstone, while the dogs in all the farms and hamlets that they passed barked and howled, catching the scent of trolls, sensing the chill of ghosts.

"At least the dwarves have further to go than us," said Garvon Hael as they toiled along, cloaks pulled tight against the wind.

"But dwarves don't need to keep fording rivers and sloshing through bogs," said Henwyn, stopping for the hundredth time to tip muddy water out of his boots.

"Dwarves have nice clear tunnels to travel through, and giant moles to ride on. They're probably back at their burrows in the Bonehills, planning their attack on Clovenstone."

He did not know how right he was. But there was nothing they could do about it. They kept on sloshing through the bogs and fording the little streams and rivers of the moor, and before too long they came over the last steep ridge and saw the plain of Dor Koth to the north, and the great ruinous ring of battlements and watchtowers that was the Outer Wall of Clovenstone.

"We're home!" said Skarper, pricking up his ears, surprised at how happy he was to see the old dump again.

"We are," said Henwyn, and he felt it too: Clovenstone, where so many adventures had befallen him, and he had learned so much. It was his home too now, and he frowned as he studied the distant view, fearing any sign that the dwarvish onslaught had begun. But no: there was no trace of the flames and fighting he had glimpsed in Madam Maura's bathtub, and those clouds that hung behind the central towers were marsh mist, not the smoke of battle.

"Is that it?" asked Cribba.

"There's trolls there?" wondered Torridge.

"And the Houses of the Dead. . ." said Zeewa.

They came down off the moor's edge and crossed the plain, the road winding between the mounds where bodies had been piled and burned after the great battle long ago. It was late afternoon, and in the low light Zeewa's train of ghosts showed pale and vaporous, like a scrap of moor mist that had followed her down from the hills. They reached the massive, crumbling Outer Wall, and Henwyn was just shoving a pathway through the brambles and weeds under the arch of Southerly Gate when a voice shouted, "Who goes there?" and with a slither and clatter of rusty armour a score of goblins leapt out of dark doorways and other hidey-holes, pointing spears and hefting axes.

"It's all right! It is only us, come home from Coriander!" Skarper yelled, before Zeewa could draw her short stabbing spear or the three trolls could start lobbing rocks about.

The goblins peered at him, and realized that he was who said he was, and that what he'd said was true. "Pity," said one, lowering a huge, spiked club. "I could just have done with bashing somebody."

"Couldn't we bash them anyway?" asked another. "Just for practice?"

"I'll bash you if you don't shut your cakehole," said the leader, pulling off his spiky-snouted helmet. He was Libnog, Skarper's own batch-brother, and he looked around expectantly as he came out to greet the travellers. "You saw the High King then? He sent warriors? An army? Where are they?"

"Here," said Henwyn. "The High King would not send his heroes, so I found heroes of our own."

Libnog stared. "A girl, two old men, and a bunch of rubbish trolls?" he said weakly. "What good are they going to be?"

"We're not rubbish," mumbled Torridge, but he and his brothers all looked a bit afraid of the goblins.

"There are ghosts, too," said Skarper. "They might not be able to fight, but they can frighten the dwarves away, perhaps. They're dead scary."

"Wooooooo!" suggested Kosi, spookily, materializing above Zeewa's head.

"Stop it!" said Zeewa. "You're just embarrassing yourself."

"Goblins are not afraid of the ghosts of men," said Garvon Hael, looking on with that faint, mocking smile of his. "And nor will dwarves be, I dare say."

Torridge, Cribba and Kenn were all trying to hide behind one another. Dr Prong was peering curiously at the goblin guards, as if he still half hoped to find a way of proving they did not exist.

Henwyn looked at Skarper, and sighed. It was

not much of an army they had brought home with them, but it would have to do. "They are not great in number," he admitted, "but their hearts are true."

What does that even mean? wondered Skarper. *It won't matter how true our hearts are if a million dwarves come charging at us.* But he didn't want to make Henwyn look foolish (at least, not any more foolish than he usually looked) so he said nothing, just followed with the others as Henwyn led them through the Southerly Gate and on up the road towards the Inner Wall on its high crag.

Several times along that road they were stopped by goblin patrols, all dressed up in outsize helms and hauberks from the armouries, playing at soldiers among the ruins. There were listening posts down in the cellars of the old buildings too, for everyone knew that the dwarves were more likely to launch their attack under the ground than over the Outer Wall. "We can hear them," said a Redcap, when they stopped beside his cellar. "We puts our ears to the ground and we hears scratching and thumping and stuff going on. It's worse round the east side. That's where they'll come from, probably."

There were fewer goblins in the woods –even in these times, the people of the trees distrusted them – but when the road came out of the trees near the base of Meneth Eskern they were everywhere, marching around in clumsy battalions on the weed-grown old drill yards and building crude catapults on the tops of ancient bastions. There were so many of them that Skarper started to feel a little happier. Goblins were good at fighting, after all. They always had been. All right, so this lot weren't as rough and tough as King Knobbler and the big bullies of years gone by, but surely they could see off a gang of pathetic dwarves?

They climbed to the gate in the Inner Wall and went through it. Princess Ned was standing in a wild part of her new garden, watching Fentongoose order a regiment of young hatchlings around. At first the hatchlings looked impressive enough, the thicket of their tall spears catching the last of the sunlight as they marched through their manoeuvres. But goblins are not clever creatures (Skarper was probably one of the cleverest goblins there had ever been, and he didn't feel particularly bright) and inevitably it all went wrong. "Right TURN!" bellowed Fentongoose, and half the goblins turned right while most of the rest turned left and a few just went round in circles, quite bewildered. They tripped over each other's feet, over spears and shields, over their own too-big armour, and went down with a clatter in a squabbling heap, while loud fights broke out over whose fault it was.

While Fentongoose tried to stop a brawl developing, Princess Ned came hurrying to greet the new arrivals. Even she was wearing armour; a silvery breastplate from the armouries was strapped on over her faded gardening dress. It did not suit her; she did not look like a warrior princess, more like a slightly ill-at-ease guest on her way to a costume party.

"Henwyn!" she said (taking his hands). "And Skarper..." (tickling behind his ears in just the way he liked). She looked questioningly at the strangers ranged behind them. Zeewa's cloud of ghosts were showing up quite clearly now in the twilight, and even Princess Ned quailed a little at the sight of them. And trolls too! But Garvon Hael stepped forward and bowed, and said, "We are your army, Lady of Clovenstone."

Princess Ned narrowed her eyes. "You are Garvon Hael!" she said. "I remember you! You came to Lusuenn once, when I was a girl."

Garvon Hael nodded. "More than once. And a loud, foolish, boastful, brash young fellow you thought me, I am sure."

"Well," said Ned, blushing a little, "I wasn't going to say anything, but..."

"But I was," said Garvon Hael. "I remember seeing you there. Like a meadow flower growing in an overtended garden, I thought you. And when the giant Fraddon stole you away I was one of the heroes who came to try and rescue you. But Fraddon set me right; told me you were happy enough and sent me on my way. I was young and full of wind and spoiling for a fight, but I could not fight him: he picked me up between his finger and thumb and hung me on a tree. I was so ashamed that, when I finally climbed down, I took ship for Far Penderglaze, in the Autumn Isles. A fight with the pirates there soon knocked some sense into me. There is nothing quite like a battle for knocking the wind and bluster out of a man."

"Garvon Hael was the only one of the High King's warriors who would come to help us," explained Henwyn.

"And we are very happy that you have, Garvon Hael," said Princess Ned. "Although I fear that Clovenstone may be a lost cause. . ." She glanced over her shoulder at the goblins, who were picking themselves up and brushing dust off their dented armour, still busy bickering about what "right" and "left" meant. Fentongoose had given up trying to instruct them and was sitting on a heap of dropped shields with his head in his hands.

"That, we shall see," said Garvon Hael. "I had an

army of farm boys and fishermen at Far Penderglaze, and they started not much better than this rabble you have here. Let me be your general, Lady of Clovenstone, and I shall knock them into shape for you."

There was a feast that night in the great hall at the foot of Redcap Tower. Princess Ned was good at organizing feasts, and she had been expecting a whole horde of heroes, not just Garvon Hael and a couple of hangers-on, so there was plenty to go round. Stew and dumplings, flavoured with the fierce scarlet peppers that the Redcaps grew in Clovenstone's ancient glasshouses; a giant apple crumble for afters, with dollops of clotted cream.

Then there was singing, and games, and a burping contest, and Princess Ned told the tale of Prince Brewyon and the Loaf of Doom. Fentongoose explained to Zeewa that the Houses of the Dead was an old name for the great complex of tombs and burial mounds in the north-eastern part of Clovenstone, and promised to show her the way there next morning. Garvon Hael drank a lot of wine from some cobwebby old bottles that someone unearthed from the cellars, and made a rousing speech in which he told everybody that this was the last fun they would have for a long time: the next morning he was going to set about turning them into an army. The new hatchlings, who were growing tired of people telling them that they shouldn't fight, were very taken with this grizzled old warrior, who not only told them that they should but promised he would show them how to do it really well. A speckled, scaly one called Soakaway used a plate as a shield and a fork for a sword and Garvon Hael taught him how to thrust and parry while the others crowded close to watch and learn. It wasn't long before Soakaway was able to catch the warrior's sword blows on the plate and Garvon Hael's quilted breeches were full of fork holes. "See?" shouted Garvon Hael. "Who says that goblins will be no match for dwarves?"

"Hooray!" cheered some goblins.

"Clovenstone for ever!" howled others.

"Anchovies!" yelled Skarper's batch-brother Gutgust. ("Anchovies!" was the only thing Gutgust ever said, and nobody ever knew why.)

Dr Prong was the only one who did not join in the party mood. He sat in a corner, looking on in nervous amazement as goblins fought and burped, danced wildly to the rough music of tooting goblin horns, and formed themselves into giant pyramids that teetered right up to the rafters before collapsing amid shrieks of goblin laughter. Eventually he seemed to decide that it was all too much; with a muttered "Excuse me!", he hurried outside and up on to the battlements.

But if he had hoped to escape from the strange sights and citizens of Clovenstone, he was in for a disappointment. Just outside the Inner Wall, where the woods began, a huge figure stood in the moonlight, taller than the tallest beech trees. The giant's face was as weathered as an outcropping of upland stone, his hair was grey as lichen, and his tusks glinted in the moonlight as he chuckled softly at the prickly, twiggy beings who were clambering over him.

"Dr Prong?" asked Princess Ned, coming up to stand beside the startled philosopher.

Dr Prong pointed weakly at the scene below. "Is that. . .?"

"That is Fraddon the giant. He is a very old friend of mine. It was he who carried my ship to Clovenstone, many years ago, with me inside it. I am very glad he did. I have never once regretted coming here."

Dr Prong made a strangled sound that might have been meant as a laugh. "I am regretting it already!" he said. "What can I do here, among goblins and giants and trolls and . . . what are those bushy creatures?"

"Twiglings. They live in the trees, and are great friends with Fraddon."

"Ah. . ." said Dr Prong. "You see, my lady, I have

spent all my life disbelieving in such things, and trying to learn the rules that govern the world. Now all the rules are torn up: wild magic is loose again, and there is no place for me."

"Oh, do not say that!" said Princess Ned. "There are rules to magic, even if they are strange ones, and hard to understand. But tell me. . ."

She hesitated a moment, and Prong turned to look at her.

"They call you Dr Prong," she said. "Does that mean that you know something of medicine?"

"I am a doctor of philosophy," said Prong primly. "But I do know something of the healing arts."

"Then you must stay!" said Princess Ned, with a smile. "There is no doctor in Clovenstone, and we are in need of one, for the goblins are forever injuring themselves, and one another."

"Well, certainly I know how to splint a broken leg, or bandage a broken head. Even a broken goblin head. . ."

"And it is not just the goblins who will need you," Ned went on. "Take me, for instance. I am not what you would call a *young* princess any more. I have dizzy spells, and get out of breath after even the least bit of exercise."

Dr Prong bowed. "I shall examine you in the

morning, if you wish, and perhaps prescribe some herbal remedy."

Ned beamed at him. "There! You see? You have found your place after all! Welcome to Clovenstone, Dr Prong!"

It was long after midnight that Skarper scrambled back up the many stairs of Blackspike to his own little chamber and snuggled down in his old, familiar nest. Outside, drunken goblins caterwauled around. The burping competition seemed still to be going on – or maybe it was just ordinary burping now. Skarper couldn't hear any judging, although there were still rowdy outbursts of applause after the loudest burps.

For the first time since the coming of the dwarves, Skarper felt quite hopeful. There might not be many of them, the little army of heroes he and Henwyn had brought back from Coriander, but perhaps what Henwyn had said was right: their hearts were true. Give us a couple of weeks, he thought, as he drifted off into a deep and dreamless sleep, and we'll be more than a match for those blimmin' dwarves. . .

*

But as it turned out, they did not have a couple of weeks. They did not even have a couple of days. They did not even have a couple of hours. In the hour before dawn, while most of Clovenstone was sleeping soundly with its belly full of stew and crumble, the dwarves began their war.

DWARF ATTACK!

Henwyn's bedroom was one of the spare cabins of Princess Ned's ship, up on the top of Blackspike Tower. He had a comfy bed there, and he had been glad to crawl into it after days on the road and then that long and happy feast. He was fast asleep, snuggled up on his side under the thick coverlet, when the braying of a goblin war horn reached down into his dreams, hooked him like a fish, and dragged him, spluttering and groaning, back into waking life.

He lay there a moment, unsure where he was. Slowly it came to him that he was home; he recognized the familiar timbers of the cabin roof, and the sampler that his sister Hirda had stitched for him hanging on the curved wall. He was a bit alarmed to find that the old ship was swaying and turning round in giddy circles, until he realized that that was just an after-effect of the wine he had drunk at the feast. But a glare of reddish light was coming in through the porthole, and he was pretty sure *that* didn't have anything to do with the wine. Also, there was that dreadful yowling noise. . .

He rolled out of bed and wobbled his way to the porthole. Outside, on the battlements of the Inner Wall, goblins were running about with flaming torches, and one was blowing steadily on a huge brass war horn. BWAAAAAAT! it went.

Being used to goblins, Henwyn assumed this was just mischief. But as he turned to go back to bed, there came a panicky hammering on his bedroom door, and the voice of Fentongoose. "Henwyn, awake! The dwarves are upon us!"

"Argh!" said Henwyn. He stumbled around the cabin, pulling on his boots, his tunic, his sword belt, pulling his boots off again so he could get his trousers on, and eventually opening the door and barging out into the ship's main cabin. Fentongoose and Dr Prong were there, still in their nightshirts, and Princess Ned was buckling on her breastplate. "Fetch Garvon Hael!" she said.

"I knocked on his door a few minutes ago," said Fentongoose.

"Then knock again!"

"I'll try!" said Henwyn. It was he who had brought Garvon Hael here, after all; he felt responsible for him.

The old warrior had been given one of the spare cabins to sleep in. Henwyn blundered through the snaky passageways of the ship and banged loudly on the door. From outside came the screams and shouts of goblins. What was happening out there? Henwyn thumped on the door again, then shoved it open.

Garvon Hael was asleep face down across his bed. It looked as if he had started to get up, and even got as far as pulling his trousers on, before falling back to sleep. He was snoring quite loudly.

Henwyn shook him. "Garvon Hael! Awake! We have need of you!"

"Gffuffgtherguerr," said Garvon Hael, half-opening one bloodshot eye.

"We are under attack!"

Garvon Hael sat up. "Pirates again, is it?" he slurred. "I'll show them. . ."

"It is the dwarves!" cried Henwyn. "You are at Clovenstone! Do you remember? You said you'd help us!"

Garvon Hael stared blearily at him. He pointed a wavering finger. "Now listen to me, you young whippersnapper: I don't like people who take that kind of tone with me. . ." He stopped, looking confused, and belched – not loudly enough to win a goblin burping competition, perhaps, but he would certainly have been awarded a place among the top three runners-up. His breath stank of stale wine. Henwyn remembered what Carnglaze had said. *He crawled into a wine jug, and he has never come out again.* How many bottles had Garvon Hael downed at the feast last night?

From outside came a mighty boom, a crash and slither of falling masonry, the squeals and shrieks of goblins. The war horn had stopped.

"Get dressed!" shouted Henwyn, heaving the drunken warrior to his feet. "Gird on your sword and come with me! There is a battle to be won!" He strode across the cabin and snatched up Garvon Hael's sword. When he turned back to the bed he saw that the warrior had slumped across it again, singing a melancholy song about a worm who accidentally fell in love with a piece of string.

"Oh," said Henwyn, "this is useless!" He dropped the sword and ran back to the main cabin. The others had already gone outside, and he followed them, out into the grey, cheerless, predawn light; out into the fire-glow and the smoke of war.

It had begun with molehills. Among the ruins which lay between the woods and the Inner Wall, flagstones had begun to tremble; walls had toppled. Up through the earth and the crusts of masonry the Lych Lord's builders had laid upon it, the diremoles came nosing, lifting tall cones of rubble and wet earth into the starlight. How many of these mounds there were, nobody was certain. Most of the goblin sentries who had been standing guard that night had sneaked off to the feast, and those that had stayed behind had mostly persuaded their mates to bring back some wine and food for them, so they were sleeping as soundly as the rest. It was young Soakaway, wandering out on to the battlements for a pee, who eventually noticed something moving down among the old buildings. He strained his sharp, night-seeing goblin eyes and saw the starshine glint upon a diremole's armoured nose.

That was when the panic began. The few goblins who were awake ran frantically in every direction, kicking their friends out of their nests, grabbing weapons and armour, falling over, getting up again, forgetting everything that Fentongoose and Princess Ned had tried to teach them. "The dwarves!" they shouted. "The dwarves are here!" In the confusion a few goblins were mistaken for dwarves themselves, and terrible fights broke out. It was minutes before anybody thought to start blowing the war horn.

Down in the woods, the giant Fraddon woke. He

picked up a club he had fashioned for himself out of a fallen oak and strode towards the Inner Wall. He looked about, and saw the dark mounds growing, the earth tumbling down their sides. Wherever an armoured mole-nose gleamed he brought his club down, smashing the diremoles back into the tunnels they had made, stunning or killing the ones which had already started to heave themselves free of their hills.

But moles were rising everywhere, and as the huge creatures kicked their way free of the earth and rubble, the dwarfs emerged behind them. These were not dwarf miners, like the ones Henwyn and Skarper had encountered. These were warriors, their faces hidden behind blank iron visors, their tough bodies armoured with coats of iron scales. Wielding hammers, axes and spears they marched towards the Inner Wall, urged on by their commanders, who rode in little castles mounted on the backs of the moles.

Skarper slept through all of that. Growing up in the noisy chambers of the Blackspike had given him an ability to sleep through almost anything, and no one had thought to come and tip him out of bed. He only stirred when a huge blow shook the tower, and half the ceiling caved in. Luckily it was not the half that he was sleeping under, and the crash of the falling timbers startled him awake. He sat up, and found that his nest was hanging halfway out of a big hole which had appeared in the wall. Below him, among the ruined buildings at the base of the wall, he saw firelight glittering on the armour of marching dwarves.

"Oh bumcakes!" he gibbered, scrabbling his way to the door just as whatever mighty engine of war the dwarves had brought with them launched another huge missile at the Blackspike. The crash as it landed sent him somersaulting out into the corridor, and a tide of squealing, yowling goblins carried him out on to the battlements.

The first thing that he noticed there was that Growler Tower had lost its top.

The second was that Redcap was on fire.

The third was Henwyn, running madly towards him, shouting, "Come on! We must drive them back!"

"What? Must we? Why?" asked Skarper, suddenly very wide awake, and very aware that he did not want to go and meet a whole bunch of dwarves with pointy things. "Can't we just hide? They can't really get through the Inner Wall, can they? Can't we just pretend we're not in?"

"Fraddon is out there," said Princess Ned (Skarper had not noticed her till then). "And the guards at the outer gates may be beset, and trying to fight their way back. Besides, we cannot let them batter down the gates; if they get inside the Wall they will be able to reach the lava lake. That is their plan, I expect! Come, we shall make a sortie, and drive them off."

"No!" said Henwyn, catching her by the elbow as she turned to go. "I mean – not you. It is too dangerous! You might be hurt!"

Ned looked strangely at him. "Of course it is dangerous! That's why I am going, to share in the danger. I will not skulk here while others fight."

Henwyn would not let go of her. He couldn't shake off the memory of the dreadful thing he'd seen in Madam Maura's vision. "You must not!" he said. "Imagine if you were harmed. What would the goblins do without you? What would any of us do? You are the Lady of Clovenstone. . ."

"I'm sure you'd manage," she said, shrugging him off. But she looked thoughtful. "Very well; I shall stay here. We must organize some catapults of our own to answer all these brickbats which the dwarves keep hurling at us."

"Yes," cried Henwyn, "yes! You do that! Let Skarper and me go forth and fight!"

"Now hang on a minute. . ." said Skarper, not at all sure he felt like fighting, and wondering if Princess Ned needed help with the catapults. But Princess Ned had help already; the three trolls had just emerged blinking from whatever hole they'd slept in and she snapped her fingers at them and shouted for them to follow her as she strode away. Skarper gulped. There was nothing for it but for him to follow his friend.

They started down one of the long, winding stairways which led down inside the Inner Wall. Henwyn was in the lead, with Fentongoose and Dr Prong close behind them, and then a great mass of the braver goblins, their war cries and the clatter of their rusty armour making a terrible din in the narrow, low-roofed passage. Close to the front were the new hatchlings, with Soakaway brandishing his sword in just the way that Garvon Hael had shown him – he had not had time to find himself a shield, though, and was still using a plate instead.

"Where is Garvon Hael?" shouted Skarper, thinking that he and Henwyn really weren't qualified to lead a war-band. But no one answered him.

Outside, the dwarves were dragging all manner of interesting objects out of the holes their moles had made. Giant catapults and bolt throwers, battering rams, and long hoses of jointed metal with dragon heads which sprayed jets of liquid fire. These they turned on Fraddon, driving him backwards towards the woods, where the treetops were full of leaping twiglings, terrified by the flames. Meanwhile the rest of the dwarven host tramped with their battering ram towards the great gate in the Inner Wall, while missiles whooshed over their heads to burst on the battlements, scaring away any goblins who might have tried to drop stones and boiling oil down on them.

But the Inner Wall had many gates; all sorts of secret ways which the goblins had made for their own comings and goings. One of these opened now, and out rushed Henwyn, with sword in hand and a horde of goblins at his heels.

He had been frightened on the way downstairs, but now, facing the enemy, he was not afraid at all; everything seemed to be moving too quickly for there to be any time for fear. He flourished his blade, and was about to shout something encouraging and historic-sounding, but before he could think of anything the goblins surged forward, carrying him with them. All the discipline that Fentongoose and Princess Ned had tried to drum into them was forgotten; they attacked the dwarves pell-mell, shouting wild war cries and whirling flails and clubs around their heads. They were almost as much danger to each other as to the enemy.

The dwarves around the main gate were taken by surprise. They gave way a little as the goblin charge slammed into them. The goblins, encouraged, scrambled over each other's heads in their eagerness to bash dwarves.

Meanwhile, high on the battlements, Princess Ned had found her way to the bratapult. The ancient war machine had once been mounted on top of Blackspike, where it had been used to fling cheeky hatchlings to their doom. It stood on an out-jutting of the battlements now, and had not been used since Princess Ned arrived. Now she set the three trolls to work heaving it to a better position, and told them, "Bring me rubble!"

Luckily there was no shortage of that – Clovenstone was probably the rubble capital of the whole Westlands. While Ned gathered passing goblins to help her operate the bratapult, Torridge, Cribba and Kenn found a huge fallen granite slab and dragged it over, lifting it into the bratapult's cup. Ned's goblins had already wound the rope tight. At Ned's command, Torridge pulled the lever which released it. The slab was heavier by many times than a hatchling, so it did not fly far and free as hatchlings did; just somersaulted clumsily over the wall and dropped. Down it went, punching through rags of cloud and the veil of smoke which hung above the battle. The dwarves below looked up and saw it falling. They scattered away from their battering ram just in time as the slab smashed and splintered it, and the goblins cheered and pressed in even harder.

For a while then it looked as if the counter-attack would succeed. But after a few fierce seconds the dwarves rallied and started to push back. Their armour was tougher than the goblins' armour, their blades were sharper, and they fought with a cold ferocity that the goblins found unnerving. There were no war cries from the dwarves, just the odd grunt of effort as they swung their big axes or threw their spears. Worst of all, they had a strange habit of changing places with one another: when a dwarf warrior grew weary of swinging his axe or hammer he simply stepped sideways and another took his place from the rank behind. This meant that, while the frantic goblins got achey arms and repetitive strain injuries from wielding their swords, the dwarves they faced were always fresh and rested.

It was more like fighting machines than living beings, although not many of the goblins knew what a machine was, so the thought did not occur to them. Anyway, they were too busy fighting to think. So was Henwyn, beset on every side. Luckily his sword was a good one, taken from one of Clovenstone's oldest armouries; it had belonged to some great captain of the Lych Lord once, and it hewed easily through the half-moon-shaped shields the dwarfs held up, and clove their helms in two amid bright showers of sparks. Even so, he was tiring quickly.

Down among the knees of the fight, among the dropped weapons and dying bodies, Skarper scrabbled about, tripping dwarves whenever he could, but mainly just trying to avoid getting bashed, spiked or speared himself. He wasn't a very large goblin, and he'd never been much of a fighter; he soon found his way back towards the door in the wall. Fentongoose and Dr Prong had already retreated to it, after learning in a few terrifying seconds that they were not cut out for battles either. Instead they were doing their best to tend the wounded; those poor goblins who were limping out of the melee with arms and legs missing, dripping dark goblin blood and grizzling loudly.

Fentongoose was struggling to staunch the flow of blood from Yabber, who was shouting angrily, "That dwarf chopped my tail off! They take ages to grow back!" when two of the littlest hatchlings appeared, dragging Soakaway.

"Fetch water!" shouted Dr Prong.

"It is no use!" said Fentongoose, bending over Soakaway. "He is stone dead!"

"Fetch water anyway!" said Dr Prong. "There will many more wounds to wash before this night is out."

As he spoke, a discarded dwarven helm went rolling

by. It looked a bit like a bucket, and Skarper decided that it might as well serve as one. Snatching it up, he went scampering down the steep, narrow paths between the ruins, heading for a place he knew where a clear stream spilled down the side of the crag. But just as he neared the spring, a movement caught his eye below. There, in a flat space between two ruined houses, the old flagstones were wobbling and rising. As he watched, the nose of an armoured diremole came pushing up into the firelight.

Skarper had forgotten how horrifyingly huge the creatures were. The pavement burst upwards, allowing the diremole's shoulders and its huge, pale hands to force their way out amid a tumble of dark, wet earth. As it heaved itself free of the ground its masters climbed up out of the hole it had made, seized handholds on its armoured flanks and scrambled up on to its back. Skarper heard them shouting to each other, and saw them point. He could see that they were going to guide the creature up the crag's flank, to attack Henwyn and the goblins from the rear. He turned, shouting, "Help! Here! Help!" into the din of the fight going on above him, knowing that no one would be listening.

The diremole was starting to scrabble its way up the hill. It didn't like being out in the open air. It tossed its huge, blunt head from side to side, firelight flashing in the dark bulbous goggles which hid its eyes. It whined shrill protests, but the dwarves on its back struck at it with goads and long leather whips and it crawled forward, starting up the slope.

Surely someone will see it? thought Skarper, crouched by the stream with the helm in his trembly paws. *Surely someone will hear?* Surely they would not leave it up to *him*?

But the goblins above him were hard pressed, the fight spreading along the base of the Inner Wall. A Redcap's lopped-off head came bounding past Skarper like a lost football, still wearing its chilli-shaped hat. It set off little avalanches of small stones as it bounced by, and somehow the dwarven mole riders heard it and looked up.

A flaming missile from a catapult hurtled overhead just then, on its way to smash against the Blackspike. Skarper crouched there quivering, bathed in the passing light with his shadow stretching and shifting around him. The dwarves on the diremole couldn't miss him.

Eek! thought Skarper, and *Poomonkeys!* He turned to run, but the idea of scrambling back up that slope with the dwarves behind him, probably aiming crossbows and fire-spout-thingies at his fleeing bottom, wasn't pleasant. So instead he did something that must have looked quite brave to the dwarves, although all he was really doing was trying to buy time, in the desperate hope that somebody might come and rescue him.

He drew his spindly little sword and stepped into the diremole's path. He shouted, as loudly as he could, "Stop!"

Whatever the dwarves thought of him, it made no difference. The diremole kept coming. Its snuffly, stinking breath jetted out through holes in its armour, smoky in the cold night air, as if it were more dragon than mole. Skarper ran as close as he dared and jabbed his sword through one of the nose holes. "That's for Soakaway!" he shouted. The mole squealed and reared back, the dwarves on its back shouting and lashing at it. Skarper jumped backwards too, feeling rather pleased with himself. It was only a silly old overgrown mole, after all! "Come on!" he shouted, beckoning to it, readying his sword to strike again. "Come and have another taste of goblin steel!"

Unfortunately the diremole took him at his word. It had been startled when he first appeared, jabbing that sharp spike into its nose. Now it was angry. Shoving itself uphill with its strong pink hands, it lunged at him. Skarper's courage vanished as quickly as it had come. He dropped his knife and ran, but something tripped him. He hit the ground, rolled over, and looked up into the mole's mouth, which hung above him like a hot cave, with two long teeth poking from its roof like stakes of pale wood, poised to crash down and impale him.

But they didn't. Instead, the mole flinched backwards, It scrabbled back a little way down the hill. Skarper half rose, tremblly, looking up at the dwarves on its back. They were cursing the creature, jabbing their goads down into its fur. One saw Skarper staring up at them and snatched up a throwing axe, but before he could throw it a spear sprouted suddenly and mysteriously from his chest and he dropped the axe and came tumbling down the mole's side. The creature seemed terrified now, squealing and panting as it struggled to turn. Skarper knew he wasn't that scary. He looked behind him to see what had frightened it.

Zeewa was striding down the hill towards him, and all around her her ghosts ran and flew and bounded, like a zoo made of moonlight. The ghost of Kosi flung phantom spears at the dwarves, which, unlike Zeewa's spear, passed through them without doing harm. But the diremole was as frightened of the ghosts as all the dogs and horses in Coriander had been. Ignoring the angry shouts and snapping whips of its drivers, it turned and started lumbering back towards its molehill.

"Hooray!" shouted Skarper, doing a little victory dance and making rude gestures at the mole's retreating rear. He waved at Zeewa. "Thanks!"

The girl nodded. "It was Kosi who heard your cries, goblin," she said. "The ears of the dead are sharp." She looked with a kind of grudging affection at the young man's ghost. Skarper was about to thank him too, when suddenly something tightened around his ankle and yanked him off his feet.

"Oof!" he said. And then, "Aaargh!"

Trailing from the back of the mole's armour was a long chain. What it was doing there, Skarper couldn't imagine. Perhaps it was meant to be coiled up in the castle on the mole's back and the panicky crew had dropped it. Perhaps the mole had been meant to tow something, or the dwarves had been planning to hook their chain to the gate and have the mole pull it off its hinges. The one thing it probably wasn't intended to do was to catch goblins, but that was what it had done. The snaking iron links had knotted tight around Skarper's left ankle, and as the frightened mole went scrambling back into its burrow, it dragged him with it.

"Help!" shouted Skarper, bouncing over the broken paving slabs. He clutched at a clump of dead thistles, but they tore free of the ground. He grabbed at the hand of the dead dwarf Zeewa had speared, but the dwarf's iron gauntlet came off in his paw. "Ow! Ooh! Oof!" he complained, as the mole started to tug him up the side of its hill. Above him he could see its giant bum up-reared against the stars. Head down, forepaws furiously digging, it spattered him with clods of wet earth. Zeewa came running, shouting, "Take my hand!" But her ghosts could not help coming with her, and that only made the terrified mole dig faster. Although Zeewa took hold of Skarper's paw with both hands, she could not hope to win a tug of war with the gigantic creature.

"Arkkk!" shouted Skarper, afraid that he was going to be pulled in two. "Find an axe! Cut the chain!"

"No time!" grunted Zeewa.

"We must chop his leg off!" said Kosi, swinging his sword at Skarper's shin. But it was a ghost sword, of course, and no sharper than smoke, and Zeewa's spears were made for throwing or for stabbing, not for chopping.

"I'm sorry!" she said helplessly, as Skarper's paw slipped from her hands.

He had a last glimpse of her standing there, dark against the pale crowd of ghosts, as he went bumping up to the summit of the molehill. Then the soft, crumbly earth closed over him, and he was following

the mole down through choking blackness, back into
the underground world of the dwarves.

AFTER THE BATTLE

Zeewa stood staring at the place where he had vanished, until another flaming missile roared overhead and burst against the Inner Wall. The bloom of light reminded her that the battle was still raging. From here on the molehill she could see the struggling mass of dwarves and goblins at the main gate. The goblins were falling back now, scrabbling up the wall to vanish in through windows and squeeze through arrow-slits. Henwyn's sword still flashed, and his fair hair gleamed, in the midst of a fierce battle near the gate, but he and the goblins who stood with him were surrounded by dwarves, and a line of the great diremoles was tramping up the road to help them.

"The battle is lost!" whispered Kosi.

"What do you know about battles?" asked Zeewa

163

crossly. "You were only ever in one, and you got killed. Come on!"

For the first time she felt glad of her ghosts. They ran with her as she sped towards the fight, and the dwarves who saw them coming were startled and not sure who to aim their darts and axes at. She tore through a small rank of them, bowling over two, spearing one who tried to cut her down. Then the road was ahead, and the lumbering diremoles sensed the ghosts and started to squeal and fidget like the first.

Looking over the heads of his fearsome but short-legged foes, Henwyn saw what was happening. He was the sort of person who always hoped for the best, but during those last few minutes even he had been starting to think that things were looking a bit gloomy. Now, seeing the huge moles rear up in terror, seeing their crews tumble off them, he found all his natural optimism returning. "Clovenstone!" he shouted, picking up a startled dwarf and flinging him bodily into the rank of dwarfs behind him.

"Er . . . Clovenstone!" hollered the half dozen goblins who still fought beside him. And away in the darkness Fraddon, emerging from the woods again, took up the cry and shouted, "Clovenstone!" in a voice like a gale among the treetops, bringing his club down with a splintering crash on one of the dwarven catapults.

The tide turned then. Stampeding diremoles crashed through the dwarf lines, flattening some of them, ruining the battle plans of all the rest. Henwyn and his goblins charged downhill to help Zeewa, who was holding off a ring of angry dwarves. Other goblins, who had fled the fighting earlier, looked out from the cracks and crannies of the Inner Wall, saw which way things were going, and decided to join in again, scampering down to harry the dwarves as they fell back. Here and there among the ruins and the clumps of trees small groups of dwarves rallied and made a stand, but Zeewa and her ghostly menagerie kept herding the diremoles back towards their burrows, and after a while the dwarves gave up and followed them, scrambling up the dark mounds and vanishing back into the earth.

By first light the battle was over. Fraddon strode about like a gigantic gardener, stamping molehills flat and trampling in the runs which led to them.

The sun came up bloody behind veils of smoke. The road to the inner wall was littered with dead dwarves, dead goblins, mole droppings, and here and there the carcass of a diremole. Fires still flickered among the towers. The dwarf battering ram lay where they had dropped it. Goblins were busy picking up fallen helmets, shields and swords, and checking the pockets of the dead for valuables. Henwyn, wandering homeward through the wreckage, remembered something Garvon Hael had said. *A battle is a dreadful thing, Henwyn of Adherak, even when you win.* But the thought of Garvon Hael jolted him out of the mood of weary sadness which had settled on him at the battle's end. A fat lot of use that so-called hero had been!

Near the gate he saw Garvon Hael himself, looking grey-faced and groggy, leaning on his sword while Princess Ned talked to him. Henwyn went towards them, and was grimly pleased to see the old hero turn away in shame as he came near. He started to think of something really cutting to say about people who woke up and pulled on their fighting trousers only when the battle had been won, but before he could get the words quite straight in his head he noticed that Princess Ned was also looking pale, and clutching her side with one hand.

"Are you all right!" he shouted, bounding up to where she stood. "Oh, have you been wounded?"

Ned looked almost crossly at him. She hated people fussing over her and treating her as if she were made of porcelain. "Oh, Henwyn," she said, "you are like a mother hen! I have pulled a muscle, that is all."

"Would you like me to look at it?" asked Dr Prong, who was crouched nearby with Fentongoose, wrapping bandages around a goblin's head. "Perhaps a nice hot poultice would help?"

Ned waved him away. "No, no; it is just a twinge and it will pass; there are others hurt far worse than me." She looked again at Henwyn, and suddenly she was laughing. "We saw them off!" she said. "All their tunnels and moles and war machines, and yet we sent them packing!"

Henwyn grinned too, because although it was sad to see Clovenstone all covered with molehills and the smoke drifting from the damaged bits of the Inner Wall, it wasn't as if the place had not been a ruin to start with. He had not expected the dwarves to be beaten back quite so fast.

"It was too easy," said Garvon Hael.

Henwyn glared at him. "How can you say that? I did not see you doing any fighting! You just lay in your bed, drunk! You let the rest of us risk our lives, and now you have the nerve to come and tell us it was easy!"

"Henwyn. . ." said Ned gently, laying a hand on his arm.

"I am sorry that I was not with you," said Garvon Hael. "But the fact remains, it was too easy. This is not ended. They are playing at something, these dwarves. Testing your defences maybe, drawing your attention in one direction while they make their real attack somewhere else. You should beware."

"Round on the north side, maybe," said Ned. "Perhaps they have found a way through the bogs, or under them. Perhaps even now they are making tunnels beneath the Inner Wall there. It seems strange that folk so keen on tunnelling should come trying to break our gate down."

Henwyn almost glared at her, too. Why was she trying to belittle the victory they had won? But he had to admit she might be right. He said, "As soon as we have breakfasted, Skarper and I will go and look along the north side."

"Where *is* Skarper?" asked Fentongoose. "I haven't seen him since I sent him to fetch water for us, in the midst of all the tumult."

"He is around somewhere. . ." said Henwyn, and then realized that he hadn't seen Skarper since the height of the battle. "Look," he said, "here comes Zeewa: perhaps she has seen him."

But Zeewa brought only bad news. When they asked if she'd seen Skarper she stood there silently amid her cloud of ghosts and said, "He is gone. One of those mole creatures dragged him down with it into the underworld. I am sorry, Henwyn. Your friend is dead."

*

Dead. I'm dead. That was what Skarper thought, when he woke. He was in darkness, buried under soft earth and heavy stones, with the stink of diremole all about him. At least, if he *wasn't* dead, he was pretty sure he would be soon. Slowly, he started to remember how the mole had dragged him down inside its hill, the hill collapsing on top of it as it went. How it had fled along twisting miles of tunnel with Skarper bumping and barrelling behind it, its huge, panic-stricken body knocking pit props aside, bringing down whole sections of the roof. How the dwarves had shouted and snapped their whips, seeking to calm it and only making it more frightened. How, when it finally stopped, Skarper had found the strength to untangle the chain that was around his ankle before slumping back unconscious amid the rubble of the fallen roof.

More of the roof must have come down later, hiding him. Loose earth shifted and sloughed off him as he stood up. Most bits of him ached, but they were all still attached, and none seemed to be broken. His goblin eyes were growing used to the dark now, and he peered warily about.

In one direction a tunnel stretched away in darkness. In the other direction . . . well, more tunnel: more darkness. He looked up at the roof, and wondered what lay above it. Was he still beneath Clovenstone?

It seemed unlikely: he remembered being dragged for miles through the dark. He must be somewhere outside, in some dwarven burrow under Oeth Moor or the Bonehills. . .

"Oh bumcakes," he said, and started walking.

The three trolls, Torridge, Cribba and Kenn, had done their bit to win the battle, dragging huge bits of rubble to the bratapult, and they proved themselves just as useful in its aftermath. They worked tirelessly that day, clearing wreckage and gathering the dead bodies into one great big pile, which Princess Ned set a torch to.

The smoke of the pyre drifted across Clovenstone on the south-west wind, and Henwyn saw it blowing past as he and Zeewa started to pick their way along the foot of the Inner Wall, round on its marsh-bound northern side. They were looking for any sign that dwarves had been at work there. Above them, on the battlements, a gang of goblins led by Libnog kept pace with them, ready to throw ropes down and haul them up at the first sign of any dwarvish mischief.

In some places the bogs reached right up to the foot of the crag on which the Inner Wall stood, and Henwyn and Zeewa had to pick their way across the bleak, black pools on the lumps of fallen masonry which lay scattered in them like stepping stones. In others, they scrambled over stony ridges, or through abandoned, weed-grown buildings. Always they kept watch for any sign that dwarves had been there, but they saw none. Zeewa's ghosts drifted and tangled with the mist.

Eventually they reached the foot of Growler Tower. A mass of rubble and roof slates lay there, which had been Growler's top until one of the dwarven war machines lopped it off. Small, wet splay-toed footprints covered the fresh-fallen stones. Henwyn looked at them, and shuddered.

"What is it?" asked Zeewa. "Have dwarves been here?"

"Not dwarves," said Henwyn, studying the froggly prints. "Boglins! They live out there in the swamp. They captured Princess Ned once, and me and Skarper had to rescue her. They are wicked creatures. They had a huge monster called the dampdrake living in one of the meres, and they planned to give Ned to it for its supper. . ." Then, fearing that he might be frightening Zeewa, he added, "Of course, they are more frightened of us than we are of them. We've had no trouble with them since the Keep came down."

Zeewa wasn't really listening. She was staring out across Natterdon Mire. Far away, beyond the mires and the rotten, subsiding buildings, the land rose again, climbing towards the northern circuit of the Outer Wall. A shaft of sunlight struck down through the mist there and lit up a scattering of square, pale buildings on a hill.

"What are those?" she asked. "Are they the tombs which Fentongoose spoke of?"

"Yes," said Henwyn. "There are acres and acres of them. Big burial vaults where the Lych Lord's captains and their families were buried."

"Do ghosts walk there?"

"I've never seen any," said Henwyn. "But I've only ever been near the tombs in daylight, and then only on the edges, not right in among them."

"The Houses of the Dead," said Zeewa.

"They are a bit like houses. Little windowless houses with the doors sealed up and nothing but bones inside."

She turned to him. "That's where I must go. Remember? If I am to rid myself of these ghosts that follow me."

Henwyn nodded seriously. Then he said, "What? You don't mean, go there *now*?"

"Why not?" asked Zeewa.

"It is too far," said Henwyn. "To reach the tombs you would have to go all the way to Easterly Gate, then follow the Outer Wall round almost to

Northerly Gate."

Zeewa frowned, as if she thought he might be making fun of her. "Why can we not just cut across the marshes? It does not look far."

"Well, it isn't," admitted Henwyn. "But the marshes are dangerous! Weren't you listening? There are boglins out there!"

Zeewa looked at the marshes, then at Henwyn. Her nostrils flared. "And you are *scared* of these boglins, are you?"

Henwyn was not sure what to say. Of course he was scared! Of all the adventures that had befallen him within the ruins of Clovenstone, the one he had enjoyed the least had been his encounter with the boglins, and their horrid pet the dampdrake, that great glistening underwater dragon thing which breathed wet fog and had almost eaten him and all his friends. He still had nightmares about it. But Henwyn was the sort of person who could never bring himself to admit that he was afraid of anything, especially not to a girl, and especially not if the girl was a princess, which of course Zeewa was.

So he gave a wobbly sort of laugh and said, "Afraid? Afraid of a few boglins? Me? Of course not!"

Zeewa smiled. "Then you will come with me? I'm glad."

And there was nothing that poor Henwyn could do

as she started into the mires, following the mysterious winding paths which wound between the reed beds, towards the distant Houses of the Dead.

UNDERGROUND

There was no denying it, decided Skarper. He was lost. For hours now he had been wandering in the blind dark, searching for a way out of the dwarf holes. All he had found were ways that led deeper in, and dwarves; lots and lots of dwarves. Each time he saw light ahead, beyond some twisting of the passage, it turned out to be only the light of dwarvish torches coming from some big burrow or marshalling yard where dwarf warriors were resting, or dwarf grooms feeding buckets of fat worms to tethered diremoles. In other places he came across dwarf miners, hard at work enlarging tunnels, or repairing places where the roof had caved in, or tinkering with nameless contraptions made from thick iron tubes.

If I had been going in the right direction, Skarper realized, *I'd have banged my nose against the roots of*

Meneth Eskern hours ago. But he did not know how to retrace his steps: he'd had to turn back so many times to avoid dwarf repair gangs, and dart down so many side tunnels to avoid the marching squads of warriors, he no longer had any idea which way he'd come or which way he was heading. He wondered if the battle was still going on above him somewhere. He wondered if any of his friends were still alive.

The only bit of luck he had was that no dwarves noticed him. They passed quite close sometimes, but he flattened himself against the wall, and they went by without seeing him. It was true that he was smeared with earth and much the same colour as the walls themselves, but even so, it was surprising. He guessed that the dwarves were so sure of themselves they didn't imagine a goblin could have found his way into their diggings. *Dwarves are stupid*, he decided.

Then, as he scurried on, he imagined what Princess Ned would say about that. "Not all dwarves are the same, Skarper, any more than all goblins or all men are the same. Some of them may be a little dense, but there are probably others who are as sharp as nails." And she'd be right, thought Skarper, because he'd already met one: the dwarf girl Etty. Now if only he could find her again. . .

And luckily, he *could*.

Like many goblins, Skarper had a keen sense of smell, and he guessed that Etty would not smell quite like other dwarves, not now she'd spent some time in Coriander. He started to sniff and snuffle at the air, and after an hour or so he picked up a familiar scent: the soap he remembered from Carnglaze's house. It certainly wasn't coming from him, because on the morning he left Coriander he'd rolled and rolled in the roadside grass to get the stink of it off. *Etty!* he thought. They'd used the same soap at The Sleepy Mermaid.

Nose twitching, he began to follow the scent. It was just a ghost of a scent, really, and often he lost it and had to go hunting for it again through broad drifts of furnace stink and smells of unwashed dwarf, but always he picked it up again and slowly it grew stronger and more certain, until at last it led him into a dim burrow where dwarf miners slept in cubbyholes hollowed from the walls, each screened by a heavy moleskin curtain.

The scent was strong there. Skarper went quietly from cubbyhole to cubbyhole, until he found the one where it was strongest. Carefully he lifted a corner of the curtain, reached a paw inside and shook the sleeper by a shoulder.

"Etty!" he hissed urgently. "Psst! Hey! Etty!"

"Mmmblgrff?" said the dwarf, and rolled over to reveal a beardy face with a big, bluish nose and two eyes which opened wide at the sight of Skarper. It wasn't Etty at all, but the dwarf called Langstone who'd been with her and her dad at Boskennack!

"Bumcakes!" said Skarper.

"Goblin!" gasped Langstone, springing up so fast he cracked his head on the roof of his cubbyhole. "Ow!" he shouted. "Goblin!" He jumped up to give chase, nightshirt flapping around his short, fat, hairy legs.

Skarper was already running from the chamber. Near the doorway a lot of tools had been stacked against the wall. Skarper kicked them over as he scampered past, and heard the pursuing dwarf curse as they tripped him. The whole burrow was coming awake now, grumpy dwarf voices complaining that it was not time for their shift to begin and asking what the matter was. "Goblin!" Langstone kept yelling.

Running on, Skarper rounded a corner and crashed hard into something that said, "Oof!"

"Ark!" yelped Skarper, knocked off balance, sprawling on the tunnel floor. He rolled over and looked up the fierce face of a dwarf who raised a pickaxe over him.

"Etty?" he squeaked.

"Skarper?" Her face stopped being fierce; she

lowered the pick. Behind her the tunnel was filling with lantern light and the angry voices of approaching dwarves.

"Help!" whimpered Skarper.

Etty glanced behind her. Dwarf shadows were dancing on the tunnel walls, waving shadowy pickaxes and hammers. "Goblin! Get the goblin!" their gruff voices shouted. Etty took a deep breath, and made her decision. There was an alcove in the wall nearby where tools and pit props could be stored. She kicked Skarper into it and stood in front of him as the other dwarves came rushing around the corner.

"Etty!" shouted Langstone. "There was a goblin spy! In our burrow!"

Etty shook her head. "He didn't come this way. I'd surely have seen him if he had."

The dwarves all stared at her for a moment. Then one of them yelled, "He must have doubled back!"

"After him!" roared the rest. "Get the goblin!" They turned as one, and went dashing off.

Etty stood trembling for a moment, while the noises of the wild hunt faded. A good, well-brought-up dwarf girl did not betray her own people, or help goblin spies. What had she been thinking of? But it was done now. Reaching down, she gripped Skarper's paw in her small, strong hand and pulled him out of the alcove.

He started to thank her, but she shushed him and led him quickly down tunnels and flights of stone stairs to an old, mined-out gallery where she hoped they could talk undisturbed.

"Now, what are you doing here?" she asked.

"I didn't choose to come!" protested Skarper. "There was this mole, and. . ."

"What were you thinking of, sneaking into our burrow?"

"I was looking for you! That's how I woke Langstone – I thought he was you! He had that Coriander soap stink all over him, same as you, only stronger. . ."

Etty sighed. She almost laughed. "Langstone is a very vain dwarf. He brought a whole cake of that soap home with him to wash his beard. But why were you looking for me? It's so dangerous for you here!"

"That's why I need you," said Skarper. "That's why I need your help."

"The others will kill you if they find you!"

"Yes, but *you* won't."

Etty looked at the pickaxe she was still clutching, then gently set it down with a clank on the stony floor. "No," she said. "No, I won't."

"You've got to get me out of here!" said Skarper. "I

have to get back up top. There's a battle going on up there!"

He pointed up at the cavern roof, but Etty shook her head. "No, no: Clovenstone is not up there. It's twenty miles west of here."

"Oh!" said Skarper, stunned. He had feared as much, but he hadn't realized that his wanderings in the dark had led him quite so far.

"Anyway," Etty went on, "the battle's over."

"So Clovenstone has fallen?" Skarper wailed. "They're all dead, Henwyn and Ned and the others!"

"Shhh!" hissed Etty. "No! I don't think so. Our warriors pulled back from Clovenstone."

Skarper perked up. "So we defeated you? Yay!"

"Not exactly," said Etty. "It was all part of the Head's plan."

Skarper scratched his head. He'd never heard of a battle which ended in victory for both sides. "But if your warriors were driven back. . ."

"I didn't say that they were *driven* back," said Etty. "I said they *pulled* back." She looked away, biting her lip. She had never imagined herself turning into the sort of girl who betrayed the secrets of dwarvenkind to their enemies. But she seemed to be the only one of her people who understood that not all goblins *were* enemies. Besides, what did it matter now? She said,

"That attack last night was just a diversion. It was meant to distract your attention from our real plan."

"It was distracting all right!" said Skarper, remembering the whooshing missile that had torn his bedroom wall away, the boom of the battering ram against the gate, the flash and clash of weapons in the firelight. Then he quirked an ear and said suspiciously, "What real plan?"

Etty took his paw again. "Come with me," she said. "I'll show you."

In Clovenstone, the tidying up was still going on. The three trolls were busy heaving fallen stones back up the stairways of the Inner Wall to repair the holes dwarf catapults had made, while Fraddon and a working party of goblins went about opening all the dwarf tunnels they could find and then filling them with rubble so that they could not be used again.

Garvon Hael sat beside a fallen statue outside the gate in the Inner Wall, moodily polishing his sword. He had a headache from the wine he'd drunk, and far worse, he was remembering how badly he had failed. He knew that Henwyn had been right to fling those angry words at him. *I did not see you doing any fighting! You lay in your bed, drunk! You let the rest of us risk our lives...* It was true, thought Garvon Hael. Even the goblins had fought more bravely than him.

A pattering of feet behind him, a whispering, alerted him to the presence of the hatchlings. Soakaway was not the only one who had been killed during the battle: several of the other young goblins had fallen too, and many in the little group that now approached Garvon Hael were missing paws or tails, or had their heads turbanned with Dr Prong's neat bandages. Garvon Hael rose and sheathed his sword, hanging his own head as they gathered around him. He was expecting them to blame him for the deaths of their friends.

Instead, the hatchlings said, "We're here, Garvon Hael."

"We're ready!"

"You said you'd teach us!"

"To be great warriors!"

"Like you!"

The warrior looked up, half angrily, thinking that they were mocking him. He was wrong. The ugly faces of the hatchlings were quite earnest. They clutched swords and axes, salvaged spears and dented dwarf shields.

"I'm not much of a teacher," said Garvon Hael. "Not much of a warrior either, if truth be told. It was more luck than skill that brought me victory in the fight at Far Penderglaze, and I have lived off the glory of it ever since. I'll tell you a secret, you little blighters: I was terrified that day. Only wine gave me the courage to fight those pirates. But it gave me no courage last night; just robbed me of my wits, so that I lay uselessly abed and let others fight in my place. Soakaway might be alive now if I'd gone out when I should."

The hatchlings looked blankly at one another. Then they rattled their swords against their shields and drummed their spear butts on the ground. "Teach us!" they said. "Teach us to fight, for when the dwarves return, so we don't end up getting splatted like Soakaway!"

Fentongoose went looking for Princess Ned, and found her standing with Dr Prong on the northern part of the wall, looking down into the mists of Natterdon Mire.

"Henwyn and Zeewa have not returned," she said. "They called up to tell Libnog that they were going to the Houses of the Dead. That was hours ago."

"Well, it's a long way to the Houses of the Dead," said Fentongoose.

"Long and dangerous!" said Dr Prong. "Princess Eluned has been telling me of the fell creatures which inhabit that marsh."

"They will be all right," Fentongoose said. "Henwyn is a brave lad, and that Muskish girl is braver still, if anything. Besides, her ghosts will frighten off any wild beasts that dwell in the marsh. Maybe they'll frighten off the boglins, too."

"I do hope so," said Ned.

Fentongoose hesitated. He felt almost embarrassed to lay another worry on her, but he had bad news, and he knew that she must hear it. "Princess," he said, "I have cares of my own. Will you come with me?"

She turned and looked at him, and saw the concern in his face. "Why, what is it, Fentongoose?"

"I'm not sure," he replied. "Best if you see for yourself."

So he led her and Dr Prong down to the base of the wall, and then down again by the old secret ways which led deep under the roots of Meneth Eskern. There, beneath the crag, lay the great cavern, filled with the silvery light and slow, pale roilings of the lava lake. It was very beautiful, and for a moment, standing upon the black stone shore, Princess Ned forgot her worries about Henwyn and her fear of the dwarves.

"Extraordinary!" murmured Dr Prong. (He had devoted a whole chapter of his book to explaining that slowsilver was a mythical element, made up by third-rate storytellers.)

Fentongoose, however, looked more troubled than ever. "Look," he said, pointing at a big rock near the lake's edge. The paddle which he used to scoop up new-made goblin eggs was propped against it.

"What is wrong?" asked Ned.

"The lava used to lap around that rock," said Fentongoose. "Last month when I came down here gathering eggstones I stood on top of it so I could reach out into the lava with my paddle and catch a floating one. I could not do that now, could I?"

A yard or more of bare stone separated the rock from the edge of the slowsilver. Princess Ned felt a prickling sense of dread.

Dr Prong said, "So the level of the lake is falling?"

"It is going down fast," agreed Fentongoose. "Look; I set this small stone here this morning as a marker. The lake has fallen by six inches just since then."

"It must be those dwarves and their beastly tunnelling!" cried Princess Ned.

"It could be," agreed Dr Prong. "They may have caused some fissure to open deep in the earth, like a hole in a bucket, and the slowsilver is leaking away down it!"

"And no more slowsilver means no more goblins," said Fentongoose. "Not ever."

"It's funny," said Princess Ned. "There was a time,

not so very long ago, when I would have thought that 'no more goblins' was a good thing."

"It's not, though, is it?" said Fentongoose. He looked gloomily out across the strange lake, and sighed. "No more goblins, no more Clovenstone."

THE HOUSES OF
THE DEAD

What it was in the Natterdon Mire that brewed up such mists, Henwyn did not know, but they seemed thicker by far than mists elsewhere. A few moments after he and Zeewa left the Inner Wall, he had looked back to find it already hidden by the vapours. He remembered uneasily the mist-woven traps which Poldew of the Mire, King of the Boglins, had made to snare his enemies. But Poldew was dead, and the mists which closed over Henwyn and Zeewa as they found their way slowly north were only mists; they did not cling and trap in the way the bog king's snares had done.

Behind the mist, old buildings reached up on every side of them: ruinous towers and crumbled walls, so thickly covered with moss that they looked as if they had been made out of moth-eaten green velvet.

Between them the pools and puddles of the mire lay like dim mirrors. Reeds, taller than Henwyn, grew in wide, whispering tracts, and the reed beds were full of movements: rustlings and scurryings, croaks and squeaks and splashes. Once, through a thinning of the mist, Henwyn glimpsed one of the giant grey raft spiders which haunted the mire, but it seemed afraid of Zeewa's ghosts, and skated quickly away.

"We are being watched," said Zeewa uneasily. "I can feel eyes upon us."

Her ghosts were uneasy, too. They stayed close to Zeewa, and even the lion and the hyenas seemed wary of those walls of reeds and the things that hid in them. Only Kosi dared to go ahead, drifting like mist through the mist and the reeds, spying out paths for the wanderers and reporting back. And with his help, to Henwyn's surprise and relief, they crossed the marshes without making a wrong turning, and came before too long to a place where the land rose up, and the air was clearer. The sun showed itself again, a pale, cool disc behind the thinning mist, and then broke through in places, scattering dapples of golden light on the short green grass of the little hill they stood on. All over the hill, like the houses of an empty town, the silent tombs stood, little low buildings, ivy covered, carved with inscriptions in dead alphabets, decorated with gargoyles, and statues of the shrouded dead.

Henwyn drew his sword and went uphill between the tombs, through the shadow of trees which had been planted beside them. Zeewa followed him, and her ghosts followed her like a streamer of marsh mist, except for Kosi, who ran lightly ahead.

"Are there ghosts here?" Zeewa asked. Her words fell flatly, not echoing as they should among the tall walls of the tombs. Even the air of this place seemed dead.

"I cannot feel them. . ." said Kosi. "But there is something – I do not know what. . ."

At the hill's top stood a ring of stones, older than the ornate tombs which surrounded them, not carved or dressed but set upright rough and shapeless, just as they had been found. Lichen and moss had grown on them; a buzzard had used one for a perch and left white streaks of bird poo down its sides. On all sides of the ring the hill sloped away, covered with tombs, so that it was like looking down over the rooftops of a miniature city whose only inhabitants were statues.

Kosi slipped between two of the standing stones and floated into the centre of the ring. Some of the animals followed him, sniffing at the stones, nibbling hopefully at the thick, short grass which grew around them.

"I can *smell* something. . ." Kosi said, sounding excited.

"What is it?" asked Henwyn, who could smell only wet earth and the scent of the marsh.

"I don't know," the ghost replied. "That's not the point. The point is that I can smell anything at all! I have not smelled anything, tasted anything, touched anything, not since Zeewa split my heart with her spear."

"All right, I've said I'm sorry, haven't I?" grumbled Zeewa.

But Kosi hadn't been trying to make her feel guilty. He wasn't even looking at her. He was turning around and around in the heart of the ring of stones, his head up, his nostrils flaring, trying to catch the mysterious scent again. Around him, the ghost animals seemed excited too; the gazelles pranced, and the hyenas stuck their spotted noses in the air, sniffing deeply. Even the ghost flies seemed to buzz more happily.

Henwyn went to follow Kosi, but as he passed between two of the stones a thin, chilly clang resounded, like the tolling of a lonely bell. From the green grass at the centre of the ring a dark vapour arose, and shaped itself into the form of a cloaked and hooded figure. Zeewa cried out in alarm. Henwyn, aghast, stumbled backwards, bumping against one of the standing stones. The wraith swirled towards him, raising its bony hands. One clutched a goblet, the other a half-eaten chicken leg. (This seemed an odd detail to Henwyn, but he was too busy being terrified to pay it much heed.)

"Who dares to trespass among the Houses of the Dead?" the phantom asked, in a cold and dreadful voice. "Only the dead live here, and the living should leave us in peace, or. . . Ow! Stop it! Get off!"

Busy looming over poor Henwyn, the phantom had not noticed all the ghostly animals, twitching their noses at the smell of the phantom food it held. Tau the lion was the first to spring. The phantom gave a yelp as the great jaws closed on his chicken leg, and if he hadn't drawn his hand back quickly he would have lost that too. "That's mine!" he said, but Tau had already gulped the chicken leg down and was looking eagerly for more. The phantom scowled at Henwyn. "You interrupted me in the middle of my dinner," he complained.

"How can this be?" asked Zeewa, stepping between the stones and confronting the phantom, her hands on her hips. "How can ghosts taste, smell, eat dinner? I thought they could do none of those things."

"Ah, well, they can't," agreed the phantom, fishing a couple of ghost flies out of his wine goblet and taking a quick slurp. "It's a nothing-y sort of place, the afterworld; very grey and uninteresting. But here at the Houses of the Dead we have made special arrangements."

"What do you mean, 'special arrangements'?" asked Henwyn, who was recovering his courage, and trying to look as if he had never been scared of this ghostly presence in the first place. "How can ghosts make special arrangements?"

"Ah, we who dwell at the Houses of the Dead are not just *any* ghosts," the phantom said. "It's very exclusive. Those who were buried on this hill were among the greatest sorcerers the world has ever known: seers and necromancers in the service of the Lych Lord. We looked ahead. We made plans to keep ourselves in old age, and beyond. While we still lived, we summoned the spirits of the dead, and learned from them what a cheerless, uninviting time awaited us, as ghosts in the world to come. It sounds bad to you, I expect: being see-through, unable to touch anything, to smell or eat or feel. Think how much worse it seemed to us, who were among the great lords of the world, used to eating the finest foods of every land! So we resolved to do something. With spells and incantations we opened a way into the afterworld, and set about improving it. In olden times great kings and princes were buried with their best belongings, believing that they could take such treasures with them. We found a way to actually do it: our furniture and favourite clothes, our pets and pastimes, came with us as ghosts to decorate our homes in the afterworld. We filled our tombs with food and finery, and as these things rotted here in the living world, their ghosts appeared in ours. And they never run out! That chicken leg your cat just ate will reappear as succulent as ever on the ghost plate in my ghost larder, where it has sat these many centuries. Yes, on the whole it is a nice life, being dead."

Zeewa looked the phantom up and down. "If you have such fine clothes, why do you dress in these gloomy robes?"

The phantom shrugged. "These old things? To be honest, I put them on to scare you. That is my job, you see; to scare away robbers and intruders who might disturb the peace of this place. They call me the Gatekeeper."

"We are not robbers!" said Zeewa.

"Though I suppose we are intruders," admitted Henwyn.

"I came here because I was told that you might rid me of my ghosts," said Zeewa.

"Yes, you do seem to have rather a lot," said the Gatekeeper, turning to gaze upon the crowd of animals that filled the ring of stones.

Kosi turned to Zeewa. "Princess, if we are to leave you, then this is the place where we would best like to be left. To smell and taste and touch again! It will be better than the world of shades which G'angooli's spell dragged us from!"

"Ah," said the Gatekeeper. He put one bony hand into the shadows of his hood to scratch his ghostly nose. "Well, it's not so easy as that; the spells which created this afterworld of ours were most specific. Not just *any* ghost is allowed entry. It is only the dead of Clovenstone who may enter. That's the other part of my job, you see: I have to keep out those ghosts who do not belong. Not that it wouldn't be nice to have a few lions and antelope and things about the place! And you too, young fellow. . ." He nodded at Kosi's ghost. "We've grown rather stuffy and set in our ways over the years; a few new ghosts would brighten up the place no end. But rules are rules, and you can't go meddling around with spells – at least, we can't, not any more, being dead. So I'm afraid you cannot join us. Not unless you are from Clovenstone."

Zeewa shook her head. "Kosi comes from the Tall Grass Country, West of Leopard Mountain. Half the world away."

"Hmm," said the gatekeeper sadly.

"I am from Clovenstone," said Henwyn. "At least, I live here. Would I do?"

"Admirably," said the gatekeeper. "But you are not dead. If you were, you would be welcome in a flash, and you could bring this young man and these animals as your retinue. I suppose if the young lady were to kill you. . ."

"No!" cried Zeewa. "That seeress at Coriander said nothing about killing anyone! She told me that I should come to the Houses of the Dead and there I would be freed of my ghosts. She did not say that anyone had to die!"

"Hmm," said the Gatekeeper again. "Perhaps she was not a very good seeress; even the best of them overlook these minor details sometimes."

"Minor details?" gasped Henwyn, who was rather afraid that Zeewa might be tempted to do him in, if it would rid her of her ghosts.

"Very well," said Zeewa. "I have had a wasted journey. I shall return to the Inner Wall, and talk to the wise ones there; to Princess Ned and Fentongoose and Dr Prong. Perhaps they will know some way to alter these spells which bind you, Gatekeeper."

"I hope so," agreed the Gatekeeper, and he bowed low, like a column of smoke wavering on the wind.

"Come, my ghosts," said Zeewa, turning away. Kosi followed her. The animals did not want to leave, but they had no choice; they were dragged after her like iron drawn by a magnet, funnelling away between the standing stones and back down the slope of the hill.

Henwyn lingered there on the hilltop. As the phantom gatekeeper began to fade he called out, "Wait!"

"What?" the phantom replied. "Only, the rest of my dinner's getting cold, you see. . ."

"What about goblins?" Henwyn asked. "Do they come to your afterworld? There is one who was a friend of mine, who was lost in the battle with the dwarves. I wondered if you might have seen him at all?"

"I'm sorry," said the Gatekeeper. "There are no goblins at the Houses of the Dead. They have their own afterworld, I believe. A noisy, smelly place. What goes on there, who the latest arrivals are. . ." He gave a ghostly shrug. "I'm sorry. But good luck to you, young fellow; to you and your princess from the Tall Grass Country, west of Leopard Mountain. I hope to see her ghosts again. And, of course, I shall see you again, sooner or later, for all the dead of Clovenstone come here. I'll look forward to having a nice long chat, when you join us."

He sank back down into the earth, and Henwyn, with a shudder, turned away. For a moment, as he looked downhill between the old stones, it seemed to him that lamps were burning in the tombs, and that he could see the dead walking to and fro between them, and riding by on ghostly horses, as if this town of tombs was a real town, and the air was full of faint voices, laughter, and the ghosts of smells. Then it faded, and there was only the hillside, and the silent tombs, and Zeewa going back down towards the marshes with her ghosts behind her.

UNDER THE MOUNTAINS

The tunnels down which Etty led Skarper were busy with bustling dwarves, but she found him an old cloak and a spare miner's helmet, and they did not give him more than the briefest of glances as he hurried along at her side. Etty was more worried that they would notice her: the red tabs on her cloak collar marked her as a member of the night shift, who were all meant to be sleeping at this hour.

Luckily the passing dwarves had other things to think about. The Head had set them a challenge. It was the biggest feat of engineering that dwarves had undertaken in that age of the world. They were all busy making sure it worked.

Etty led Skarper out of a side passage and into a wider tunnel; a big delve that ran straight as an arrow for as far as he could see in either direction. A fat pipe ran along it, much like the pipes which he had glimpsed earlier in other tunnels, further west. The pipe passed through a stone-built shed in which a diremole trotted endlessly in a big wheel, turning a series of cogs and shafts.

"That's a pumping station," said Etty. "There are dozens of them, one every few miles. This pipe goes under the roots of the Bonehill Mountains all the way to Delverdale."

"So if it ends at Delverdale," said Skarper, "where does it start?"

"At Clovenstone," said Etty. "In the slowsilver lake beneath Meneth Eskern. The attack last night was staged to stop you hearing our diggers and diremoles at work as they drove their last mine through the crag and tapped the slowsilver. Now all Clovenstone's slowsilver is being pumped north to Delverdale."

Skarper gawped. He tried to imagine the slowsilver gushing and gurgling through that pipe. He couldn't. Slowsilver wasn't like other substances. Slowsilver was magic. It did what it wanted, not what you told it to. It spat out eggstones, or formed itself into shimmery firefrost stairs.

"You can't pump slowsilver!" he blurted.

"Dwarven iron is proof against all magic," Etty said. "Dwarves learned that long ago. So you see, we have got our slowsilver after all, and there will be no need for more fighting."

"But ... but ... but..." Skarper hopped and jittered like fat in a hot pan. "You can't! You mustn't! Slowsilver is the heart of Clovenstone! It's where goblins come from! If you take our lava lake away, you're taking our whole future from us!"

Etty bit her lip again. "It's the Head's orders, Skarper, and the Head knows best. The Head probably has a much better use for all this slowsilver..."

"What, better than making goblins?" asked Skarper. "We don't live for ever, you know. A hundred years or so and then we crumble back into stone. That's if we don't get stabbed or strangled or squashed or splatted first, and stabbings and stranglings and squashings and splattings happen to goblins a *lot*; we're very accident prone. What will happen when all the goblins living now are gone, and there isn't any lava lake to spit out eggstones and make new goblin hatchlings? There won't be any goblins left! What sort of a world will it be without goblins?"

"A better one, of course," Etty started to say, because that was what she'd been taught to believe, all her life. The trouble was, she didn't really believe it any more. She'd been told that goblins were mindless, savage monsters, but Skarper wasn't mindless, or savage, or even particularly monstery. *The Head Knows Best and the Head Knows All*, she told herself. But it seemed the Head didn't know all about goblins.

She looked down at her feet and listened to the soft, sad sighing of the pipe as it carried Clovenstone's lava lake away.

"I'm sorry," she said.

"Well, sorry's not much good!" complained Skarper. "Sorry won't fetch our slowsilver back! We have to do something! You have to stop it! Block the pipe, or make it flow the other way or something!"

"I can't!" said Etty. She drew Skarper aside into the shadows near the tunnel wall as a gang of dwarf workers came by, listening to the pipe with long brass ear trumpets to check that the stuff inside was flowing smoothly. By the time they had gone past, Etty had made another decision.

"We must talk to the Head," she said. "You and me, Skarper. We'll go to Delverdale and tell the Head that goblins these days aren't like the goblins of old. Perhaps . . . perhaps the Head doesn't understand how things have changed."

Skarper pricked up his ears and nodded cautiously. He thought it might be worth a try. After all, if these dwarves were stupid enough to do whatever a big brass head told them to, maybe a really cunning goblin like him could trick them somehow. He'd creep inside that head and say loudly in a head-ish voice, "Goblins are all right! Put that slowsilver back where you found it!" Or he could just grab a hammer and smash the head to bits. Goblins were good at smashing stuff to bits.

"How far is it to Delverdale?" he asked.

"More than a hundred miles," said Etty.

"And over the mountains!" Skarper's ears drooped. "That will take weeks!"

"Under the mountains," Etty corrected him. "And it won't take more than a day, not if we go by railway."

Her eyes shone. It could be done; she was sure it could. Every dwarf had the right to lay their troubles and complaints before the Brazen Head, and although she had never actually heard of any dwarf who'd done so, she was sure the Head would hear her, and decide what was best for dwarves and goblins.

Skarper just looked blank. "What's a railway?" he wondered.

Slowsilver was not the only thing the dwarves were sending home to Delverdale. Wherever they went they sought out veins of ore, seams of coal, diamonds, crystals, and all the fruits of the underworld. Some of these things they used in the places where they were mined: coal to heat their furnaces, iron to make new tools. Most was sent north, however, to the great smithies and storerooms of Delverdale. To make this easier, they had a built a railway. A set of iron rails snaked under the Bonehills, and along these rails there trundled carts full of ore and precious stones. On the uphill stretches the carts were hooked to winches powered by diremoles. On the downhill sections they rolled free, and gravity did the work. The dwarf engineers were so clever that very few diremole winches were needed: the track had been planned in such a way that the carts picked up enough speed on the downhill stretches to carry them up all but the steepest inclines.

The railhead was in a huge, noisy cavern, into which a dozen tunnels opened. Ore and coal from all the mines of the Bonehills were brought there, and tipped into little high-sided wooden carts which waited on the rails. When eight or ten carts were filled they were linked together by dwarf labourers and shoved off down the track, vanishing into the low, dark mouth of a tunnel which opened at the cavern's end.

It all looked like chaos to Skarper, but Etty understood the system well enough. She led him quickly through the toiling gangs of workers, between the waiting heaps of coal and ore. A train of carts was being linked together by big metal hooks.

Etty and Skarper hung back watching, waiting nervously for the right moment. Above them, hanging from the cavern's roof, a huge banner with a likeness of the Brazen Head stared down, rippling in some underground breeze.

As they watched, the last cart was filled with ore and linked on to the train. Dwarfs took hold of handles on the sides of each cart and started to wheel them down the track. "Now!" said Etty. She grabbed Skarper's paw and they ran forward together. The railway dwarves, used to their steady, unchanging routine, were too confused to do anything but keep pushing as the goblin and the girl ran past them and scrambled up on to the leading cart.

"Hey!" said one of the dwarves. "Get off there! That's not allowed!"

"No!" said Etty. She started to throw chunks of ore over the cart's side, making a nest where she and Skarper could sit on the knobbly cargo. The dwarves pushing the cart along shouted again, but there was nothing they could do; the heavy carts were moving under their own momentum now, coasting down an incline towards the tunnel mouth. The ones shoving Etty and Skarper's cart along did their best to slow it, but it was too heavy and moving too fast, and the dwarves holding the handles of the carts behind kept pushing, breaking into a run as the carts moved faster and faster.

"Etty!" roared a voice, louder than the rattle of the wheels on the tracks.

"Oh crikey!" said Etty.

Her father had arrived in the cavern. He was running along beside the rumbling carts, with Langstone and and another dwarf puffing and panting behind him. "You come down off of there, young lady!" he bellowed.

"I can't, Father!" Etty shouted back.

"She can't," agreed one of the dwarves pushing the carts. "It's moving too fast. Won't stop now till Moledale Steep."

"Etty!" yelled Durgar.

"I'm sorry, Father!" she called back.

"Etty, DUCK!" her father shouted.

Etty and Skarper both looked round, and saw just in time what he meant. The mouth of the tunnel was rushing towards them. It was a low tunnel, just high enough for a fully laden cart of ore to pass through. The dwarves had hacked it through the living rock of the mountains, and they hadn't wasted any effort by making it higher than it needed to be: high enough to take a fully laden cart with a goblin and a girl on top, for instance.

Squeaking with fright, Skarper and Etty threw

themselves flat on top of the ore and tried to press themselves down into it. Everything went black as the cart rushed into the tunnel, and all the noises of the cavern, the shouts of Durgar and the other dwarves, were suddenly cut off, replaced by the echoing rattle of the wheels on the tracks.

FETTER OF THE MIRE

Henwyn and Zeewa set off again across the marshes, but although they followed the same track that had brought them to the Houses of the Dead, something had altered, and they were soon lost. The mist swirled around them again, thicker than ever. The path twisted and turned in ways that it had not that morning, as if the whole dank maze of reed beds, pools and ruins had rearranged itself while they were talking with the Gatekeeper. Within twenty minutes, Henwyn no longer had any idea of the way to the Inner Wall, nor could he have found his way back to the Houses of the Dead.

Of course, he could not admit that to Zeewa.

"It's perfectly all right," he said, pulling his boot out of a black, sucking mudhole which had almost swallowed him. "Wrong turning. We'll bear left a little.

Soon hit higher ground, and maybe this mist will clear."

Zeewa did not look as if she believed him. "I am certain we have passed that building before," she said.

They sent Kosi on ahead as path-finder again. Being a ghost, he was able to float above the travellers and spy out the way, but being tied to Zeewa by the wizard's curse, as if by invisible string, he could not float very far above them; not high enough to see over the mist and tell them if they were still heading towards the Inner Wall. Several times he found good, broad tracks leading through the reeds and ruins, but each time the path petered out and vanished after a few hundred yards.

Then, at last, they struck one which did seem to be going somewhere, following the route of an old paved street, now half swallowed by the mire. The ground seemed to rise beneath Henwyn's and Zeewa's feet as they hurried along it, Kosi gliding in front of them, the storm of other ghosts following close behind. Ahead, through the mist, the shape of a large building loomed.

"Have we walked in a circle?" asked Zeewa. "Is that one of the Houses of the Dead?"

"It could be," said Henwyn, although it looked a bit too lumpy to be a tomb. Then he stepped through a last veil of mist and saw it clearly, and realized just how lost they were. The winding paths they'd followed had led them into the heart of the mire. He stood staring at the crumpled ruins of the boglin king's hall, Bospoldew, with the wide dark mere in front of where the dampdrake dwelled.

"We have come the wrong way!" he said. "This accursed mist. . ." He remembered the strange traps and snares which Poldew of the Mire had woven from the marsh mists. Poldew was dead, but maybe other boglins had power over the mists as well. As he thought back, it seemed to Henwyn that ever since they left the Houses of the Dead the mist had been misleading them; hiding the right path and herding them along the wrong one, until it had brought them here.

Zeewa kicked angrily at a tussock and crouched down, weeping with frustration. Her ghosts fluttered anxiously, and Kosi went close to her and tried to lay a hand on her shoulder, but of course it slid straight through. Looking at his pale, transparent face, Henwyn realized that the young ghost was in love with Zeewa. He felt rather pleased with himself for noticing that, because he didn't usually understand other people's feelings very clearly. Then he felt sorry for Kosi, because it must be sad to be in love with somebody who was alive when you were just a ghost and couldn't even hold her hand.

Tau the ghost lion growled suddenly, soft and low, and Henwyn drew his sword and spun around, eyes on the reeds and the ruined hall, thoughts of love forgotten. "This is a bad place," he said. "We must go at once!"

Kosi said suddenly, "There are creatures moving. All around us."

"Where?" asked Henwyn. He sensed the cold black eyes of boglins watching him, but he couldn't see anything.

"Behind the mist," said Kosi. "Behind the reeds."

Zeewa stood up, pulling her stabbing spear from its quiver, shrugging her shield off her shoulder.

The reeds rustled, and the boglins were there. They had surrounded the travellers, making a ragged circle which slowly shrank and tightened as they came out of their hiding places and stalked forward. Froglike they were; speckled and bow-legged, with broad mouths and bulging eyes, and they moved like frogs on their long web-toed feet. But in their hands they carried glass knives and stone-tipped spears, and some wore armour made from old roof slates. They looked curiously at Zeewa's ghosts, and a few flicked out their long sticky tongues trying to catch phantom flies, but they were not afraid. One, a little larger than the rest, hopped right up to Henwyn and stood sniffing at him.

"We mean you no harm," said Henwyn. "We are lost, and found our way here by accident. We were looking for our way home from the Houses of the Dead, but we took a wrong turning in all this mist and came by chance to Bospoldew."

"Not called that any more," croaked the boglin. "It's Bosfetter now. That's my name, see. Fetter of the Mire. I'm king in the reed maze now. Got any crumbles?"

"What?" said Henwyn.

"Crumbles," said the boglin, and licked his lips. "The lady leaves it for us sometimes, down by the Inner Wall. Tasty."

Henwyn remembered the morning – it seemed like years ago – when he and Skarper had talked to Princess Ned while she sat watching for boglins, with a dish of fresh apple crumble cooling on a tussock. How the boglins had made off with it so slyly, while no one was looking. He said, "I don't actually have any with me now, but I'm sure that if you let us go. . ."

"So you been to the Houses of the Dead," said Fetter. His big golden eyes peered up intently at Henwyn's face. "We saw you. We watched. Nothing at the Houses of the Dead but old bones, old moaning ghosts. Why do you want to go there?"

"My friend Zeewa wished to talk to those ghosts," said Henwyn. He glanced behind him, past the hall, towards the mere. He was afraid that while Fetter kept him talking, the dreadful dampdrake might be rising again, ready to gobble him up and Zeewa too.

Fetter of the Mire guessed what was on his mind, and gurgled with laughter. "Scared, are you, warmblood?"

"Well," said Henwyn, "it's just that last time I was here, your dampdrake. . ."

Fetter's long mouth turned downwards in a sad frown. The other goblins muttered dolefully. "Dampdrake all gone," said one.

"No more dampdrake," said another.

"It is the burrowers," said Fetter. "They have driven him away, our dear, darling dampdrake."

"Burrowers?" asked Henwyn. "You mean dwarves? They have been tunnelling here, too? Under the mire? I should have thought they would have drowned!"

"Under the mire is the stone," said Fetter. "Under the stone the burrowers dig their holes. Bash, crash, shake, shudder. The dampdrake doesn't like it. He has gone; left us and swum away, through the secret waters, away into the big marsh in the north."

"Good riddance!" said Henwyn, very relieved, and then hastily added, "I mean, what a terrible shame!", because he knew the dampdrake was important to the boglins; it was their god and their pet, and they loved it.

"Burrowings must stop," said Fetter.

That reminded Henwyn of the dwarves. What were they doing under this part of Clovenstone? There had been no attacks on the northern stretch of the Inner Wall. He had seen no sign of molehills rising in the north. "They must be very deep," he said aloud. "I wonder what they are doing down there?"

"Tunnelling," said Fetter. "Just one tunnel they have been making; very long, very straight. Boglins listen. We puts our ears to the floors of the meres and we hears. Clanging things they have down there; bong, clong. Bangings and hammerings, and diggings. They came from the west, and they made their burrow long and straight, and last night, while you warmbloods were busy fighting, they dug through the foot of the crag to where the lava lies. Like poking a hole in a wineskin; like sucking broth through a straw. You go back to your princess lady, warmblood. You tell her that. Tell her she must stop the burrowings. Also, send more crumbles, please."

Fetter stepped backwards, and as he did so the mist seemed to thicken, swallowing him and all the other boglins. At the same time, a patch on the far side of the hall thinned, and sunlight shone there, lighting up the entrance to a broad track that led away through the reeds.

"Fetter!" shouted Henwyn.

There was no answer. The reeds rustled. The boglins were gone.

Zeewa looked uneasily towards the gap in the mist and the path through the reeds. Kosi said, "Is it a trick? Are they hoping to trap you?"

Henwyn shook his head. "If they had wanted to kill us they could have done so easily. I think he was granting us safe passage. What did he mean, 'sucking broth through a straw'?"

"Does he want Ned to send him soup as well as more crumble?" wondered Zeewa.

Henwyn shook his head. The Muskish girl had never seen the lake of slowsilver lava under Meneth Eskern. Henwyn had, and he was starting to get an unsettling idea about what the boglin king had meant.

"This is important!" he said. "We must warn Ned and the others at once!"

"Why? What is it?" asked Zeewa, running beside him as he turned and hurried towards the path which Fetter had revealed. It stretched away ahead of them through the reeds, with thick walls of mist towering up on either side, and at its far end, very dimly, the sun was shining on the battlements of the Inner Wall.

"I'm not certain," said Henwyn. "But I think . . . I think all our battling was in vain. I think the dwarves have won!"

WORMSLAYER

Onwards and onwards raced the cart, rattling and swerving through the tight, black bowels of the Bonehills. At last Skarper found the nerve to open one eye and peer upwards. Not even goblin eyes could see anything in that inky, roaring darkness, but he could imagine the low, jagged rock of the tunnel roof speeding by just inches above him.

"I don't think this was such a good idea," he told Etty.

"Perhaps it will get better. . ." Etty started to say.

But it got worse. The dwarves who built the railway had planned it so that their carts would pick up plenty of speed at the beginning of their journey. As Etty spoke, the track seemed to drop away beneath the cart, and it went plummeting down, down, down through the dark. Sparks flared wildly from the wheels, lighting up the rushing tunnel walls.

"Aaaaaaaaaaargh!" screamed Etty and Skarper together, and the long echoes were torn away behind them.

Then the echoes changed. The cavern widened, and there was light again as the carts reached the bottom of that long drop and went rattling across a rickety-looking bridge above a glass-clear, glass-still, underground lake. The light came from the torches of dwarves on a road that ran beside this lake, threading its way between stalagmites and tall, slender columns of stone. The dwarves had heard Etty and Skarper's screams, and stopped to stare as the train of carts went clattering by. In the front one Etty and Skarper busied themselves throwing out more chunks of ore so that they could burrow down deeper. The ore fell with white splashes into the water below, and the spreading ripples broke and scattered the reflections of the watching dwarves and their torches, freckling the cavern walls with shifting light.

The railway curved, and the cart started to gather speed again, descending towards the entrance of another tunnel. "Etty!" called a voice from behind. Skarper looked back and saw Durgar and Langstone scrambling over the ore in the last cart.

"Look!" he said, tugging at one of Etty's braids to catch her attention. "They must have jumped in as we were leaving!"

"Oh, Father!" said the girl.

Ignoring the wobbling and juddering of the carts, old Durgar clambered unsteadily to his feet and sprung across the gap which separated his cart from the one in front of it. "Never fear, Etty!" he shouted. "I'll save you!"

"He must think I've kidnapped you!" said Skarper.

"I'm not afraid!" Etty shouted back. "Eeeeek!"

They were in darkness again, plunging through another rock-walled tube, the cart leaning so far to one side that Skarper felt sure it was going to fall over, but it was kept on the rails by its own rushing weight. He thought of Durgar and Langstone, just seven carts behind, but the sparks which kept flashing from the wheels showed him that the tunnel roof had closed down again; there was not even room for him to raise his head above the brim of the cart, let alone look back. That meant the two dwarves could come no closer: they'd be cowering in their own cart for the moment.

On and on the carts went thundering, slowing now as they climbed long, shallow inclines, then gathering more speed as the track sloped downwards again.

Several times the tunnel opened into wider caverns, and once by spark-light Skarper and Etty saw Durgar jump from the seventh cart to the sixth. The cart rattled across sets of rusty points where other rails joined the main one, branch-lines coming in from other mines. Once it crossed a bridge which seemed to span some unimaginable abyss: Skarper had a sense of a great space opening below him, and thought he saw red veins of molten stone glowing sullenly, miles below. For the most part, though, the headlong journey was spent in blind, black darkness. After a while Skarper grew so used to the careering of the cart that he stopped being scared by it. Carts of ore must come this way every day, he told himself. These clever old dwarves wouldn't have made the bends and drops of their railway sharp or steep enough to derail their trains and spill their precious cargoes. He snuggled down into the ore next to Etty and tried to relax, telling himself that the only things they had to fear were Durgar and Langstone, and there was little chance of them making it all the way to the front cart at this rate.

"I never realized there was so much going on down under the mountains," he said, having to shout a bit over the thundering wheels and their echoes. "Railways and stuff, and these great big holes."

"We are deep in Dwarvendom now," said Etty, close to his ear. "Some of these caverns we pass through are old mines, dug when the world was young, before Men came to live in it. Things were better then; when dwarves ruled above the land as well as beneath it. . ."

And then, as people in the Westlands so often did when they started thinking about history, she began to sing:

It was an age of gold and stone
The dwarvenking sat on his throne
In Dwarvenholm where halls were hollowed
By the first dwarves, and those that followed
Had dug them deeper, made them fine
With silver's glimmer; diamond's shine.
Said the dwarves,
"By land or sea, there are none mightier than we."

Dwarves were lords of all things then,
Until into the land came Men
The Dwarvenking heard of their fleet,
He said I shall go forth and meet
These strangers: at my feet they'll fall,
For I am so strong, so very tall.
Said the dwarves,
"By land or sea, there are none mightier than we."

This great king stood full four feet tall!
Proudly he ventured from his hall;
He did not think to find that Men
Were half as tall as him again.
And when they met him, looking down,
They laughed, "A king? This little clown?"
Then cried the dwarves,
"Across the sea have come some mightier than we!"

The pride of Dwarvendom was gone
And many a mirthless, bitter song
Tells of the mockery Men brought
Of how they pointed, called us "short"
And crueller names, the least of which
Were "half-pint", "stumpy-legs" and "titch".
Now groaned the dwarves,
"By land or sea, there are none lowlier than we."

And so in darkness dwarfkind dwells,
In halls and delves beneath the fells,
Waiting for the great day when
Dwarves will look down again on Men.

"So is that why dwarves are so grumpy, then?" asked Skarper, when she had finished. "Because you're short?"

"We aren't grumpy!" said Etty. "And WE ARE NOT SHORT!"

The cart shot out again just then into a larger stretch of tunnel, and her voice echoed loudly from its curving walls and roof: "SHORT . . . ORT . . . ORT. . ." This cavern was lit by mole-dung lamps, which burned outside a little building beside the tracks ahead. The cart veered around a series of tight bends towards it, the rails snaking through a forest of huge stalagmites and stalactites, some of which had joined in the middle to form wasp-waisted pillars. Clinging on tightly to Etty as the cart threw him them from side to side, Skarper looked nervously behind him. Old Durgar was springing nimbly from the sixth cart to the fifth, the fifth to the fourth. Langstone followed behind him, but failed to notice a low-hanging stalactite. "Oof!" he shouted as it swiped him, and he tumbled down out of sight below the tracks.

"Oh, poor Langstone!" gasped Etty.

Skarper was more worried about poor Skarper. Durgar had ducked the stalactite, and was now poised to jump from the fourth cart to the third. He had pulled a big, two-headed axe out of his belt, and he was eyeing Skarper as if he meant to use it.

Desperately, Skarper looked round, hoping that there might be another low tunnel ahead. There wasn't. But there was something else; something which scared him even more than Durgar's axe.

"Dwarves are not *short*!" Etty was saying. "It's the biglings who are too tall! Everyone knows that!"

"Etty!" Skarper shouted, pointing, and she looked, and saw what had frightened him.

About one hundred feet ahead of them, just beyond that brightly lit building, the track started to rise; a gentle slope, up which the carts would easily be carried by their own momentum. Except that halfway up, a large chunk of the rails was missing. There was a hole in the cavern roof there – a sort of raggedy, melted-looking hole, not at all like a tunnel dwarves would make – and the tracks beneath it seemed to have melted too, the spindly viaduct that supported them collapsing to leave a wide gap in the railway.

"Oh!" said Etty, staring at it. "A tunnel worm!"

"A what?" yelled Skarper. They shot past the lamplit building, and he caught a glimpse inside, of overturned chairs and tables, fallen tools, the place deserted. And now the cart was starting uphill, slowing a little as it hit the incline, but not enough that he could see any hope of stopping it before it reached that damaged section.

From behind him came a crunch as Durgar leaped

and landed in the second cart. "I have you now, goblin!" he gloated.

"Oh bum –" Skarper started to say, and the cart was suddenly off the rails and spinning through empty air, ore, girl and goblin spilling out and tumbling down among the roots of the stalagmites. Skarper clamped his dwarf helm down tightly with his paws and felt chunks of ore and other debris rattling against it. "– cakes!" he said. He scuffled into a niche between two stalagmites and peered back to see the carts come crashing down off the broken track one by one. The enormous din of their falling made his teeth rattle.

"Etty?" he shouted, through the rolling echoes. "Etty?"

"I'm all right!" she called, standing up nearby, caked with dust and touching her forehead, where a small wound dribbled blood.

"I have you now, goblin!" roared Durgar again – he seemed to think it was a pretty good line, and worth repeating. He came stumbling out of the wreckage with his axe agleam, and his eyes gleamed too, focusing on Skarper. "Sneak into our delves, would you, stone-born scum? Kidnap my daughter? Sabotage our railway?"

"But I never. . ." Skarper whimpered, drawing his

short sword and thinking how little use it would be against this strong, angry dwarf with his dirty great big axe.

"Skarper didn't do this, Father," Etty shouted. "Don't you see the signs? That hole above us? 'Tis a tunnel worm!"

"A worm?" Durgar looked suddenly uncertain.

"What's a tunnel worm?" asked Skarper.

As if to answer him, a long, terrible shape burst from the shadows where the wrecked carts lay. It was a serpentlike thing, as thick around as the pipe that was drinking Clovenstone's slowsilver.

"Oh, right," said Skarper.

"Moawwrr!" roared the worm, opening its vicious beak and lunging at Durgar. The dwarf, taken by surprise, had no time to turn and face it. His axe clattered uselessly to the ground as the creature seized him round his middle and lifted him high into the air.

"Father!" screamed Etty.

"Run, Daughter!" Durgar cried, kicking his short legs as the thing shook him furiously from side to side. His helmet flew off and fell among the stalagmites with a clatter like a dropped pan. "Run, Etty! Save yourself!"

Near Skarper's foot the fallen axe glinted, catching the faint lamplight which filtered between the stalactites. Not quite sure what he was doing, nor why he was doing it, Skarper threw his sword aside and picked the axe up. The tunnel worm was sliding backwards, dragging Durgar with it into another of those melted-looking tunnels, which opened in the cavern floor between the supports of the dwarves' viaduct. Durgar was grabbing at anything that came in reach – wrecked carts, stalagmites and bits of spilled ore – but the worm was stronger, and it plainly meant to drag him back into its lair.

"Father!" wailed Etty again.

Skarper lifted the axe, and brought it down hard on the worm's neck, just behind its outsized, ugly head. There was a splatter and fountaining of dark blood, and the head, with Durgar clamped in its beak, dropped off. The bleak light faded from its eyes. Durgar wrenched the beak open and stumbled free, staring at Skarper in astonishment.

"Skarper, no!" shouted Etty, scrambling over the heaps of tipped-out ore to support her father as he stumbled and almost fell. "You don't chop off a worm's head!"

"Why not?" asked Skarper, who had been feeling rather pleased with himself.

"You'll just make it angry!" Etty cried.

Skarper booted the huge head. "I don't care how

angry it is," he said. Then he looked at the rest of the worm, slumped in the entrance to its hole. Blood had stopped flowing from its severed neck. In fact, the worm's flesh had closed over the wound. As he watched in horror, the stump bulged in two places. The bulges grew, swiftly developing eyes, nostrils, beaks and expressions of extreme annoyance. The corpse twitched, wriggled, and rose up, two-headed now, both heads hissing and growling, "Moawwrr!" as it writhed towards Skarper, hungry for revenge and goblin flesh.

"Now that's why we don't deal with tunnel worms by chopping off their heads," said Durgar. "Chop a tunnel worm's head off and two more grow in its place, see?"

Skarper ducked under the worm's heads as they lunged at him. "Henwyn told me a story about a creature like this!" he shouted, sidestepping as the beaks snapped fiercely at him. "Some hero killed it with fire! You burn the stump before new heads can grow!"

He nipped behind it, stepped up on its slimy back and swung the axe again, lopping off both heads. Almost instantly, four heads emerged from the stump of the creature's neck. They looked even more annoyed than the previous two.

"But we don't have any fire!" said Durgar.

"We can make it!" said Etty. "Give me your tinderbox, Father!"

Skarper jumped out of the way as the worm's four new heads twisted round, searching for him. "Moawwwrrr!" they all screamed, in unison. But the "Moawwwrr!" was higher-pitched than before, because the heads were smaller. They had to be. How else could they have fitted on the worm's neck? Each new pair of heads that grew were about half the size of the one that they replaced. Encouraged, Skarper swung the axe again. The four heads fell; eight more shoved their way out of the stump, glaring at him with sixteen angry eyes.

Meanwhile, Etty was crouched over a little pile of kindling, striking sparks with the flint and iron from her father's tinderbox. But it is not easy to make fire at the best of times, and here in the cavern, with her hands trembling and Skarper fighting for his life, it was almost impossible. Red-gold sparks showered on to the kindling, but they did not catch. Even if they had, what else could she find that would burn, in this lifeless cave?

Skarper's arms were getting tired, and the raging tunnel worm now had thirty-two heads.

"Here, Daughter!" called Durgar, dragging himself

closer. He had taken out his knife, and he used it chop off the end of his beard. He handed the tuft of hair to Etty, and when the sparks fell on it it kindled quickly. She pulled her cloak off, wrapped it around a metal bar that had come loose from one of the wrecked carts, and thrust it into the flames.

"Stand back!" she shouted, turning to run to Skarper's aid.

"Eh?" Skarper was leaning on his axe among a pile of lopped-off worm heads, quite exhausted. The tunnel worm roared its anger at him; tiny thin howls of "Moawwwrr!" from one hundred and twenty-eight tiny heads. It was starting to look a bit embarrassed. None of its new heads was much bigger around than Etty's little finger, and although the little snapping beaks looked like they might give a nasty pinch, they didn't hold any real terror any more. Two hundred and fifty-six baleful little eyes winced as Etty came nearer and the torchlight fell upon them. The worm slithered backwards, and vanished into its hole.

"Phew!" said Skarper. "Good riddance!"

"Skarper, you were wonderful!" said Etty.

"Aye," agreed Durgar, looking the goblin up and down. "That was bravely done, goblin. I owe you my life, it seems." He looked almost as embarrassed as the worm had. It did not come easy, giving thanks and praise to goblins. He shook his head and tried to stand, but the worm's beak had bruised him badly and the pain made him slump down again. "That damned worm must have eaten all the dwarves who manned the way station here." He kicked one of the chopped-off heads as if it were a football. "Worms were rare till lately, but there are more of the foul creatures since the Lych Lord's star returned. They come up from the under-underworld, melting their way through the rock with a noxious vitriol that oozes from them. The dwarves of old tried taming them and using them to mine, but they are savage beasts, and quite untameable. So they roam wild, a menace to dwarves and dwarvish works alike."

Skarper looked down at the axe in his hands. Its blades were notched from slicing through so many wormy necks, and etched with odd scars and scorch marks, perhaps from the vitriol that Durgar spoke of. (Actually, Skarper himself had been spattered with the stuff; there were little singed patches on his clothes and skin.) He went to where Durgar sat to give the axe back to him, reflecting that a proper goblin would have chopped the old dwarf's head off too. But Etty would not have liked that, and anyway, he sensed that he had won Durgar over when he saved him from the worm.

But just as he held out the axe, something struck

him a terrible blow on the head. "Arkle!" he cried, collapsing. If it had not been for his tough dwarven helmet and the thick goblin skull beneath it, his story would have ended there.

Langstone, who had crept up behind Skarper and belted him while he was talking to Durgar and Etty, gave a shout of triumph and waved his dented war hammer in the air. Behind Langstone a whole crowd of other dwarves came scrambling through the stalagmites, armed with all sorts of weapons. "Where is it?" they shouted, and "Let us at it!" They were the dwarves from the way station, who had not been eaten by the tunnel worm at all; they had simply run off to fetch help and equipment when the worm appeared, and Langstone had bumped into them as they were returning to deal with it. They had overcome their fear of the creature and were eager for a fight, and they stopped and stared in bewilderment when they saw all those severed worm heads, in assorted sizes, scattered on the cavern floor. "By all the gold in Delverdale!" they muttered, and "Flippin' Ada!" A burp of fire escaped from somebody's flame-hose and set light to somebody else's beard.

Etty flung herself down beside Skarper and gently rolled him over, crying out, "Oh, Skarper! Skarper!"

"Steady on, Etty!" said Langstone. "The foul goblin

may not be dead yet. Stand back and I'll give him another bash."

"Then you'll have to come through me to do it," said Durgar, and he stepped between Skarper and the other dwarves, gripping the axe which Skarper had just returned to him. "This goblin saved my life," he said gruffly. "He single-handedly saw off a tunnel worm that would have taken ten dwarves to deal with, and without the use of fire, either – a very interesting technique. Oh, and my daughter seems fond of him. I think at the very least we owe him a chance to explain himself."

The dwarves all glanced uneasily at one another. Let a goblin explain itself? This was unheard of. But Durgar was a surveyor, and senior to them, so they dared not argue.

Skarper sat up, rubbing his head. He twitched his ears a bit, one by one, just to make sure that they were still attached. He blinked his eyes, and counted his teeth. He didn't feel ready to speak yet, but he didn't need to, because Etty was speaking for him.

"It's wrong for us to be taking all the goblins' slowsilver!" she said loudly. "We can't need all of it. Those gallons and gallons all gushing through the new pipe back to Delverdale. . . What is it all for? We should take what we need, and leave the rest for the goblins."

"Stone-born hooligans!" growled one of the dwarves (he was the one whose beard had caught fire, and he was still smouldering a bit, which may have been why he was in a bad mood).

"They are not hooligans!" said Etty firmly. "Not all of them, anyway. Skarper isn't."

The dwarves looked uneasily at Skarper, remembering what Durgar had said about him saving his life and defeating the tunnel worm. "The Head Knows All. . ." grumbled one.

". . .and the Head Knows Best," the others agreed.

"But what if it *doesn't*?" asked Etty. "How can it know all, unless we tell it when new things appear? Goblins have changed; there's no need for us to just fight them any more. That's why I'm taking Skarper to Dwarvenholm, so that I can bring him before the Head and explain."

"A goblin in Dwarvenholm?" shouted one of the dwarves.

"Never!" cried another.

"The girl has a right to take her troubles to the Head if she so wishes," said Durgar firmly. "That is the right of all dwarves."

"But I've never heard of any dwarf actually doing it," said Langstone. "None but overseers dare enter the hall of the Head usually, and as for goblins. . ."

"Nevertheless," said Durgar, "'tis Etty's right, and if that is what she wants to do, I shall not stop her."

The dwarves muttered and shuffled. "Well," said one, "if the goblin really did save you from the worm. . ."

"If you're sure it's not all some goblin trick. . ."

"Etty," said Langstone sternly, "no good will come of this troublemaking. The Head Knows All and the Head Knows. . ."

But Etty, ignoring him, was helping Skarper to his feet, and Durgar, stuffing his axe back into his belt, called loudly, "Right, lads; how long will it take us to get these rails repaired?"

DWARVENHOLM

It did not take very long at all. Dwarves might be annoying, hairy, set-in-their-ways, axe-happy killjoys, thought Skarper, but they were hard workers, and well organized. Ask a bunch of goblins to repair a broken railway and they'd just bicker for a while and end up hitting each other with the bits; the dwarves, under Durgar's supervision, went to work like the pieces of one big, beardy machine. Before Skarper's ears had quite stopped ringing from that hammer blow the railway was repaired, and he was back in a cart with Etty, Durgar and Langstone, rumbling towards Dwarvenholm.

The caverns through which the railway led were larger now, and more often lit by mole-dung lamps, or the furnaces of smithies and smelting works. This part of the Bonehills had been home to dwarves for long, long centuries, and it looked much grander and more settled than the newer tunnels which lay closer to Clovenstone. Multi-storey dwarf burrows had been hollowed from the cavern walls, huge stalagmites had been wrought into frowning likenesses of the Head, and above the mouths of tunnels big runes were carved, spelling out encouraging slogans like DELVE FOR VICTORY or KEEP CALM AND QUARRY ON.

Soon the railway was rising steadily, and the carts no longer rumbled along under their own momentum but were hauled up a series of steep inclines by mole-powered winches. At the top of the last of these steeps spread a broad marshalling yard, where carts from all over the dwarves' underground empire arrived to be unloaded. The travellers disembarked here, and even with his dwarven helm and cloak Skarper drew more wide-eyed stares than ever he had from the people of Coriander. "Goblin!" The word ran ahead of him through the bustling streets of Delverdale like a fire through dry grass, until everyone in the great cave city seemed to know. "A goblin has come to Dwarvenholm!"

Along the vaulted streets they went, lit by hanging lamps like pocket suns. Up broad stairways carved from living rock, and across bridges which arched above chasms and cataracts. Here and there teams of harnessed moles turned enormous gears, working pumps which carried clean air down from the world above. Outside the warrens and the factories, dwarves gathered to stare and point, murmuring "Goblin!" as Skarper passed. Dwarf children toddled out into the roadway to peer at his face and see if he was as scary as the goblins were in stories, and their mothers snatched them out of his path as if they feared he might eat them. Young dwarves threw pebbles and pasty crusts at him, and earned themselves hard stares from Etty and her father. Older ones demanded, "What is he doing here, Durgar?" and "How dare you bring one of our enemies into Dwarvenholm, Langstone?"

Langstone could only shrug, and say, "It wasn't my idea."

Durgar said, "Etty and I are taking him to the Head. It's the Head who will decide if he's our enemy or not."

They climbed a long, curving stairway, and passed beneath the shadow of a richly carven arch. Two dwarves with staffs stood guard there and stepped out to bar the way, but Durgar said, "My daughter has come to lay her grievances before the Head, as is the ancient right of every dwarf."

"But that's not a dwarf, Durgar!" said one of the sentries, jabbing his staff at Skarper. "That's a goblin!"

"You think I don't know that?" said Durgar angrily. "This goblin is the subject of Etty's complaint to the Head. Now, will you let us pass, Slab Stonethwaite, or will you break the oldest custom of the dwarves?"

Slab Stonethwaite mumbled something about the other oldest custom of the dwarves being not to let goblins go wandering about inside Dwarvenholm, but Durgar's fierce glare silenced him, and he and his companion stepped aside. Durgar, Etty, Skarper and Langstone passed between them, and entered a huge space: a hall hollowed from the heart of the mountain, ringed with pillars and pierced screens of living rock as delicate as lace.

In the centre of that hall, in a pool of light cast by lamps which hung on long chains from the high ceiling, there stood the Brazen Head. It was a handsome dwarf head, wrought from dull, aged bronze, and the size of a large house. There were gaps and openings in it – at its temples, and in its sunken eyes – and through these holes Skarper could see big, toothed wheels turning amid a complicated tangle of pipes and tubes. These inner workings had a silvery sheen, an owl-light glow that Skarper knew meant they were forged from slowsilver.

All around the Head, and up and down ladders and walkways which spidered over it, there hurried important-looking dwarf overseers in purple robes. Some climbed up to feed small, polished stones into its brass ears; some stood ready to catch other stones which emerged from its open mouth and slid down the flutings of its beard into their waiting hands. The stones being fed in had questions on them, runic letters carved by dwarves who sat in rows at low stone benches. The stones coming out bore the answers. The dwarves who caught them shouted out these answers to young dwarf messengers who waited eagerly in the shadows around the edges of the hall. "Excavations in the Elkendelve shaft are to proceed; send three squads of miners there. . ."

"Level Fourteen of the mine at Boldventure is to be abandoned before the yield drops any further. . ."

"Cardle's mole cavalry may withdraw from Clovenstone."

Awed by the ants'-nest bustle of the place, Skarper hung back in the shadows near the entrance until Etty took him by the paw and led him forward. "The Head must get a look at you!" she said.

"No!" said Langstone. He had been uncomfortable about her wild plan all the way from the worm's hole, and now the looming presence of the Head so overawed him that he was trembling. "Don't do this! I will not be a part of it! I am going to fetch Overseer

Glunt; I shall tell him that this is all your idea and nothing to do with me."

He reached out to pull Etty back, but Durgar thrust him away. "Fetch Glunt, if that's what you want," he said. "No doubt he'll be down here soon enough anyway. The whole of Dwarvenholm is buzzing like a kicked hive with news of our coming. Etty, lass, if you're sure you want to do this, do it quick."

Langstone made an exasperated, strangled noise, then turned and went running from the hall. As his footsteps faded, Etty squeezed Skarper's paw and led him on across the hall, with Durgar. Slowly the shouted orders, the pecking of the question-carvers, and the clumping footsteps of the departing messenger-dwarves fell quiet. Only the Brazen Head kept clanking and rattling and chunking, as it had clanked and rattled and chunked for centuries. The gears revolved behind its empty eyes. All other eyes in the hall were turned upon Etty and Skarper.

"Hello!" said Skarper, trying to sound friendly, and he waved a paw at the nearest overseer. The dwarf just stood glaring at him with an unread answer stone clenched tightly in his trembling hands.

"What is the meaning of this intrusion?" another overseer demanded, his long white beard quivering with outrage.

"I have a question for the Head," said Etty.

The question carvers looked nervously at her, then at the Head, wondering what to do.

"Certainly not!" blustered the white-bearded overseer. "This is a time of great deeds and mighty undertakings. The Head is busy with important computations. It is not to be bothered with questions from a girl-child and a goblin!"

"Yet it *is* her right," said another overseer.

"The right of every dwarf," agreed a third.

"Hurry up and tell us your question, girl," said a fourth, and signalled to the oldest of the question carvers that he should write it down.

Etty coughed twice to clear her throat. She was not used to having quite so many eyes upon her, quite so many ears waiting to catch her words. She said, "I want to ask the Head, does it know that goblins no longer want to be our enemies? And, if it does, why is it that dwarves and goblins may not live in peace?"

The question carver plucked two fresh stones from the basket that stood at his side. (Like all the question stones, they were flat, black pebbles, smoothed and rounded in the River Blindwater, which ran through deep caves far beneath Dwarvenholm.) Quickly the carver's chisel pecked out Etty's questions, one on each stone. Then an overseer gathered them up, climbed the spindly ladder to the Head's ear, and fed the stones in, one by one.

The Head quivered. Clank, it went. And rattle, and chunk. Reflections of the hanging lamps danced in the flutings of its beard where the bronze had been worn smooth and bright by all the answer stones sliding down. Clank, rattle, chunk – and out came another stone; a single answer to Etty's two questions. It dropped into the hands of a waiting overseer, who raised it and read it aloud.

"The Head says, 'Goblins have always been the enemy of dwarves. Goblins will always be the enemy of dwarves.'"

Clank, rattle, chunk, went the Head, but no more stones emerged.

"Well, lass, you tried," said Durgar, placing a fatherly hand on Etty's shoulder. "The Head has spoken, and now we must leave. . ."

Etty shook herself free of him. "But it didn't answer my question!" she said angrily. "I asked if it knew goblins had changed. I asked why goblins must be our enemies. It's not good enough, just to say that they always have been and they always will!"

"But the Head knows all. . ." said one of the question carvers.

Etty strode to the overseer who had read the answer

stone and snatched it from him. She hurled it at the floor, where it shattered, and the shards went skitter-skating across the marble and away into the shadows. "It doesn't really know anything, does it?" she shouted, pointing up at the great, impassive face of the Brazen Head. "You ask it questions and it gives you answers, but it doesn't know anything! It still thinks things are as they were all those years ago when it was made. It's just a clanking, rattling, chunking *contraption*!"

All around her, overseers gasped, while messengers and question carvers covered their ears to try to stop themselves hearing any more of her terrible, blasphemous words. One messenger fainted. Another said, "How could she?" Even Durgar muttered, "Steady now, lass."

"But it's true!" shouted Etty. "We've all known it's true, haven't we, really, for years and years? It was just easier to pretend that the Head knows all!"

Not many of the dwarves in the hall were listening to her any more, and it wasn't just because half of them had stuck their fingers in their ears and started going, "La-la-la. . ." There was a commotion going on outside: a blur of voices and a tramp of iron-shod shoes. Skarper, who had been thinking of slipping quietly away while Etty's angry outburst was distracting the overseers, turned to find that his way was barred. A squad of armoured dwarves was marching into the hall of the Head, forming a line across the entrance with their spears levelled.

"Who are they?" asked Skarper nervously.

"Those are the tallboys," said Durgar grimly. "The tallest dwarves of each generation are picked to serve as defenders of Dwarvendom and bodyguards for the overseers. . ."

Skarper gulped, looking at the barrier of spears. The bosses of the tallboys' shields and the visors of their helmets were forged in the likeness of the Head, and some of them were very tall indeed, real giants of dwarves, almost four and a half feet high.

Their ranks shifted slightly, and out between the spears stepped a shorter figure; one that Skarper knew. It was Overseer Glunt, whose ugly head he'd landed on when he first fell into the dwarf tunnel in the Bonehills, all those weeks before.

"All right, Durgar, this nonsense has gone far enough!" Glunt announced, with a nasty sneer. "Langstone has told me the whole sorry tale. To think, a surveyor of your age and standing, doubting the wisdom of the Head! And you, Etty – conspiring with goblins and biglings against your own people! It's Dungeon Crag and the Bright Bowl for all of you."

"What's that mean?" asked Skarper. "Is it bad? Is it an actual bowl? How bad can a bowl be?"

His friends did not answer, but they did not really need to. Skarper could see the look of dumbstruck fear that had settled upon their faces. It told him that whatever this Bright Bowl was, it was something very bad indeed.

THE GIANT DWARF

The hollow mountain that housed Dwarvenholm was high and stark, and its western face fell almost sheer, a black cliff with its feet in the stony fields of Delverdale. In this cliff there was a vast door, with ramplike roads zigzagging up to it, but it was shut and barred, and had not opened since men first came into the Westlands and the dwarves retreated in a huff into their caves.

There were other doors, though, further down the mountain, and out of one of them the tallboys led their prisoners, out under the light of a bone-pale moon. Looking back, Skarper saw the huge, shut door of Dwarvenholm towering above him, and looking ahead he saw Delverdale spread out below; the big fields divided by stony walls, the barns and pigsties clustering around windowless, turf-roofed farms from which dwarf farmers would emerge at night to plant their crops and tend their animals. Dwarf chimneys poked up everywhere, a forest of tall stone stacks that sucked in air and breathed out the smoke of the teeming city hidden beneath the fields.

But Overseer Glunt and his tallboys were not leading their prisoners down into the dale. Instead they turned south, along a narrow path whose paving had been worn smooth by the feet of many such processions. Up and up the thin way wound, to a place where a tall crag jutted out of the mountain's flank, sharp and jagged with the moon behind it, and as black as a goblin's toenails.

"Dungeon Crag," said Glunt. "You may not have heard of it, goblin. To dwarves it is a name of terror; something for dwarfwives to scare their naughty children with."

Skarper looked up critically at the crag. What did the dwarves do to their prisoners there? Chuck them off the top? His ears curled at the memory of his long-ago fall from the top of Blackspike Tower, but he did not want Glunt to have the satisfaction of seeing how afraid he was, so he shrugged and said, "I've been thrown off taller things than *that*."

Glunt looked narrowly at him, and then laughed. "Who said we were going to throw you off it? We're going to take you up there and leave you there, you and these traitor friends of yours. Of course, after a day or two, you may *wish* we'd thrown you off!"

And his nasty laughter echoed off the rocks of Dwarvenholm as he led the tallboys and their prisoners up the steep stair to the summit of the crag.

Dwarves do not build dungeons. Even in the olden days, before they started to live underground, they felt at home beneath the earth. The darkness of an underground cell holds no terrors for them, and they would probably manage to tunnel out of it quite quickly anyway. So, long ago, the Dwarvenkings had commanded the building of a sky dungeon: the dreaded Bright Bowl, a deep, steep-sided hollow which dwarf stonewrights had carved into the summit of Dungeon Crag. There traitors and murderers could be cast and left to rot. Its sides were as smooth as glass, and shone dimly with reflected moonlight as the prisoners arrived, panting, on the narrow path which circled the bowl's brim.

There, Etty turned to Glunt and said, "Please, Overseer; my father and Skarper have done nothing wrong. It is I who should be punished, not them."

Moonlight silvered the masks of the tallboys, and made Glunt's ugly sneer of triumph uglier still. "Skarper is a filthy goblin," he said. "As for your father, you should have spared a thought for him before you started shouting insults at the Head."

"It is nothing but a machine," said Etty. "How can I insult it?"

Those tallboys who stood close enough to hear her muttered dark mutterings behind their visors, outraged that, even here, on the brim of the Bright Bowl, she should still be telling her dreadful lies about the Head. But Overseer Glunt just leaned close to her, and winked. "A machine it may be," he said softly, "but it shall be the salvation of Dwarvendom. The dwarves who made it were very wise, and they gave it one mission that is more important than any other: to restore the pride of dwarves. But the magic was failing in those days, and there was not enough slowsilver left in the world to make it work, so it was never finished. They did not know of the great lake under Clovenstone, or perhaps they did not think that they could drain it. Well, I, Glunt, have succeeded where they failed! The Clovenstone slowsilver is flowing to Dwarvenholm now, and the Head shall be finished at last."

"Finished?" said Durgar. "Finished how?"

Glunt chuckled. "There was a time when our kind did as we liked in the Westlands, before the biglings came. That is how it shall be again, when the Head goes forth. The time is coming, very soon, when we shall look down in scorn upon men."

"'When the Head goes forth'?" asked Etty. "How can it go anywhere? It's just a head!"

"Why don't you think about that," suggested Glunt, "while you wait to die?" And with that he reached out and shoved her in the chest. He did not push hard, but she was caught off guard, and she stepped backwards, slipped on the sleek stone of the bowl, and went slithering helplessly down. With armoured fists and spear butts the tallboys shoved Skarper and Durgar after her. Even Skarper's sharp claws couldn't find a purchase on that glassy slope, and he went skidding down to land with the others in the bottom of the bowl.

They lay there, hearing Glunt and the tallboys leave, then nothing but the soft moaning of the wind as it blew around the bowl's brim, far above them.

Something was digging into Skarper's bottom. He wriggled round and pulled the object out from under him. It was a bit of somebody's skeleton, and looking around he saw that a litter of bleached bones filled the bottom of the bowl. Skulls grinned sheepishly at him in the moonlight.

"So I suppose there's no way out of here?" he said.

"No prisoner has ever escaped from the Bright

Bowl," said Durgar doomily, which was exactly what Skarper had been afraid he was going to say.

"So why do they call it the Bright Bowl?" he asked. "It sounds quite cheerful. And it doesn't look very bright to me."

"Not now it isn't," Etty said. "But wait till morning. When the sun comes up its light will shine into the bowl, and we must lie in it till we are blinded and burned and shrivelled up. Dwarves are shy of sunlight. We have dwelled too long in shadows."

"Oh," said Skarper, remembering how the tallboys had stripped Etty and her father of their black glass goggles before they brought them to the bowl. Then he brightened. "Still, goblins don't really mind the sun," he said.

"Then you will lie here till you starve," said Durgar. "Or die of thirst. Whichever comes sooner."

He turned his back on Skarper and cuddled up to Etty, leaving the goblin to stare up miserably at the cold, mocking twinkle of the high stars.

"Maybe it will rain," Skarper suggested hopefully. "Then there'll be something to drink, and the clouds will shield us from the sun. Then we'll have time to think of a way out. Princess Ned says there's always a way if you just think hard enough."

But the dwarves did not answer. Maybe they

were asleep, or maybe they were just too miserable. Skarper lay awake, thinking hard for a long time, but he couldn't think of a way out, and above him still the cold stars shone, promising a cloudless day to come.

Towards dawn, Skarper fell into a fidgety sort of a sleep. Bad dreams came to him; of moles and dampdrakes and long drops. He woke with a start. He was lying beside Etty and Durgar in the bottom of the Bright Bowl. Above him the sky was like another bowl, harebell blue and upended over him. It was completely clear. Soon the sun would be up, and Skarper was not sure how long Etty and Durgar would be able to withstand its scorching gaze. He wasn't sure how long he could withstand it, come to that – goblins did not mind the daylight as much as dwarves did, but it was going to grow hot here, with no shade, no water, and the sunlight reflecting off the polished stone. He licked up some of the dew that had formed on the bowl's sides in the night, then made another scrabbling attempt to climb out. He soon slid back again. He seized one of the dwarf bones that lay in the bowl's bottom and tried using it as a pick, but it soon splintered on the hard stone.

Durgar, who was awake and watching him, said, "It

is useless. We tried while you were sleeping, me and Etty."

"There is no hope for us, Skarper," Etty said sadly, hugging him. "We can only wait, and hope that the Overseers of the Dead find good work for us when we reach the afterworld."

Skarper scratched his head. "What? You dwarves have to keep on working even after you're dead?" he asked.

"Of course!" said Etty. "The dwarf gods are building a vast castle in the afterlife to keep out the ghosts of men. There is much to be done there!"

Skarper didn't fancy that. Goblins were a bit vague about what went on in the afterlife, but he'd always imagined it would be a chance for a nice long rest, with maybe a bit of wafting about and scaring people like those ghosts of Zeewa's, to stop it getting boring. It seemed to him that if he died here with these dwarves there was a good chance he would end up in the dwarf afterlife by mistake, and be set to work building their ghost castle.

More desperate than ever to escape, he looked up at the sky again. Black dots circled up there; carrion birds whose sharp eyes had spotted the three prisoners waiting in the bowl. Over to the east there hung a little puffball cloud, the first he'd seen, but it was not big enough to blot out the sun for long. Then, as he looked at it, Skarper realized that Etty had been wrong. There was hope after all!

The dwarves looked on in bewilderment as he jumped up and started shouting. They'd never paid much attention to the sky. They'd never looked with any interest at clouds, and had certainly never noticed that some clouds didn't always go where the wind blew them. They'd never guessed there were such things as cloud maidens, air-headed spirits of the skies who travelled the world aboard their magic clouds and who could sometimes be persuaded to take passengers.

"Cloud maidens?" growled Durgar, when Skarper tried explaining. "Are they friendly?"

That made Skarper hesitate for a moment. Cloud maidens weren't exactly friendly; not really; not to goblins. The first time he'd dropped in on them, they'd been ready to hurl him off their cloud, and when the fall proved not enough to kill him they had chased after him, slinging lightning bolts and hailstones. No, you couldn't really call them *friendly* at all. But they were the only scrap of hope he had, so he went on leaping up and down, waving his paws and tail in the air and shouting, "Hello! Over here!" They were flighty creatures, but there was always a chance that they might decide to help. And if they didn't, well, it would probably be better in the long run to be roasted quickly by a thunderbolt than slowly by the sun. . .

Etty joined in, waving her short arms and yelling, and eventually Durgar started shouting too. The dwarf sentries at the foot of Dungeon Crag looked up and shook their heads and grinned, imagining that their captives were screaming for mercy as the sun rose. But at last the cloud seemed to swivel a little in the air, and then it drew closer, as if blown towards them by a wind they could not feel. As its shadow fell over the Bright Bowl, the wispy faces of the cloud maidens appeared around its edges, looking down. Their high, fair voices carried clearly on the morning air.

"It's that horrible goblin again!"

"What is he doing here?"

"And some dwarves. . ."

"Come, sisters, let us leave this dismal place. I told you there would be no princes here."

"No!" shouted Skarper, as the cloud began to rise again. "Don't go! Please help us! We'll die if we stay here!"

"Then you shouldn't have climbed up there in the first place, should you?" said a cloud maiden tartly. "You have only yourselves to blame, you know."

"Please!" begged Etty.

The cloud came down again, but only so that the

cloud maidens could peer at Etty. They hadn't realized she was a girl until she spoke, and they wanted to make sure that she was not prettier than them. When they saw that she wasn't, they giggled at her.

"Have you heard what has happened at Clovenstone?" asked Skarper slyly. "There's been a great battle there! Henwyn led a charge against the dwarves!"

Just as he'd hoped, the cloud maidens stopped tittering and stared at him. They were all crazy about Henwyn.

"Is he. . . Is Henwyn all right?" they asked.

"Oh yes," said Skarper, hoping it was true. "You know Henwyn: brave as a lion and twice as clever. He defeated the dwarves. But now they are planning some new trouble; building a great engine of war or something, and there's little doubt they'll use it to take Clovenstone by force."

"Oh! And dear Henwyn would sooner die than let that happen!" wailed one of the cloud maidens.

"That's why I need you to help us, see?" insisted Skarper. "We have to get home and warn him."

"Oh, sisters," said Rill, the kindest of the cloud maidens, "we must do as the goblin asks."

"But why?" asked the others. "He's horrid and he'll get our cloud all dirty. We can fly to Henwyn faster if we are not weighed down by nasty goblins."

"But think how cross Henwyn will be if he hears you've left me here to starve and parch!" said Skarper.

"Oh, that's true," admitted a cloud maiden. "Remember, sisters, Henwyn is fond of the ghastly creature for some reason."

"Oh, very well," said the others.

"And my friends must come too," said Skarper, pointing to Etty and Durgar. "I can't leave them behind."

If the cloud maidens had thought about it for a moment they would have realized that all they needed to do was fly away: if Skarper was left behind to die, how would Henwyn ever know that they had even spoken to him? But the cloud maidens weren't all that bright, and at the moment there was not much room in their cloudy heads for any thought except Henwyn. Most of them were just staring into the middle distance with soppy smiles upon their faces, imagining his blue eyes and blond curls. "Mmm, he's so dreamy!" they murmured, while their cloud drifted sideways on the morning breeze.

"Come on then!" shouted Skarper, before they blew away entirely, and Rill and a few of her sisters came to their senses and lowered cloud ladders for the prisoners to climb aboard.

"You must all take your boots off," they said. "We don't want grubby footprints all over our cloud."

Meanwhile, two of the dwarf sentries down at the foot of the crag had decided that they really should investigate the conversation that was going on above, and the strange cloud that was hovering above the Bright Bowl. They hurried up the long stair and emerged on to the bowl's brim just in time to see their prisoners climbing up a cobwebby ladder which had descended from the belly of the cloud. Their eyes went wide behind their black glass goggles. They shook their halberds in a threatening way and shouted, "Stop!" but the prisoners just kept climbing. Then the sentries did the only thing they could think of: they shouted to their friends for help, then jumped into the bowl and went slithering down into its middle, where they grabbed at the bottom of the cloud ladder and started climbing it.

But the cloud maidens were unhappy about letting two dwarves on to their cloud; they certainly weren't going to welcome any more aboard. As Durgar clambered up to sit panting beside Skarper and Etty on the cloud's cushiony top, the maidens let their magic ladder melt back into plain ordinary cloud. The dwarves below yelled in anger and surprise as the woolly rungs which they'd been climbing turned suddenly to mist. They yelled again, in pain mostly, as they dropped heavily down on to the heap of dry bones in the bottom of the bowl. The cloud twirled above them, scattering maidenly laughter, and the last Skarper saw of them they were trying desperately to scrabble back up the bowl's sides and calling out to their friends to bring them ropes and real, solid, metal ladders.

But their friends were not paying them much attention; they stood on the bowl's brim and on the stairs that led to it, staring north towards the doors of Dwarvenholm, and as the cloud rose and flew out across Delverdale Skarper stared with them, for something was happening in the country of the dwarves.

The road which led up to the great doors was lined with onlookers. Streams of dwarves were pouring out of all the little hidden doors which speckled the lower slopes of the hollow mountain. They kept to the shadows where they could, but where they could not they braved the sunlight, shielding themselves with umbrellas and moleskin screens. Like the guards on the crag, they were all staring towards the main doors, which Skarper now saw were swinging open.

"Hang on!" he told the cloud maidens, who had lifted their cloud up into the clear, cold river of wind which swirled over the mountain's shoulder, and were starting to steer it towards Clovenstone. "Wait! What's going on down there?"

"Oh, what now?" tutted the cloud maidens, but when they looked where Skarper was pointing they fell silent too, and watched. It was not every day that the Doors of Dwarvenholm were opened.

The great burnished metal plaques which sheathed the doors flashed and rippled with sunlight as they swung wide. Behind them lay shadows: a dark opening leading into the heart of the mountain, like the earth's mouth. Then, in the darkness, Skarper started to make out the twinkle of dwarf lamps, and the glint of light on the armour of marching dwarves. Hundreds of warriors were coming up out of the deeps, up the great paved way which led to the doors, and out into the morning sunlight. Banners with the device of the Brazen Head flapped in the breeze, and so did the broad moleskin awnings which the marchers on the edges of the column held up to shade their comrades.

"Marching above ground?" said Durgar, frowning at the spectacle below. "It don't make sense. Why send an army marching in hot sunlight when we have tunnels and delves below ground that will take us all the way to Clovenstone?"

But behind the marching warriors, something else came striding: something far too big to fit in any delve or tunnel. It was the shape of a dwarf, but as tall as the tallest giant, and it was made all of shining metal. On its shoulders sat the Brazen Head, and as it stepped out through the open doors and started to follow the army down the road that led through Delverdale, the Head swung watchfully from side to side, as if it were gazing down upon the dwarves who lined the way.

"They have built a body for the Head!" said Etty, clinging to the thick, cottony cloud-stuff and leaning far out over the edge to stare down.

"So that is what that maggot Glunt meant!" said her father. "I have heard stories of storerooms deep beneath the mountain where mighty limbs were stored; legs and arms, built out of iron. So they were meant for the Head, and Glunt and his friends have assembled them, and now he has slowsilver enough to set them moving. . ."

"The Head walks! The Head walks!" dwarves were chanting, down in the valley, their massed voices loud enough to be heard clearly on the cloud. The cloud maidens steered it lower, and soon Skarper and the others could make out the tubby form of Overseer Glunt, standing with some other dwarves upon a railed platform which circled the Head's brow like a crown. Glunt had a huge brass trumpet in his hands, and when he bellowed through it his words came out loud enough to be heard even over the chanting.

"Behold!" he announced. "The Giant Dwarf! The slowsilver of Clovenstone runs in its veins! The magic of our spell-smiths makes it move! No army can defeat it! No wall, no tower, no bastion raised by men can stand against it!"

"That's Clovenstone done for, then," said Skarper sadly, ears drooping.

"Poor Henwyn!" whispered the cloud maidens. "It will stamp him flat!"

"The day long foretold has dawned at last!" Glunt roared. "The day when dwarves look down again on men! They called us short! They laughed at us! We'll see who laughs last when they look up and see the Giant Dwarf coming to trample their palaces underfoot! To Coriander!"

"To Coriander!" shouted all the dwarves in the valley – at least it sounded like all of them; their voices merged into one vast voice which echoed and re-echoed from the steep sides of Delverdale.

"Did he say Coriander?" asked Skarper.

"So they aren't going to Clovenstone at all!" sniffed a cloud maiden, looking disdainfully at the footprints the passengers had made in the cloud. "The goblin lied to us!"

"I thought they were!" said Skarper. "I thought. . . Why do they want to go to Coriander?"

"To drive men out," said Durgar. "To open up the mines of the sea coast again. To take back what was ours in the long ago. Dwarves were wronged, and the wrong must be righted."

"But not this way!" cried Etty. "Not this monstrous thing, trampling folk and bringing death and disaster! Dwarves should be makers, not breakers of things!"

"We must still take word to Clovenstone!" said Skarper. "Henwyn should hear about this, and Fentongoose, and Princess Ned. . . Maybe they'll know what to do. . ."

Just then the shadow of the cloud fell over the Giant Dwarf. Glunt looked up and saw the faces of the cloud maidens and their passengers peering down at him. He shouted something that they could not hear. Dwarf crossbowmen on the Giant Dwarf's shoulders raised their weapons. A flight of darts went chirring into the sky like starlings, and thudded into the underside of the cloud. They did no harm, except to make it look rather odd, like a flying pincushion, but the cloud maidens quickly took it higher and, flinging a storm of hailstones down at the dwarf army, soared up into the river of wind again and let it carry them west, away over the empty valleys and stony summits of the Bonehills, whirling towards far-off Clovenstone.

COUNSEL AT CLOVENSTONE

A dreadful noise filled the cavern beneath Meneth Eskern, echoing and re-echoing from the stony ceiling. *SQUksWKSwKKRKkkkggKKrrrrRRRggKK* it went, rather like the noise you get when you're drinking milkshake through a straw and reach the bottom of the glass, or when the last of the bathwater goes gurgling down the plughole. The pipe which the dwarves had driven through the crag had finally drained the last of the slowsilver from the lava lake.

Princess Ned and Fentongoose, standing on the beach, looked down into a broad, empty pit where the slowsilver had been, and saw the mouth of the dwarf-pipe far below them. A few small pools and puddles of the magic metal still glimmered in crevices of the stone around it, but they had lost their silvery glow, and showed no sign of spitting out any eggstones.

They had known of the pipe's existence – or at least guessed it – ever since Henwyn and Zeewa came back out of the marshes with the tale of their strange meeting with the boglins. Fentongoose and Dr Prong had spent a long time hunting for it, hoping that it could be blocked. But they had soon realized that the pipe must open at the very bottom of the lake, and there was simply no way to reach it. Slowsilver is not like water, or even like ordinary lava; it is more magical and mischievous than that. The hooks and poles which the two philosophers lowered into the lake in the hope of finding the pipe dissolved in puffs of steam, or froze and shattered. A goblin called Spurtle, who was helping them, fell into the slowsilver by accident and was instantly transformed into a small sofa. The pipe remained hidden. It seemed immune to the strange powers of the slowsilver. It kept on sucking and sucking away, invisible down there in the depths. Every half-hour Fentongoose checked the stones he had set on the beach to mark the edge of the slowsilver, and every half-hour he found that the level had dropped. It had gone down with horrifying speed, and now the lake was empty.

"That is that," said Fentongoose sadly. He was thinking of all the eggstones he had collected on the lakeshore, and how he had kept them warm and helped the hatchlings inside them to emerge (and forgetting how the hatchlings had hit him with planks and bitten his fingers). "It is the end of Clovenstone!" he said.

"There must be some way we can get our slowsilver back!" said Princess Ned. "What if we sent some of our smaller goblins along that pipe? Perhaps they could find whatever tank or reservoir the dwarves have taken all our slowsilver to, and – oh, I don't know – reverse the flow somehow? Pump it back to us?"

Fentongoose shook his head. "I do not think so. Apart from anything else, the pipe will be smeared with slowsilver. It must have been wrought by spell-smiths out of dwarven iron to be proof against the slowsilver's effects. Our goblins are not, and they would probably be transformed into frogs or puffs of smoke before they had crept more than a few feet along it. Remember what happened to poor Spurtle. . ."

"Of course. How is Spurtle?"

"Oh, he is comfortable enough. We just have to plump up his cushions from time to time. But Ned, these dwarves do not do things for fun. I daresay they have plans for our slowsilver. They are probably putting it to use already."

"But to what use?" wondered Princess Ned.

Flat feet flapped on the stone floor of the passage

behind her and a panting goblin came running up to her. It was Yabber, and he had news. "The cloud maidens are back!"

"Oh, that is all we need," groaned Fentongoose, who had always found those airy young ladies most annoying. But Yabber hopped up and down and waved his paws excitedly. "They ain't alone! Skarper's with them!"

"Skarper?" cried Fentongoose and Ned together, and they went hurrying up the long, winding passageway and out into the afternoon light.

It was a cloudy day at Clovenstone, and for a moment it was quite difficult to make out which of all of those clouds was the exciting one. Then they saw it; there was Skarper, dancing up and down on top of it as it came slowly down to brush against the battlements of the Inner Wall. A huge crowd of goblins had already gathered there to greet it. Others, who had been practice-fighting with Garvon Hael in the old tilt yard behind Growler Tower, were running up the stairways in a yowling, cheering throng.

Outside the wall, Henwyn heard the cheering, but he was busy helping Cribba, Torridge and Kenn block up dwarf tunnels, and he did not see the cloud descend. *Stupid creatures*, he thought bitterly, listening to the whoops and howls of the excited goblins echo among the ruins. That was a bit unfair, but it was certainly true that most goblins weren't all that bright. *How can they be celebrating*, thought Henwyn, *when Skarper is dead, the slowsilver lake is being drunk dry and goblinkind is facing its doom?*

"What's that?" asked Torridge just then, pointing up.

"It's a cloud, stupid," said Cribba.

"But it's got people on top of it!" said Kenn.

"Henwyn!" shouted Zeewa, running through the ruins with her tangle of ghosts behind her. "Henwyn! It is Skarper! He is alive! He has come home!"

They ran towards the wall together, Henwyn and Zeewa, the trolls and the ghosts, almost getting stepped on on the way by Fraddon, who had come up from the woods to see what was happening. Rushing inside the wall and shoving their way past the yapping, yahooing goblins who clogged the stairways, they reached the battlements just as the cloud bumped gently against the top of Blackspike Tower. Skarper jumped off, followed by Durgar and Etty, who looked about uncertainly at the goblins who surrounded them and peered down at them from the Blackspike's mossy roof. The whole cloud blushed sunset pink as the cloud maidens spotted Henwyn: they waved shyly, and shook their hair out into long cloudy streamers, which they hoped he'd think pretty. But Henwyn wasn't paying them any attention at all; he ran straight to Skarper, picked him up, and swung him round and round.

"You're alive!" he shouted.

"I know!" Skarper shouted back, and also, "Put me down!", because he was hoping to *stay* alive, and being whirled round and round on top of a crumbly battlement with a long drop on each side didn't seem like a good way to make that happen. "Stop! Put me down! Listen! The dwarves have built a body for their Head. A Giant Dwarf! I saw it come stomping out of Delverdale, high as a mountain. That's what they drained our slowsilver for! That's what it runs on. . . "

"It's true!" said Durgar, and Etty added, "It's huge! Nothing can stand before it!"

A sort of silence fell over the crowd, broken only by a low murmuring as goblins tried to work out what this would mean.

"Is it coming here, this Giant Dwarf?" asked Fraddon.

A score of goblin voices echoed him. "Is it coming here? Is it coming to Clovenstone?"

"Coriander," said Skarper. "They're taking it to Coriander."

"Yazzay! Yibber! Hap!" the goblins screamed

throwing hats and helmets, spears and clubs into the air in their excitement. "We're saved! Clovenstone is saved!"

"No, no!" shouted Durgar. "You don't understand!"

The goblins fell quiet again, except for the occasional "Ow!" and "Argh!" as the spears and clubs fell back on to their owners.

"The Giant Dwarf is meant to restore the pride and standing of the dwarves," Durgar said. "They are taking it to Coriander. They mean to defeat the High King and his armies."

Even the "Argh!"s and "Ow!"s had stopped now: the goblins frowned and scratched their heads, trying to work out what this news meant for them. They didn't care about Coriander. They didn't much care about softlings, except for the ones they knew. This Giant Dwarf could stomp the High King flat for all they cared.

But Princess Ned had heard all this as she came slowly up the stairs with Fentongoose, and she saw at once what it would mean. "If the dwarves take Coriander, then no kingdom can stand against them. They will rule over the Westlands again, as they did in days of old. We must warn the High King!"

The goblins rumbled, mumbled, grumbled. They

had all heard how it had gone when Henwyn and Skarper asked the High King for help. They still didn't really see why they should help him. They were goblins, after all: it wasn't their style. They rather liked the idea of his majesty getting stomped on by a Giant Dwarf. It was just the sort of thing that appealed to them.

Princess Ned sat down on a small sofa which someone had left there on the battlements, then sprang up again and said, "Oh Spurtle, I'm sorry! But please think, all of you. If the dwarves control the Westlands, do you really believe they will let us live on here in peace? Of course not. They have already made sure that there will be no new goblins. They will come and deal with the rest of us at their leisure. They already have our slowsilver, but there is much else at Clovenstone that dwarves would value, and they will not want goblins here. This giant dwarf is as much a danger to us as it is to Coriander."

Henwyn had been thinking, too. He was imagining a map of the Westlands, with Dwarvenholm in the north-east, Coriander in the south-west. An old straight road ran from one to the other, and it passed through Henwyn's own hometown.

"Adherak!" he gasped. "The Giant Dwarf will have to pass through Adherak!"

That changed things. The goblins knew people from Adherak. Henwyn's father and mother had visited Clovenstone, along with his sisters, Herda, Gerda and Lynt. They'd helped set up the Clovenstone Cheesery, and taught the goblins how to make Clovenstone Blue. None of the goblins thought it would be funny if *they* got stomped on.

"We must do something!" said a voice out of the throng.

"We must stop it!"

"Anchovies!"

"Could Fraddon fight this thing?" demanded Fentongoose.

Etty looked at Fraddon and shrugged. "It is taller than your giant. And it is made all of metal, and slowsilver runs in its veins instead of blood. I do not think that anything could fight it."

"Goblins can!" the goblins yelled. They waved their spears and clubs and rusty old swords. Even the sofa rustled its cushions in a warlike way. "We'll bash it in!" they hollered. "We'll smash it up! Nothing's ever been built that goblins can't smash up!"

"Garvon Hael taught us to fight!" shouted Libnog. "We'll just fight at Adherak instead of Clovenstone, that's all!"

"To Adherak! To Adherak!" other goblins shouted.

"Stop the Giant Dwarf!" And raggedly and out of tune, they began to chant the ancient goblin war song:

> Goblins come!
> Goblins come!
> From Clovenstone with horn and drum!
> To the Lands of Man with fire we come!
> Over the mountains,
> Over the moor,
> Goblins are marching,
> To war! To war!

It was like the turning of a tide: a great swirl of motion, surging down the stairways of the Inner Wall towards the armouries below. The goblins had grown so used to the idea of fighting dwarves, and so eager for revenge, that once the idea of going to Adherak was sown in their brains it sprouted swiftly.

> Goblins go!
> Goblins go!
> With things to thump and things to throw!
> To smash that Giant Dwarf we go!
> There and back,
> There and back,

Goblins are marching,
To Adherak!

On the battlements, Ned struggled through the current of departing goblins to reach the waiting cloud. "Oh, cloud maidens, do be dears and fly to Coriander with this news!" she said. "And to Adherak as well, to let them know that we are coming. . ."

"Not we, princess," said Dr Prong, quite sternly. "Do you not remember when you asked me to be your doctor? Well, as your doctor, it is my medical opinion that you must rest, and not exert yourself."

"Oh yes!" said Henwyn eagerly, because he had suddenly remembered his vision in the bathtub, and was wondering if it was on one of the green fields of Adherak that he had seen the princess laid out dead. "You should stay here. Someone must stay behind to keep an eye on Clovenstone; to make sure the boglins do not try anything while we are away, and to organize a last defence if we fail and the dwarves come here."

"Henwyn, I am not an invalid!" said Ned quite crossly, because it seemed to her that her place was at the front of this boisterous army, not skulking at home. But then she looked at them, pouring down off the Inner Wall, grabbing pikes and shields and banners from the armouries, and it struck her what a long way it was to Adherak, and how fast the goblins would cover that distance if they did not have an elderly princess to delay them, and she had to admit that what Henwyn and Dr Prong had said was right.

"Well," she said, determined to be of some use to the expedition, "you cannot just set off now, all higgledy-piggledy, without a plan of campaign or any provisions. We must organize you."

Ned was good at organizing. As soon as she had waved the cloud maidens off on their mission to Coriander she made Fentongoose and Dr Prong sit down with some old maps from the bumwipe heaps and plan the shortest route to Adherak and the best place to try to stop the Giant Dwarf when they got there. Meanwhile, Henwyn and Garvon Hael ran around making sure that all the goblins at least had weapons and shields, and Fraddon lifted the Bratapult down off the battlements and replaced its creaky, half-rotten wheels with some new iron-bound ones from one of the wrecked war machines the dwarves had left behind. And while they were all busy, Princess Ned gathered the best goblin cooks, lit fires under the great cauldrons and kettles in the scoffery, and set about cooking up an enormous stew, so that the army would not have to set out for Adherak on empty stomachs.

That was not all she cooked. She also made a

big dish of crumble, and later, when the rest were eating, she asked Fraddon to carry it for her, and led him around the Inner Wall and down to the edge of Natterdon Mire. It was almost dark by then. Everything was grey: grey ground, grey sky, grey ruins, and the paler grey of the shifting mist. Here and there a marsh light flickered, drifting eerily above the meres; here and there a bittern boomed, and unseen creatures splashed and rustled in the reeds.

"O boglins!" called Ned, feeling a little silly to be talking to a marsh. "Boglins of Natterdon! Thank you for warning us about the dwarves. We are going out to find and fight them, to try and put things right again. There are not very many of us, and we are not sure that we can do anything, but we have to try. And you could help us. You could weave mists that would hide our little army, so that the dwarves would not see how few they are. You could go with the goblins to Adherak, and help save Clovenstone, and all the Westlands."

She stopped and listened for an answer, but none came; only the wind, sighing through the feathered reed tops, stirring the water in the secret pools.

"Well," said Ned, motioning for Fraddon to set the crumble dish down on a flat stone near the mire's edge, "here is some crumble for you, anyway."

"Do you really think they'll help?" asked Fraddon.

"Boglins have never been helpful yet. They only told Henwyn and Zeewa of the dwarves because their precious dampdrake had been scared away. Boglins don't care for anyone but boglins."

"Maybe not," said Ned. "But much has changed in the world: perhaps boglins have changed a little too." She sighed. "I wish I could go with Henwyn and the others! I feel so useless, staying here! It is dismal, growing old. If I were as young and strong as Zeewa I would be leading the army, not Garvon Hael."

She heard Fraddon's huge face crease into a smile in the darkness above her. "And if I were three hundred years younger," he said, "I would walk to Delverdale in ten great strides, squeeze the slowsilver out of this giant dwarf like wringing water from a dishcloth, and carry it home to you. But I am not. All things grow old, and that's as it should be. There comes a time when we must let the young take over."

He reached down his hand, as big and comfortable as a favourite armchair, and Princess Ned sat down in it, and let him carry her home to her ship.

All was quiet in Clovenstone by then. The only sound was the soft rasp of metal on stone, coming from the armoury, where Zeewa sat by the light of the dying fire and sharpened her spears, all alone with her ghosts.

She had been thinking hard since she'd spoken to the Gatekeeper. It seemed to her that she owed it to her ghosts to leave them in that afterworld, beneath the green hill at Clovenstone, where they could taste and smell and touch. It was not fair to keep dragging them around after her, and she was tired, so very tired, of being haunted. So it seemed to her that the best thing would be if she were to die in this battle. She had talked of it to Fentongoose, without admitting what she was planning, and he had agreed that someone who fell fighting for Clovenstone would surely be allowed to enter the Houses of the Dead. She would die then, and lead her ghosts after her down into the grass.

The night passed, and as the sky grew grey again above the crumbled spines and spires of Clovenstone the goblins stirred, grumbling and stretching, yawning and farting, and gathered themselves into the order that Garvon Hael had decreed. War horns were blown, startling sleepy birds out of the ruins; the gate in the Inner Wall was opened, and the first goblin army since the Lych Lord's time went marching down the long, rubble-strewn road to the Southerly Gate. Garvon Hael led the way, mounted on his grey horse, and behind him came the oldest, toughest goblins. Henwyn and

Skarper were in the middle somewhere, trying to keep order among the hatchlings, and beside them strode Zeewa, her ghosts mingling mistily with the marchers. Behind her walked Fraddon, carrying the bratapult in one hand and his tree-trunk club in the other, and on his broad shoulders rode Etty and her father. It seemed a strange thing for dwarves to be marching with a goblin war band off to make war on their own people, but Ned had persuaded them to go: they understood this Giant Dwarf better than anyone, and perhaps, with their help, it would be possible to defeat it without too much loss of life. At the rear came Fentongoose and Dr Prong, along with Torridge, Cribba and Kenn. The trolls were carrying the two philosophers' bags of bandages and medicines, and as the day wore on they ended up carrying the two philosophers as well, for they were not young men, and found it hard to keep up with giants and goblins.

In the pale grey dawn as the first birds were stirring the host passed beneath the trees of the great woods which filled the southern parts of Clovenstone. Twiglings kept pace with them, scampering through the branches over their heads, their woody feet sending down a rain of autumn leaves, red and gold and brown, which fell like tears on the goblins. Looking up, Skarper saw that most of the twiglings carried sharp spears, and their eyes glinted fiercely in the half light, but their anger was not directed at the goblins. Fraddon had spoken with them in the night, and they knew what was at stake; for once they were happy to let goblins pass through their woods. They would have liked to join the army themselves, and go to fight the dwarves whose tunnels had harmed the roots of so many fine trees, but they could not survive for long in treeless country, and the moors between Clovenstone and Adherak were bleak and bare.

As for that other inhabitant of the woods, the old troll who lived under the crossing of the River Oeth, he had never heard so many pairs of feet go tramping over his bridge. He was quite alarmed, and sank deep down into his pool, only emerging when the army had passed. He peeked out through the hart's tongue ferns that grew from the buttresses of the bridge and was just in time to see the last of the rearguard marching away through the trees on the south bank. *Ooh, trolls!* he thought, recognizing the lumpy, lumbering shapes of Torridge, Cribba and Kenn as things like him, and for a moment he was tempted to scramble up the riverbank and follow them, but he was a solitary old stone, and he stayed where he was.

At the southern edge of the woods the twiglings stopped, and the goblins looked back to see the treetops bristling with them, spears and twiggy hands upraised in salute. Voices like the wind in dry leaves called out to them, wishing them good luck and a safe return, and promising, "We shall keep Clovenstone safe while you are gone: woods, waters, stones and all!"

And then, quite quickly, they were at Southerly Gate, and setting out across the wide, brindled hills, and very soon Clovenstone was lost behind them, hidden by low cloud and the folds of the land. The black banner with its silver comet streamed out on the moorland wind, and the road swung east and south to Adherak.

GOBLINS ON
THE MARCH

Adherak lay cupped between green hills, on a curve of the River Sethyn, where the road from Coriander crossed the road to Lusuenn. It had been a walled town once, but the Softlands had been so peaceful for so long that the town had spread far beyond its walls, spilling down the hill to the river, where the boats and barges of the floating market moored.

Except that now, most of those boats and barges had gone, slipping their moorings and drifting away downstream. Many of the houses had been hastily shuttered too, and the people who lived in them had taken to the roads, heading south to stay with friends and relatives in Nantivey or Chinnery. News came early to a crossroads-town like Adherak, and for some days now frightened people from the northland farms had been crowding down the Old North Road with their tales of the Giant Dwarf. Not all the stories were accurate, because the farmers and their families had left their homes in too much of a hurry to study the approaching terror in any detail. Some said that the giant was as high as a house; some claimed it was taller than a mountain. A few said it had three heads, and sneezed fireballs. One man claimed that a whole army of Giant Dwarves was on the march. But the people of Adherak got the general idea: something bad was coming, it was coming from the north, and it would be upon them very soon.

The town emptied quickly. Even the Lord of Adherak remembered that he had important business down in Porthzafron and shut up his castle before haring off down the South Road in a carriage with smoked glass windows. Soon a strange silence settled on the once-busy streets. Only a few brave Adherakians stayed behind, vowing to defend their town against whatever it was that had come out of Delverdale.

Henwyn's mother, father and sisters were among them. They were cheese-makers, not warriors, but bravery ran in the family; that was where Henwyn had got it from. Anyway, they had a fine new cheesery, built only the previous year to replace the one that had been accidentally destroyed by a cheese monster. "If any dwarf, giant or little, thinks he can take our cheesery from us," said Henmor, Henwyn's father, "then he has another think coming!" And his wife and daughters all agreed, and busied themselves fixing cheese knives to the ends of old broom handles to make pikes.

Then came more bad news. Farmers from the west started arriving, pausing at the Adherakians' hastily built barricades before taking the road south. They told of another menace. "Goblins!" they said, breathless with fear and the effort of hauling all their best possessions on handcarts. "A goblin host is coming, pouring out of Clovenstone, just like in the bad old times! Run, friends, or you'll all be robbed and murdered!"

The Adherakians looked worriedly at one another. Were the goblins in league with the dwarves? Had some great alliance been forged among the old things of the world to overthrow human beings?

"What say you, Henmor the Cheesewright?" people asked Henwyn's father. "Your lad lives at Clovenstone, doesn't he? You've had dealings with these goblins. What does this mean?"

Henmor shook his head. "I can't say for sure. Goblins are rough, roistering types, but good cheese-makers. I don't know why would they want to go hallooing about, starting armies and such."

"Why don't you go and talk to them, Henmor?"

said his wife. "See what all this is about?'

So Henmor fetched his old dappled mare from the stables behind the cheesery, and a few of the more curious Adherakians found horses too, and soon they were riding up the narrow road to Sticklecombe, where they could see the goblin host coming over the moor towards them like dark cloud-shadow.

The goblins had been on the road for two days by then. Rainstorms had swept over them as they came down off the high moors (there was a reason why those hills were so green) and the villages where they'd hoped to find food and lodging were all shuttered and deserted. The tooting of the war horns had a weary sound, and rather than chanting war songs they were bickering, complaining about their poor tired paws, or asking in whiny voices, "Are we nearly there yet?"

The humans were just as tired, but Henwyn perked up when he recognized his father's horse on the road ahead. "Come on!" he shouted to Skarper, and they jogged on together ahead of the footsore army and met Henmor in the valley bottom, where the road forded a little river. There father and son hugged, and Henwyn explained that the goblins had not come to loot Adherak, but to save it.

The other Adherakians who had ridden out with

Henmor looked warily at the goblin army, and raised a cautious-sounding cheer. Few of them had ever seen a goblin before, and they were appalled by all the scaly, furry, fanged, ferocious faces which peered at them from behind Henwyn. They weren't at all sure they wouldn't rather just take their chances with the dwarves. But Henmor said, "You are welcome, then! You must come into the town."

"No," said Garvon Hael, riding up on his grey horse. "You are kind, but we have not time to accept your hospitality. We will make our way to the Old North Road, and try to stop the Giant Dwarf there."

A cloud, which had been hanging above Sticklecombe all this time, descended now, and the astonished men from Adherak saw the cloud maidens who rode upon it, and blushed under the gaze of their colourless hailstone eyes. The cloud maidens had delivered Ned's warning to the High King at Boskennack (in fact they'd startled him rather badly, by hovering outside the window of the royal toilet and calling in to him while he was concentrating on his morning poo). Since then they'd been riding the winds of the upper air, racing north to spy on the progress of the dwarves and then rushing back to report on it to the goblin army. Now they said, "Henwyn, the Giant

Dwarf is twenty miles from here, stomping down the road from the north and burning man-houses as it comes."

Garvon Hael shouted an order, and goblin captains ran up and down the long, ragged column of the army, chivvying back into line all those goblins who had collapsed on the roadside or gone to bathe their blistered feet in the River Stickle. Griping and complaining, the goblins went on, pausing only to scoop up drinks of water in their helmets as they splashed across the ford. To the north, thin trickles of smoke were rising up the sky.

Henwyn's father sent one of his companions galloping back to Adherak to fetch the rest of its defenders, and then he and the others joined the army, looking nervously at the goblins, and the trolls, and the giant, and even more nervously at Zeewa. Why did the air around her flicker and shift in that strange way, making their hair stand on end and causing their horses to shy? "Is that dark queenly looking lass a *witch*?" whispered Henmor to his son.

"Oh no, she's just haunted," Henwyn replied, as he hurried back to his place in the middle of the column.

"Ghosts, now?" said Henmor, trying to calm his panicky horse as Zeewa's ghosts went brushing and rushing by. "Ghosts and cloud ladies. Whatever is the world coming to?"

"Oh, you'll get used to it!" Dr Prong called happily, as he went piggybacking by on Torridge's shoulders. "Creatures out of children's tales!"

Over the hills the army wound its way, through meadows Henwyn had known since childhood. They crossed the Sethyn at Shallowford and climbed up to meet the Old North Road where it ran over Adhery Hill. There on the hill's crest, they halted. Looking north, they could see the rolling farmlands reaching away to the blue distance where the mountains rose. And there upon the patchwork of fields and commons, like a chessman on a counterpane, they saw the Giant Dwarf.

"We shall stop here," said Garvon Hael. "Climbing this hill should slow it; that's when we'll take it down. The trolls can bombard it with the bratapult from the shelter of that wall; Fraddon will do battle with it, and the rest of us can deal with the dwarves who march beside it."

"March beneath it too, maybe," said Fentongoose. "This hill may be riddled with dwarf tunnels for all we know. They could attack from beneath our feet, or burrow behind us and attack us in the rear!"

Some of the goblins put their ears to the ground, listening for signs of tunnelling, but all they could hear was the faint, far-off tramp of the feet of the Giant Dwarf.

By that time, evening was drawing on. The goblins lit campfires and brewed up horrible stews for themselves, squabbling over who got the juiciest bits of the rats, bats and slugs they'd caught on the march from Clovenstone. Garvon Hael took Fentongoose, Durgar and Dr Prong up on to an ancient burial mound which stood near the road, and Henwyn went with them, trying to look important.

"What do you make of it?" asked the grey warrior, squinting at the Giant Dwarf, which was shining golden now with the light of the low sun.

"It is at least two hundred feet high!" said Dr Prong.

"How on earth can you tell that from this distance?" asked Durgar.

"Oh, you work it out with trigonometry," said Dr Prong.

"It is coming fast," said Henwyn.

"It will be here in another hour or two, is my guess," said Fentongoose.

Henwyn glanced up at the sky. "It will be dark by then."

"The dwarves won't mind that. They fight happiest in the dark. This will be a hard battle, Henwyn."

"But we'll win, won't we!" said Henwyn bravely.

Garvon Hael looked grimly northward, and said nothing more.

Soon after that there was a clatter of hooves on the road and a group of horsemen came riding up the hill from Adherak. The goblins who had been sitting on the road moved aside to let them through, and Henwyn and the rest went to meet them, assuming they were more of his father's friends, come to help save their town. He was startled to see how elaborate their armour was, and how rich their cloaks and clothes. He was more startled still when he recognized them as the High King's heroes from Boskennack.

"What's this rabble doing all over the road?" demanded Lord Ponsadane in his high, sneering voice.

"Make way!" bellowed Kerwen of Bryngallow.

"Goblins, I'd say," observed another man. "When we've sorted out this dwarvish nonsense we should come back and put these horrors to the sword, too!"

Angrily, Henwyn stepped into the road in front of him. The man made as if to ride him down, but Zeewa came forward, and the horse sensed her ghosts and began to rear and skitter.

"We are the army of Clovenstone," said Henwyn, "and we have come here on the orders of Princess Eluned herself, to defend Adherak."

The man he had spoken to was too busy trying to control his horse to offer any answer, but the others laughed. "Very kind of you, cheesebearer!" called the one named Merion. "But you can take your tribe of boggarts and long-leggedy beasties home again; we're here to sort out these dwarvish scum."

"I thought you were frightened of fighting dwarves?" said Garvon Hael, walking over to stand with Henwyn.

"It's Garvon Hael!" said Merion. "Sounds almost sober, too!"

"Dwarves in tunnels I can't abide," said Kerwen of Bryngallow. "But these dwarves are above ground, by all accounts, and relying on some sort of clumsy war machine to scare the common folk. Cowardly lot. We shall teach them a lesson: smash their machine and put them across our knees for a good spanking, eh, friends!"

The other heroes roared their agreement. "We'll kick them like footballs back to Dwarvenholm!" shouted one.

Garvon Hael nodded, waiting patiently for the loud laughter to subside. "At least join your forces with ours," he said. "We've fought these dwarves once; they nearly destroyed us, and they didn't have their giant mannequin to help them then. Perhaps if we stand together. . ."

"Stand with goblins and drunkards?" sneered Ponsadane. "We are heroes, and we are riding north now to do what heroes do. Will you ride with us, Garvon Hael, or would you rather stay here with this menagerie of yours?"

Garvon Hael stepped aside to let the horsemen go clattering by. "My place is here with my friends," he said.

Henwyn stood watching as the heroes galloped on down the road, and were quickly swallowed by the shadows of evening. "To think I once dreamed of being one of them!" he said bitterly.

The goblins craned their necks, watching the progress of the riders. Skarper, who had always been brighter than the rest, trotted across the hilltop to where Fraddon stood, and ran like a squirrel up the giant's body to perch on his shoulder. There he found Etty, who had had the same idea and stood holding tight to the hairs which sprouted from Fraddon's huge ear. She was looking northward.

"Do you think they can fight it?" she asked.

"I think they're idiots," said Skarper. "Mind you, I think we're idiots too. Look at that thing! It's two hundred feet tall! Dr Prong worked it out with trigopromontory. Like Garvon Hael said, it was bad enough fighting them when they *didn't* have a giant dwarf. Soakaway got skewered, and I was dragged underground by a maniac mole. Now that there's the Giant Dwarf too. . . We're doomed! It will be like trying to fight a castle!"

"Nevertheless," rumbled Fraddon, "I shall do my best."

"Sorry!" Skarper squeaked. He had forgotten that he was standing next to the giant's ear. If he'd remembered, he would never have said anything so gloomy.

But Etty was feeling gloomy too. "It is horrible," she said. "All those burning houses. Dwarves should *make* things, not destroy them. I wish there was some way I could stop it, before it does any more harm and damage."

Skarper wished that too. All the way from Clovenstone, the thought had been growing in him that he really, really didn't want to be in another battle. He said, "What about those workings inside it? The wheels and levers and clockwork bits? What if someone got inside and smashed them up?"

"The dwarves are all around it," said Etty. "And the wheels and levers are dwarf-wrought, and hard to smash."

"Poke a hole in it, then: let all the slowsilver run out. . ."

But they had thought of that already, and discarded it. They needed that slowsilver, and besides, you do not simply *poke holes* in things that dwarves have made.

The dust cloud kicked up by the hooves of the heroes' horses rose up from the shadowed land into the sunlight, blushing gold. The riders were halfway to the giant dwarf now. The goblin army was silent, waiting to see what would happen when they reached it. Skarper imagined the smug smiles fading from the faces of Merion and Ponsadane as they realized just how big it was.

"What is that?" asked Etty suddenly, and Skarper saw that she had turned and was looking behind them, back the way they had come into the shadows of Sticklecombe. A mist was rising there. For a moment he was afraid that it was dwarf smoke, the signal of some sneak attack, but it was mist all right, spilling down the valley of the Stickle like cauldron smoke, just like the mists which hung over the Oeth and the Natterdon Mire at home. "It's only mist. . ." he said.

"Ooh!" cried all the goblins suddenly. "Aaah!"

Skarper forgot the mist and looked north again. Out in the farmlands the last long rays of sunlight flashed and flickered upon naked blades. More dust was rising, and it was clear now even to those goblins who had not mastered trigonometry that the Giant Dwarf was not just Giant, it was *enormous*. The sound of its huge feet stamping up and down could be heard quite clearly on the hilltop now. So could a faint clatter of dropped weaponry and abandoned shields as the cowardlier goblins started to slink away. But they did not go very far, because as they started back down the hill towards Shallowford they saw the mist coiling up at them.

"That is not just mist!" said Etty firmly.

It was thick and white and it reached like a tentacle out of Sticklecombe, feeling for the ford over the Sethyn. It found it, and began to climb the hill the goblins stood on. The goblins who had been sneaking away from the Giant Dwarf all started to back away from the mist instead, and bumped into the ones who were still on the hilltop, staring north. Consternation spread. Soon everyone was looking at the mist, and nobody even noticed the great burps of fire that shone briefly behind them in the north.

The strange mist was so dense that it was impossible to see anything through it, but now and then its edges lifted slightly from the ground, and beneath it, in the very last of the sunlight, Skarper saw little marching shapes: fat bodies with bandy legs, web-toed feet stamping up and down.

The boglins had arrived.

THE BATTLE OF ADHERAK

One small patch of mist detached itself from the rest and drifted ahead. Skarper and Etty, watching from the giant's shoulder, could see that it was like a mist umbrella, or a mobile tent of shade and dampness, beneath which three big boglins squelched along. Two clutched trailing stalks of mist to keep it from blowing away. The third was Fetter of the Mire.

Henwyn went forward to meet him. Not sure how to greet a boglin king, he held out his hand. Not sure how to greet a warmblood, Fetter stared at it for a moment, then reached out his webbed hand and shook it firmly. His touch was as cold and sticky as a slug.

"We came," he said. "We are here to help, as the crumble-lady asked."

"You are welcome!" said Henwyn. "Look northward!

There are the dwarves. Your mists will hide our true numbers from them."

Fetter turned away, shouting to the mass of boglins who were toiling up the hill. They began to move faster, breaking into different groups, and the mist went with them, rolling screens and curtains of it, wrapping the goblin army. By some magic, the boglins made little holes and slits appear in it, so that the goblins could still see out.

"Riders coming!" shouted Gutgust, from the front rank of the army.

Racing specks showed on the pale road ahead of the Giant Dwarf. The goblins drew their swords and levelled their spears as the specks grew closer, coming up the hill. But it was no dwarfish attack; it was the heroes from Boskennack returning. Nine had gone down to face the Giant Dwarf; only two came back, and three riderless horses, wild-eyed, with foam upon their flanks. The trappings of the horses and the fine clothes of the heroes were torn and scorched. Kerwen's cloak was on fire.

"That thing breathes flames!" cried Lord Ponsadane.

"Run for your lives!" shouted Kerwen. "Arrows just bounce off it!"

"What of the others?" demanded Garvon Hael, as they stopped to rest their gasping horses on the hilltop.

"Smashed! Crushed! Stomped! Burnt!" said Ponsadane, all the redness and smugness gone from his big face, which quivered like an agitated blancmange as he stared about him at the goblins. "The greatest heroes of the Westlands could not stand against it! All is lost! Flee, all of you! Save yourselves!"

"Stand with us!" said Henwyn. "We shall stop the Giant Dwarf here. Look, we have mists to hide us from it, and a giant to challenge it!"

Ponsadane shook his head. "Not likely! I'm off!" he said. He dragged his weary horse's head up by the reins and set his spurs to its dripping flanks, ready to ride on to Shallowford and Adherak and away, and Kerwen of Bryngallow did likewise.

But before they could start down the southerly slope of the hill the ground began to tremble. For a moment Skarper thought it was the footfalls of the Giant Dwarf, but no. The road across the hilltop heaved and split, shattered chalk churning like the foam of a wave. The defeated heroes' horses reared in terror, spilling their riders in the dust, as a great armoured nose came snuffling up through the rubble.

"Moles!" goblins were shouting, all over the hilltop.

Then it was mostly chaos, and running about. A

dozen diremoles must have been sent ahead of the dwarf army, and they had burrowed up through the soft chalk of Adhery Hill. They emerged all over the hilltop, white with chalk dust, dwarves upon their backs. Their plan had been to herd the goblins downhill into the path of the Giant Dwarf, like beaters driving wild animals on to the spears of a hunt, but they had not reckoned on the desperation of the goblins, or on the walls of magic mist that cloaked and screened them. Dwarves and goblins met in the mist's white corridors, and the clash of weapons echoed across the hill. Through the battle ran Zeewa, her spear in her hand and her ghosts behind her, and the diremoles sensed the ghosts and fled from them, just as they had at Clovenstone, trampling dwarf and goblin alike in their panic. Ponsadane and Kerwen realized their escape was cut off and decided they might as well fight too, drawing their swords and joining Garvon Hael. Boglin blowpipes spat drugged darts that dropped dwarfs drowsing in the dust.

Henwyn hurried through it all, shouting, "Fraddon! Fraddon!" Through rents in the boglins' mists he could see the Giant Dwarf, almost at the hill's foot now. He knew that it did not matter how well his friends fought: if the dwarves could keep them busy for a few more minutes till that monstrosity arrived, they would all be doomed. "Fraddon?" he shouted, then, "Ooof!" – he had crashed into one of the giant's big feet, which loomed out of the murk like a boulder.

The giant had a diremole in either hand, and he was busy banging their heads together.

"Fraddon! It is time!" Henwyn shouted up at him. "The Giant Dwarf comes!"

Fraddon nodded, put down the dazed moles, and picked up his club. "Good luck, little softling," he said.

"Good luck, Fraddon!" shouted Henwyn.

The giant strode downhill in the twilight, tearing through curtains of mist, which clung like cobwebs to his legs. The noise of the battle faded behind him, and the noise of the Giant Dwarf swelled ahead; the clank, rattle, chunk of its mysterious workings, the stamp of those huge feet falling. Fraddon raised his club and ran at it. Etty and Skarper, whom he'd completely forgotten, clung in terror to the hairs in his right ear. Darts whined past them as the dwarf crossbowmen on the Giant Dwarf's shoulders shot at Fraddon. The little missiles could not pierce Fraddon's thick hide, of course, but for a moment Skarper and Etty were in danger.

The Giant Dwarf seemed to grow bigger as

Fraddon ran towards it. Skarper had grown used to Fraddon himself being the biggest thing around. Now the Brazen Head on its new body loomed above him. A huge iron fist swung at him, and Fraddon sidestepped and slammed his club into the Giant Dwarf. It rocked backwards, and a dozen dwarves tumbled off its shoulders and the platforms that jutted from its chest, but the Giant Dwarf itself did not fall. A silvery glow shone through gaps and gratings in its sides as it reached out a huge hand and seized Fraddon's club, snapping it in two. Fire snorted from its nostrils, playing across the giant's broad chest and setting his shirt a-smoulder. The Giant Dwarf wasn't really breathing fire – Skarper could see two dwarves hiding up its nose with those dragon-snouted flame-hose things of theirs – but that wasn't much consolation as the flames gushed and crackled. If the jet had touched Fraddon's hands or face it might have done real damage, but luckily his shirt was thick, and before the flame-hose operators could improve their aim the Giant Dwarf was distracted by another onslaught, this time from above.

The cloud maidens, who had been watching from on high, had decided it was time to lend a hand. Black and angry, their cloud swung low over the Giant Dwarf's head, and lances of lightning crackled down, striking its shoulders and chest, playing across its great bronze face in showers of coloured sparks. Hailstones pounded it, hard enough to dent its brazen mask, and rain turned the ground around its feet to a quagmire. Above the noise, the clear voices of the cloud maidens rang out, shouting, "Go away, you big bully!" and "Pick on someone your own size!"

The Giant Dwarf raised its head. Twin jets of flame geysered from its nostrils, engulfing the cloud. "Oh poo!" and "Bother!" shrieked the cloud maidens. Fire couldn't hurt them, but the fierce heat made it impossible to hold their shape; their cloud was thinning, and they thinned with it, becoming a fine mist which blew away on the wind.

With a roar of anger, Fraddon lunged at the Giant Dwarf before it could bring its fiery breath to bear on him again. He grappled with it, grasping its metal body in a bear hug. The shock as the two huge figures collided was so great that the remaining dwarves were shaken from the Giant Dwarf's shoulders like shouty dandruff, while Skarper and Etty lost their grip on Fraddon's ear hairs and went tumbling down his scorched chest.

Skarper, who had had a lot of experience falling from great heights, knew that the thing to do was flail blindly for a handhold. He flailed, and found one. As he clung there, Etty grabbed his tail. It was not until a moment later, when the Giant Dwarf had thrust Fraddon away from it, that Skarper realized he was dangling from the handrail of one of the platforms on its armoured chest. The Giant Dwarf lurched and rolled, almost shaking Skarper loose, and Etty swung from his tail's end like a pendulum with plaits, but at last he managed to struggle up onto the platform, and heave her up after him. Then he looked round for Fraddon.

The giant was nowhere to be seen.

Skarper squeaked in alarm, looking left and right. He could see the battle raging on Adhery Hill, the dwarf host spreading up the hillside ahead of their giant contraption, but no sign of Fraddon. Then, looking down, he saw him; stretched on the fields like a fallen colossus, felled by the Giant Dwarf's fists.

Was he dead? Or simply dazed? There was no telling, in the twilight, with the great fallen figure dwindling behind as the Giant Dwarf started to climb the slopes of the hill.

"Skarper!" shouted Etty, over the rattle and clatter and chunk from inside that vast iron chest. "We can't stay here!"

As if to underline her point, a crossbow dart came whirring between them and pinged off the Giant

Dwarf's hide. The dwarves milling about its feet had seen the two stowaways, and were hurling missiles and rude names at them. Skarper looked for a way off the platform, and found one: a circular door, just big enough for a stooping dwarf to pass through. He tried its metal handle, and it opened. Dragging Etty after him, he crept into the hot, dark innards of the Giant Dwarf.

Up on the hill, the battle between dwarves and goblins raged back and forth, and always where it was at its thickest, there was Zeewa, seeking her own death. But getting killed was turning out to be surprisingly difficult. Wherever the Muskish girl went, the diremoles fled before her ghosts. Even the dwarves ran from her, because the drifting dust from all their chalk molehills had coated everyone white, goblins and boglins and dwarves and men alike, and the mists made everything appear vague and ghostly, so the ghosts themselves looked no different now to anyone else. Kosi kept leaping in front of Zeewa, shouting challenges and brandishing his ghostly spear, so that the dwarves who might have struck her down wasted their time slashing at him instead, and getting confused when their weapons passed straight through. Most just fled before Tau and the tide of charging animals. Once three fearless tallboys cornered Zeewa and she thought her end had come, but a huge chalk boulder from the bratapult flattened all three before they could land a blow. And when others tried to fight her, her instincts kept saving her; she meant to stand and wait for death to come, but she always ended up lashing out with her spear, sinking its red blade into dwarf flesh, slamming its butt against dwarf helms.

And despite all her efforts, and all the bravery of goblins, boglins and men, the dwarves seemed slowly to be winning, and the little army of Clovenstone was being driven back to make its stand on that burial mound, under the comet banner. There Fetter fought side by side with Fentongoose, while Yabber and Lord Ponsadane led desperate sorties to gather lost and wounded goblins from other parts of the hill. There Cribba, Torridge and Kenn heaved huge stones into the bratapult, and shouted "Boing!" as they sent them hurtling into the dwarvish host. There Nurdle blew his war horn, and boglin mist weavers worked their spells. There Garvon Hael rode his grey horse through the ranks of the dwarfs as if they were waves on the sea at Far Penderglaze, and Henwyn fought bravely too, and wondered what had become of Skarper.

And the ground beneath the battling warriors shook, and above the crash and cry of war they could all hear the clank and thunder of the footfalls of the Giant Dwarf.

IN THE BELLY
OF THE DWARF

Skarper had never had a chance to see inside a gigantic mechanical dwarf before, and he had to admit that it was quite interesting. Wherever he looked, huge toothed wheels were spinning, turning mysterious shafts and causing sleek silvery pistons to pump up and down. There was a smell of slowsilver in the hot air, and all around him, like iron spaghetti, a mad tangle of pipes coiled and curved. These were the Giant Dwarf's veins, along which the slowsilver went gurgling, carrying magical power to all its metal organs.

Unfortunately there was not much time to look around, for in between the pipes and wheels and shafts and pistons there were more platforms, linked by iron ladders and lit by glowing mole-dung lamps, and on every platform clustered dwarf overseers and their followers.

If they had had crossbows, or even spears, that would have been the end of Skarper and Etty. But foolishly, the overseers hadn't imagined anyone getting inside their miraculous Giant Dwarf, and so they were armed with nothing more than the spanners and wrenches they used to keep it running. All the same, the intruders were soon captured, and forced up a ladder to the highest platform of all, just underneath the Head itself, where Overseer Glunt was poring over a thick sheaf of plans.

The angry voices of their captors distracted him, and he looked up to see the girl and the goblin standing before him. "Etty!" he said, ignoring Skarper completely. "Thank the depths! Is your father with you?"

It was not the welcome they'd expected. They had both been expecting something more along "Off with their heads!" lines. But Overseer Glunt's whole manner had changed. Gone was the sleek, pompous dwarf who had condemned them to the Bright Bowl. This new Glunt looked worn with worry. His hands shook, and his fingernails were nibbled. Beside him, holding more plans, stood Langstone. His reward for turning against Etty and her father had been to become Glunt's assistant, but he didn't look as though he was enjoying it very much.

Glunt came close to Etty and spoke in a voice as

quiet as he could make it and still hope to be heard above the din of the Giant Dwarf. "This thing's mad, lass! It crushes everything in its path!"

"I thought that's what it was supposed to do," said Skarper.

"Oh, aye, it was meant to crush everything, but not to actually *crush* everything. Not literally! We want to look down again on men, we don't want them all dead, or driven away across the sea – what use are they to us then? We need people to trade with, to buy the fine things we make. How can they even afford to trade if the Head and its new body has trampled their cities flat?" He looked around him in despair at the shining pistons and the grinding gears. "It won't stop, Etty! I thought if Durgar was here. . ."

"He's not," said Etty. "He's up on the hill, and your tallboys may have killed him by now. Oh, Master Glunt, what have you done?"

"It wasn't my doing!" pleaded Glunt. "We overseers thought we controlled the Head, but no! It has a mind of its own, Etty! It has just been biding its time, waiting for us to build this body for it, and find slowsilver to fill its veins with!"

"The dwarves of old built the Head to make them great again," said Langstone. "And that is just what it means to do! We cannot stop it!"

"Why not jump out?" said Skarper, not much liking the thought that he was stuck inside a runaway dwarf. "You could jump out, couldn't you?"

"Aye," said Glunt, "but that won't stop this thing. The Head thinks for itself! It will just go crashing on!"

There was a clang from somewhere; a screech of escaping steam; shouts and running footsteps. The smell of slowsilver in the tight, lurching space grew stronger. An overseer came up the ladder and pushed past Etty and Skarper to tell Glunt, "Another of them! And Feldspar thinks some may be collecting in the S-bend behind the right hip!"

"Well get them out!" shouted Glunt, waving his short arms in fury.

"What is it?" asked Etty, as the other overseer scampered back down into the Giant Dwarf's depths.

Glunt would not answer her, but Langstone said, "Things keep appearing in the slowsilver. As if it is solidifying. They are blocking its passage around the dwarf's veins. Our spell-smiths can't explain it."

"But that's good, isn't it?" asked Etty. "If the slowsilver stops flowing, the Giant Dwarf will stop too, won't it?"

Glunt shook his head. "It's not that simple, lass. The slowsilver rushes through these pipes under great pressure. A blockage could lead to terrible disaster. A magical explosion! We could all be drenched in slowsilver. There have already been a couple of serious leaks. Look at what happened to Overseer Bendick here."

"Ribbit!" agreed a bearded frog, hopping across the pile of plans which Glunt had thrown aside.

"We have to open the pipes as carefully as we can and fish these stones out," said Glunt. "It's dicey, dangerous work while the Giant Dwarf keeps moving, but the alternative. . ."

"Stones?" said Skarper. "You said *stones*?"

Glunt looked at him. "Aye, goblin. Stones. That's what these things in the pipes look like."

"Show me!" said Skarper.

Langstone led the way, and Etty went with him. On a high, narrow platform behind the Giant Dwarf's beard stood a barrel. It was almost full of eggstones. Some were fresh, with the veins of slowsilver still glowing on their surfaces; others had cooled, and were dark as cannonballs.

"We store them here," said Langstone. "They are too valuable to throw overboard. See how the slowsilver shines in them. . ."

"There must be dozens!" said Skarper. His mind raced. The slowsilver lake had not been due to cough up any eggstones yet. But what if the business of piping the slowsilver north to Dwarvenholm and then decanting some of it into the veins of the Giant Dwarf had made it produce eggstones early? Perhaps that was the slowsilver's way of trying to escape; turning itself into goblins, who could run away. . .

He thought some more. "Fire!" he said. "We need fire! What about those flame-hose thingies up in the nose? Can we bring one down here?"

Langstone looked uncertain. "What are you planning?"

Skarper thought it better not to say. He didn't need to, anyway: Etty took Langstone's hand and, shouting "Come on!", led him up a ladder into the dark, turning shadows of the Head. A moment later they were back, uncoiling the long, snakey metal tube of a flame-hose behind them. A dwarf in scorched leather armour came with them, lugging the fat metal bottle which held the flame-hose's fuel, and grumbling, "What's all this then? Goblins?"

"Just do as he says!" ordered Etty, and Skarper said, "Pour fire on that barrel!" and jumped aside as the hose roared, wrapping the barrel of eggstones in gaudy flames.

At Clovenstone, eggstones took days to hatch. They sat beside Fentongoose's fire, gentled in its warmth, until the hatchlings inside them woke and bashed their way out. But Skarper didn't have time for that. He hoped this would work instead. Shielding his face from the flames with both paws, he went as close as he dared. The hose roared, the barrel burned, the fire crackled. Inside the fire the eggstones cracked and banged like popcorn.

"Stop!" shouted Skarper, adding his own voice to the voices of dwarf overseers, who had come running to see which idiot was letting off a flame-hose inside the Head.

The flames subsided, leaving only the fires of the burning barrel. In the heart of the heat, something moved. Skarper blinked away bright after-images, edged nearer – and a new hatchling, slightly singed, came tumbling out of the heap of flame-wrapped stones and landed at his feet.

"Urple!" said the hatchling, coughing smoke. Two more followed. Then suddenly there were hatchlings everywhere, and like all goblin hatchlings they were spoiling for a fight. Some snatched up still-burning barrel staves; some simply used their fists. One picked up the flame-hose (he didn't know what it was for; he was just planning to use its heavy iron nozzle to thump his batch-brothers with). But as he swung it at them he overbalanced, and plummeted with a yelp over the edge of the platform (being even littler than a dwarf, he fitted easily under the brass handrail).

With a shriek, the unlucky hatchling dropped down into the Giant Dwarf's innards; into the rolling wheels, the sliding gleam of pistons. He was still clutching the flame-hose, and as it went slinking, link by metal link, over the platform's edge, it began to tug the big iron bottle that held its fuel after it. "No!" shouted Langstone, reaching for it – but by then the hose's end was caught in the teeth of great gears far below, and although the operator and other dwarves joined him in trying to hold the bottle back, it was a tug of war that they were doomed to lose.

Over it went, and away into the depths. Skarper and the dwarves on the platform all stared at one another, appalled. Even the hatchlings stopped fighting for a moment.

A terrible red glare came up out of the dwarf's belly, and a boom. Shadows of the machinery went wavering over the faces of the watchers on the platform. The glare faded, and for a moment it seemed that all was well below. Then, echoing up through the innards of the dwarf, they heard the gush of spilling slowsilver, and the pop and crack of eggstones.

Panic took hold then. "Abandon Dwarf!" screamed

Overseer Glunt.

"Run for your lives!" suggested Langstone.

All hope of salvaging the Giant Dwarf was forgotten. The overseers ran hither and thither, up and down the iron ladders, making their way to whatever doors and hatches and openings they could find. They jumped over the squabbling hatchlings, who were spilling all through the Giant Dwarf's interior. The ones Skarper had hatched in the barrel were ganging together to fight new hatchlings, who came spidering up the ladders from below. It seemed to Skarper, looking back as he reached one of the hatches, that all the slowsilver gushing from the Giant Dwarf's severed veins was turning into eggstones, and all the eggstones were hatching instantly in the heat of the fire that had started down in its belly. Even the whirling wheels and gears, which had been forged from slowsilver long ago, were developing odd warts and pimples which swelled and burst and spat out hatchlings. The clank and rattle and chunk of the magical machine was almost drowned out by the squealing voices of new goblins.

Then Etty pulled him through the hatch, and they followed the escaping dwarves, scrambling perilously down the Giant Dwarf's armour until they were low enough to jump the rest of the way to safety.

"Ghooooof!" said Skarper, landing next to Etty in a hedge. He scrambled out in time to see the Giant Dwarf reach the hilltop. The fighting there had stopped: dwarves and boglins, goblins and men, all stood amazed, gawping up at the mighty figure. But instead of raising its huge feet to trample the enemies of Dwarvendom, it stopped and stood there. Weird groans and gurglings came from its insides. If it hadn't been a two-hundred-foot-tall magic-powered mannikin, you would have said that it had terrible indigestion. A moment more, and the Brazen Head began to wobble and rattle on its shoulders like the lid of a saucepan coming to the boil.

"Get clear!" Overseer Glunt was yelling, running towards the motionless armies. He was shouting it at the dwarves, but the others heard him too, and all began to back away. "That thing's full of slowsilver! When it blows. . ."

It blew. Dark shards of its iron body went howling over the watchers' heads, and sank like blades into the ground. But no rain of molten slowsilver came spraying out. What came instead, still bickering and squabbling, were hundreds of hatchlings. A scrambling scrum of little goblins came pouring out of the holes in the Dwarf, and as they clambered down its huge legs to the ground the whole figure overbalanced and toppled backwards, crashing down in ruin on the hill.

Around it, the hatchlings started to pick up the fallen weapons of the battle and attack each other. "Stop!" shouted Henwyn, pushing his way down the old mound. The dwarves, meanwhile, looked on in amazement. Some had panicked and run when the Giant Dwarf fell; others were crowding round the Brazen Head, waiting for it to tell them what to do, but there were still some – the armoured tallboys mostly, a few surviving diremoles and their crews – who held their ground and held their weapons. The hatchlings were too busy hitting one another to be any threat to them. Their commanders ran up and down their lines, shoving dwarves into position, urging them to attack the battered army of Clovenstone.

But then like a miracle, a horn rang out: a single, high, clear note. Even the hatchlings heard it, and looked up.

Over the hill's brow, from the direction of Adherak, came a throng of riders. For a moment, in the dying light, no one could imagine who they were. Then Skarper recognized Carnglaze riding in the front rank, with Prawl beside him, and King Knobbler in a lacy fighting bonnet with pink ribbons, swinging a huge axe. Behind them rode the finest warriors money could buy;

men of Musk and Barragan and the Autumn Isles, armed to the teeth and as ready for a fight as any hatchling.

"Thank you!" said Fentongoose, who had been appealing to the hatchlings to be quiet, completely unheard, and now found that total silence had fallen. "Now, put those swords and axes and things down, all of you. What sort of way is this to be carrying on? We are trying to have a battle here! Except I think it is over. It *is* over, isn't it?" he asked nervously, looking around at the dwarves.

The tallboys sheepishly lowered their weapons, knowing they could not fight both the goblins and their new allies.

"It is over," said Durgar, standing up from where he had sat the battle out, on top of the burial mound. "Isn't that so, overseers?"

The overseers, scattered around on the hillside where they had landed when they leaped from the Giant Dwarf, all nodded, or murmured their agreement.

"What of the Head?" demanded one of the dwarf captains, a tallboy who towered almost to Henwyn's shoulder, and others took up his call: "It's not up to overseers. What of the Head? What does the Head say?"

But the Head said nothing at all. Dwarves scrambled over the great iron carcass to examine it, but the machinery inside it had been all wrenched and ruined when it fell, and the magic which had powered it for so long was fled. Dwarves would be their own masters from now on.

GHOSTS

And that was almost the end of it. The dwarves went home to Delverdale, agreeing to pay for all the farms and villages that their Giant Dwarf had trampled on its march south, and to pump back to Clovenstone the remainder of the slowsilver they'd stolen. They were unsure who their leaders would be now, with the Head ruined and the overseers in disgrace, but many looked to Durgar for guidance, remembering how reliable he had always been, and how he and his daughter had been the only ones to question the wisdom of the Head.

Etty hugged Skarper tight before she left. "I'll come and visit Clovenstone often," she said. "I'll bring other dwarves, to repair the damage that we did there."

"And will you be a surveyor now, like Durgar?" Skarper asked.

Etty grinned. "I don't know!" she said happily. "I don't know what I'll be! I might be anything. I haven't decided yet."

The army of Clovenstone and the army Carnglaze had raised went back together into Adherak, whose people were returning home as word of the victory spread. Lord Ponsadane and Kerwen of Bryngallow rode on towards Coriander. They promised faithfully to tell the High King of the bravery of the goblins, boglins, trolls, men, ghosts, girl and giant who had kept the dwarves at bay and brought the Giant Dwarf down in ruin. "Clovenstone can take its place now among the kingdoms of the Westlands, cheesebearer," they called to Henwyn, as they rode away. "Tell your Dark Lady that, with our thanks!"

Many goblins had been injured in the battle, of course; a hospital was set up in one of the empty warehouses beside the floating market, and the women of Adherak helped Dr Prong to nurse them better. The boglins, however, vanished away in the dark on the night of the battle, and took their wounded with them. No one saw them go, but later, farmers up on Oeth Moor told of a thick mist which had drifted back up Sticklecombe and away across the hills.

Fraddon was too large to fit into the hospital, but he was not badly injured, only a little bruised and scorched. Henwyn's family mixed up some ointment in one of their old cheese vats and spread it on his burns and cuts with curd paddles.

The new hatchlings, meanwhile, were far too badly behaved to be allowed into Adherak. Fentongoose and the older goblins began to herd them home, and a slow, slow business it was. The army which had taken just three days to march from Clovenstone to Adherak would take weeks to find its way home again.

But Henwyn and Skarper were in a hurry: they knew how worried Princess Ned must be, and they wanted to get back to her as soon as they could. Henwyn had asked the cloud maidens to carry the good news to her, but although the cloud maidens had gathered themselves together and they and their cloud were almost as good as new, they were still annoyed about having been dissolved, and anyway, they were very taken with Kerwen and Lord Ponsadane; when the two heroes rode away, the cloud went with them.

"There is nothing else for it," said Henwyn. "We must carry word to Clovenstone ourselves; we can go on ahead of the army, and put Princess Ned's mind at rest."

"You ride ahead," Garvon Hael told him. "Don't worry; Fentongoose and Prong and I will bring these goblins safely home."

Fraddon was eager to leave too, for he badly missed the trees and waters of Clovenstone. So as soon as his wounds were salved and bandaged they set off, the giant limping along as slowly as he could go, Henwyn and Skarper riding horses, and Zeewa striding along behind (they had offered her a horse, but she mistrusted horses, and no horse would have let her ride it anyway, with those ghosts all around her).

A chill wind battered at them as they crossed the moor: a wind of winter, trembling the water in the puddles, blowing the dead grass flat. But no rain came, and although Skarper thought the air smelled of snow, none dropped on them during their journey north.

On a cold bright morning they came over the last ridge, and saw Clovenstone ahead of them. Zeewa was footsore by then, so Fraddon picked her up, and her ghosts wrapped themselves around his neck like a scarf. Then Fraddon broke into his rare, heavy run, and Henwyn and Skarper kicked their horses to a gallop, and they all went racing down to Clovenstone, to be greeted with whoops and friendly punches when they brought their good news to the goblins who'd been left on guard at Southerly Gate.

The guards had good news of their own. "The slowsilver's coming back! The lava lake is filling again!"

Up the long road through the ruins they all went hurrying, twiglings scampering happily through the bare branches overhead, dragonets flitting around them. The gate guards heaved the big gate in the Inner Wall wide open to let them through. "Princess Ned wasn't feeling too bright, so she couldn't come to meet you," said Spurtle (who wasn't looking too bright himself, being still half sofa). And there she was, in her old russet dress, standing waving among the fruit trees. They waved back, and Henwyn and Skarper climbed down off their horses, and they ran towards her.

And it was then that the terrible thing happened. Princess Ned clutched suddenly at her side, and they saw her face change from joy to a sort of astonishment. Then her knees gave way, and she fell, and lay upon the grass.

"Ned!" they shouted, and ran to her. Henwyn and Skarper knelt at her side; Fraddon bowed his huge head over her; Zeewa, slipping down from the giant's hand, stood watching from a little distance, with all the goblins left in Clovenstone gathering behind her in a worried, whispering crowd.

Ned's face was pale; her mouth was faintly blue. She felt as though a great weight were pressing on her, pushing her down into the grass. Dr Prong had warned her of this. Her heart was weak, he said. Too much

327

exercise, too bad a shock, might make it break. But Ned had never guessed the joyful surprise of seeing her friends come safely home might break it. She felt cheated. She reached for Skarper's paw, and Henwyn's hand. "Oh, how annoying!" she said. "Now I shall never know how everything turns out! Tell me quickly, was the battle won?"

Henwyn nodded. Skarper said, "It was."

"And Fentongoose and Dr Prong? And Garvon Hael?"

"They're all right," said Henwyn, trying not to cry. "Almost everybody's all right, and there are loads of new hatchlings. They're all coming home. They'll be back soon. Just wait till Dr Prong is here. . ."

Ned smiled at him. "I am sorry," she said. "I wish I could. But I don't think I can."

The snow which Skarper had smelled on the wind was starting to fall at last. The tiny dry flakes came whirling across the garden, settling on the dark earth of the flower beds, gleaming in Ned's strewn hair, dusting down white upon her face, catching in her eyelashes.

"This is what I saw in the oracular bathtub at Coriander!" said Henwyn through his tears. "I thought the falling stuff was ash, but it was snow."

"Oh Ned!" said Skarper, and his ears drooped.

Zeewa put her dark hands kindly on their shoulders

and said nothing, and the tears of Fraddon fell down on them all like rain.

They laid Ned in her cabin in the old ship, and lit candles around her, which was the custom of the Westlands, and sat for a long time sadly, talking about the arrangements that must be made. The goblins dug a grave for her, in her favourite corner of the new garden, where a little stream splashed down over the rocks of Meneth Eskern and made a pool. And although they none of them felt hungry, they cooked some food, and ate, and after that their talk grew strangely happy and full of laughter as everyone remembered good stories about Ned. Long after the other goblins had gone to their nests Skarper and Henwyn sat in the main cabin of the old ship, and Fraddon stood outside and looked in through the open windows, and they kept remembering stories, and telling them to Zeewa, who had hardly had a chance to know Princess Eluned.

And at last, although none of them thought that they could sleep that night, they slept, exhausted by their long journey and their grief. And in the dark of the night, when a butter-pat moon hung above Blackspike Tower, the candle flames in Ned's cabin fluttered, and Ned's ghost rose and walked.

It did not look like Ned. It did not look like

anything. No curse was laid upon this spirit. It was more like a pleasant feeling, which brought comfort to the restless sleepers in the main cabin. But Zeewa's ghosts saw it. They rose and clustered around it, and Tau purred, and Kosi said, "Welcome."

Ned's ghost still felt fluttery and unsure of herself. She looked down at Henwyn and Skarper where they lay sleeping, curled up on their chairs. She thought they might be cold, and wanted to pull a blanket over them, but of course she couldn't; she couldn't touch anything; she was a ghost. She looked out at Fraddon, asleep on his feet outside, the big, kind, ugly face she knew so well. She said, "The worst part is, I wanted to know how everything will work out. Who will look after Clovenstone now? Will Henwyn be king? He is the Lych Lord's heir, after all; it is his by right, really. . . But he is so young! Perhaps Fentongoose will help him. And Skarper too; Skarper is wiser than he looks. And what about Zeewa? Will she go home to the Tall Grass Country, west of Leopard Mountain?"

Kosi said, "She would like to stay here at Clovenstone, I think. For a while, at least."

"Oh," said Ned's ghost sorrowfully. "Am I allowed to stay here, do you think? To hang around and see what happens next? To keep watch over them?"

Kosi shook his head. "Your time is over, Lady of

Clovenstone. It is their time now."

"But you are still here!"

"Not through choice. And not for long, not now. Will you take us with you, lady?"

"Take you where?" Ned's ghost wondered. "Of course I will, if you would like me to. But where?"

Kosi smiled. He stooped over Zeewa and kissed her forehead, and Tau the ghost lion licked her face, and of course Zeewa felt nothing but a faint chill which made her frown and snuggle deeper inside her cloak. Then Kosi gestured for Ned's ghost to follow him, and stepped out through the ship's curved wooden wall. Out into the night air above the garden they flew, and Ned's ghost looked back and saw the other ghosts streaming from the old ship like smoke: the lion, the antelope, the fish, the flies. When Ned agreed to take them with her the curse had broken, and they were untethered from Zeewa. Like a moonlit mist they blew across the rocks and roofs of Clovenstone, through the stones of the Inner Wall, and out across the marshes, where lanterns burned, and boglin voices chanted. Ned's ghost looked down, and saw beneath the mist to the boglins gathered there, and beneath the waters to where the dampdrake lay, curled up at home again in its own deep mere.

The ghosts soared over it all, and descended to the

silent Houses of the Dead. Kosi led them to the hilltop, and as she stepped between the old stones, Ned's ghost suddenly felt the cold, frost-prickly grass under her feet, which made her realize that she had not felt anything till then. She looked down and saw that she was herself again, or at least a sort of see-through version of herself.

Tau the ghost lion came and nuzzled her, and she could feel the nap of his velvety nose against her fingers and smell his liony smell.

When the Gatekeeper rose out of the grass she cried out in surprise and said, "Oh, a ghost!", before remembering that she was a ghost herself, and laughing.

"Welcome, Princess Eluned," said the Gatekeeper. "Welcome to the resting place of the dead of Clovenstone."

"I have brought some friends," said Ned's ghost, letting a ghost beetle settle on her hand, a ghost bird on her head. "Is that all right?"

"We have been expecting them," said the Gatekeeper.

Ned's ghost turned and looked back towards the Inner Wall; to the towers, with their dim lights burning. She was thinking of Fraddon, Henwyn, Skarper and the goblins. "I shall miss them all so much," she said.

"I know," said Kosi.

"I'm frightened," she said.

"It is just another adventure," said Kosi. "You are good at those."

He held out his hand to her, and she took it, and together they sank down like smoke into the grass, and the ghost animals went with them, until the hill was still and silent, and the moon was gone, and the first light of dawn touched the eastern sky.

Skarper woke suddenly and sat bolt upright, wondering what was wrong. For a moment he could not think what it was. Then he realized that Zeewa's ghosts, which had been rustling and buzzing and droning in their usual way when he fell asleep, had fallen silent. The air above the sleeping girl was still. The only sound was Henwyn softly snoring. Skarper looked everywhere, but there were no ghosts.

He rose, tiptoed past Henwyn, and went to the window. Outside, the snow was falling again, proper snow this time, whirling down white against the pale sky and the old dark towers. He thought, *Princess Ned's gone, but it's still snowing. Everything is still going on without her.* And although he couldn't really imagine ever feeling happy again, he knew that one day he would, and that things would go back to normal, or at least find a new way of being normal, like a river finding a new path for itself. And he thought, *We'll be all right, Henwyn and me and the others. We'll manage.*

And the sun rose, and brought a new day to Clovenstone.

ACKNOWLEDGEMENTS

With thanks to my editors, Marion Lloyd and Anna Solemani, to Sarah McIntyre for suggesting the title, and to Sam Reeve, for listening.

Philip Reeve was born in Brighton in 1966. He worked in a bookshop for many years before becoming an illustrator and then an author. His debut novel, *Mortal Engines*, the first in the award-winning epic series, was an instant bestseller and won the Smarties Gold Award. The Mortal Engines Quartet and its three subsequent prequels cemented his place as one of Britain's best-loved authors. In 2008 he won the CILIP Carnegie Medal with *Here Lies Arthur*.

His recent works include the Railhead trilogy and a series of books for younger children, co-written and illustrated by Sarah McIntyre. A movie version of *Mortal Engines* was released in 2018. He lives with his wife and son on Dartmoor.

WWW.PHILIP-REEVE.COM